The Dagger in the Crown

By the same author from Macmillan

Enter Second Murderer
Blood Line
Deadly Beloved
A Quiet Death
To Kill a Queen
Killing Cousins
The Evil That Men Do
The Missing Duchess
The Bull Slayers
Murder by Appointment
The Coffin Lane Murders

Alanna Knight

The Dagger in
the Crown

MACMILLAN

First published 2001 by Macmillan
an imprint of Pan Macmillan Ltd
Pan Macmillan, 20 New Wharf Road, London N1 9RR
Basingstoke and Oxford
Associated companies throughout the world
www.panmacmillan.com

ISBN 0 333 90415 X

1 3 5 7 9 8 6 4 2

A CIP catalogue record for this book is available
from the British Library.

Phototypeset by Intype London Ltd
Printed and bound in Great Britain by
Mackays of Chatham plc, Chatham, Kent

For Alistair
husband, friend, reader and enabler
with love in our special year

Author's Note

For more than four hundred years historians have argued over the authenticity of the Casket Letters and who warned Lord Darnley to make his escape from Kirk O'Field (with equally dire consequences) minutes before the house was demolished by gunpowder.

This criminal investigation is fiction based on fact, using wherever possible quotations from letters and other documents, as well as reported conversations.

Among the innumerable works of non-fiction and biography read over many years I am indebted to *Mary Queen of Scots*, Antonia Fraser's incomparable biography; *Lord Bothwell* by Robert Gore-Brown; *The Queen's Man* by Humphrey Drummond; *The Tragedy of Kirk O'Field* by R. H. Mahon; and *Mary Stuart's Scotland* by David and Judy Steel. And mention must be made here of the two great historical novels of my early years which were to influence my abiding interest in Mary Stuart: *The Gay Galliard* by Margaret Irwin and *Immortal Queen* by Elizabeth Byrd.

MACBETH: . . . the murderers,
   Steep'd in the colours of their trade, their daggers
   Unmannerly breech'd with gore: who could refrain,
   That had a heart to love, and in that heart
   Courage to make's love known?

LADY MACBETH: Help me hence, ho!

MACDUFF: *Look to the Lady.*

> *Macbeth*, William Shakespeare, Act II, Sc. 3
> (The murder of Duncan)

Part One
Craigmillar Castle
near Edinburgh

'The queen is at Craigmillar, about a league from the city; she is in the hands of the physicians, I do assure you not at all well, and I do believe the principal part of her disease to consist of a deep grief and sorrow. Nor does it seem possible to make her forget the same. Still she repeats these words, "I could wish to be dead." You know very well that the injury she received is exceeding great, and Her Majesty will not soon forget it.'

– du Croc, French ambassador to the Scottish court

Chapter One

Saturday 20 November 1566. Early evening

My Lord Bothwell's mind had never been far from murder that day, but the sudden scream of mortal terror took him off-guard. As its violence shattered the blood-red calm of sunset gleaming on the castle walls, his first thought was, *The Queen – the Queen is in peril!*

His hand flew to his sword. Poised and alert for instant action, he looked towards the royal apartments where Mary had sought sanctuary from Lord Darnley, a brutal husband who would stop at nothing, not even regicide, to gain the throne of Scotland. But the lords loyal to Mary stood firm and had gathered around her in Craigmillar Castle and formed the Conspirators' Bond.

To protect the throne and the Queen's person from a husband's abuse, divorce was the matter under discussion, smoothly diplomatic and bloodless-seeming. On the surface . . .

And with more taste for Border foray than political intriguing, the faces of his fellow conspirators flashed across Bothwell's mind – arrogant Huntly, belligerent Argyll, smooth-tongued Secretary Maitland – grim accompaniment to that second cry of terror.

Dear God, what new devilment, unplanned, was afoot tonight? Alert to the silence that regathered around him, he was sure that it had been a woman's scream.

His head jerked upwards again. But there were no signs or sounds issuing from the Queen's apartments and he firmly put aside contemplation of the dreadful fate that awaited those who planned treason.

Disguise it as they would, for decency and safety's sake, a more permanent disposal of Henry Darnley was no longer a remote possibility to be toyed with. It grew daily, steadily larger, as yet unspoken but ever looming to the forefront of their minds.

And if they should fail? Bothwell groaned inwardly. A quick end with a sword was the legacy a Borderer was born to; one the fortunate would welcome a thousand times rather than the screaming agony of the rack, confession by torture, the slow horror of hanging, drawing and quartering . . .

Another shrill cry, a woman in peril. And closer at hand. Now there were footsteps, which had him turning swiftly, heart racing, sword drawn.

'My Lord Bothwell – wait!'

From the gloom of the tree-shrouded lane, a figure staggered towards him. A ragged boy, filthy-faced, his bonnet over his eyes gasped out, 'My Lord, take care. You are in grave danger.'

The youth came nearer. Breathless, he almost fell at Bothwell's feet, clutching his left arm with a right hand covered in blood.

'The woman, sir. She was following you. I watched her, staying close to the hedgerows, all the way from your house down yonder.'

He pointed back to where Bothwell and his retainers were lodged in Peffermill House, invisible behind a tracery of tall winter trees and black hedges.

'Did you not hear her cry out, my Lord? I wrested this from her,' he added proudly, and flourished a small dagger.

French or Italian, despised as a mere toy by men, this was a weapon ladies might carry to protect themselves, one to be wielded with severely damaging and even fatal results.

'She was but a few steps behind. You would have been taken unawares.'

Bothwell doubted that. Normally he would have contested such a suggestion, but he had much secret matter to occupy his thoughts besides the conspiracy. Rid of the weak and treacherous Darnley, he was growing surer that nothing stood between him and marriage to the Queen.

Discounting his mistress, Janet Beaton, of course, to whom he would always stay faithful in his fashion, there was one other impediment. His lawful wedded bride of nine months, Lady Jean Gordon, sister to one of his fellow conspirators, the powerful Earl of Huntly.

A marriage of convenience, a political expedient urged by Mary herself and, with Lady Jean making matters difficult by pining for her lost true love, doomed to failure. But even with conjugal matters more than somewhat cool between them, there was no way on earth he could imagine the chilly but dignified Countess of Bothwell, at present in attendance on the Queen herself, creeping up a dark lane and stalking him, dagger in hand.

He sighed. He liked a woman with spirit and, alas,

had she been capable of such passion for him, their marriage might well have shown signs of success. As for other women, he was puzzled. He had not formed any recent amorous attachment. At Peffermill House his Borderers brought their women with them, but wisely none that excited Bothwell enough to risk for a brief bedding the loss of some valuable fighting man's trust and respect. And it was unbelievable that any serving-wench he tumbled would have the audacity to try to kill him. In moments of anger such threats were hurled at him, even the violence of pounding fists on his person, and clawing hands at his face. But they were to be expected when he wearied of one bed and made his way to another more enticing new love, paying for his pleasures with some jewel or pretty trinket.

Before him his rescuer moved from one foot to the other, nursing his arm. The sunset's last red glow had faded, leaving the lad's features indistinguishable as the darkening sky overhead released its first heavy drops of rain.

'Are ye bad hurt, lad?'

'Nay, my Lord,' was the gasp through tightened lips. 'It is only a scratch, when I snatched the blade from her.'

Bothwell held out his hand for the dagger. A woman's plaything, small and delicately jewelled, but deadly. He had seen one exactly like it somewhere before. If only he could remember . . .

'Give it me!'

But the lad shook his head, thrust it quickly behind his back. 'Nay, my Lord, this prize is mine,' he said proudly. 'I won it and it may have value.'

'Ye say ye followed this woman. Are ye from Peffer-mill then?' Bothwell asked curiously.

'Nay, my Lord. From over there.' The lad pointed in the direction of the castle gardens.

Doubtless one of the many extra servants required during the Queen's residence, thought Bothwell. But young as he was, this one was learning fast the lessons of his elders. Never part with anything of the remotest value. Everything and every man and woman have their price.

'Your name, lad, so that I might see ye properly rewarded for your pains.'

Expression was lost beneath the ragged bonnet. 'I am but a servant. You would not know me.'

'And yet ye ken who I am.'

He thought the lad smiled. 'Everyone kens my Lord Bothwell, sir,' he said, and with a slight bow turned to leave.

And everyone kens my movements, that I walk the short distance from Peffermill, where other men might ride, thought Bothwell, as he asked, 'This woman – what manner of person was she?'

'One of the court ladies, my Lord.'

'And how looked she?'

The lad considered Bothwell for a moment. 'Of your own height, sir, tall for a woman. Dark hair, but I could not be sure, she wore a cloak. Foreign-looking, Spanish or French.'

Definitely not his wife, fair and small, thought Bothwell with a sigh of relief. The lad was proving very observant. Considering the rapidly approaching darkness, such information was surprising, but of little value. Especially as many of the Queen's French court were housed down the hill on the far side of the castle at the place they called Little France.

'She had jewels on her, as if she had lately been in good company,' added the lad, expecting gain for his information and now eager to please.

'Jewels, ye say?'

'Aye, my Lord. I fancied there was the glitter of diamonds.'

Bothwell considered him thoughtfully. 'Had ye seen her or her diamonds afore?' he demanded. The lad shrugged. 'Once, walking in the gardens with the Queen's ladies. With the Lady Marie Seton – at least I think it was she.'

'Ye canna be sure though?'

'Nay, my Lord. I rarely meet ladies of the royal court.' The lad sniffed, then wiped his nose and dirty face on a ragged sleeve. He was trembling, as if in a fever. Or from fear.

'What is your name?' Bothwell asked again.

The lad stared at him from beneath the now dripping bonnet. 'My Lord, it is Will Fellows.'

'Good Will to ye then.' Bothwell laughed and, not unknown for his sudden outbursts of generosity towards servants, handed him the warm cloak he had thrown over his velvet doublet.

'What is your wish, my Lord?'

'Take it – for your trouble, lad. With my gratitude. Ye did well.'

The astonishment with which this unexpected gift was received suggested to Bothwell that a shilling would have been adequate, a more than ample reward. Holding the cloak, Will cradled it about himself, savouring the richness and luxury of such a garment and, in wonder, stroking the woven insignia of Bothwell's coat of arms.

'Should ye see this lady again, get a message to me by one of my servants at Peffermill, d'ye hear?' And, turning on his heel, he walked away rapidly, pausing to shout back over his shoulder, 'See that ye take care of that arm too. Don't let it go bad.'

As darkness swallowed up his rescuer, Bothwell realized that, but for the discomfort of standing in the rain without his cloak, there were many questions for which he should have obtained answers before releasing Will Fellows. Such were his uneasy thoughts as he put his mind to something, sweeter by far than treason or an assassin's knife, that awaited him in the old west tower of the castle.

Janet, his beloved mistress of the past eleven years, a handfasted union formed when he was nineteen and she near forty, mother of six children and already a grandmother. Janet as lover, satisfying needs bodily and spiritual, brought illusions of security to a fighting man, enforced by her reputation as the Wizard Lady of Branxholm, dealer in magic it would ill befit any to cross.

As he entered the postern gate, Craigmillar Castle loomed far above him. Black against the sky, its battlements on fire in the last glowering splendour of a stormy sunset. Second only to Edinburgh Castle, its magnificence disguised a fortress's watchful survey south towards England, whence all dangers came. Only the Lammermuir Hills and Bothwell's fierce Borders stood between the two rival queens, Elizabeth of England and Mary of Scotland.

A thin, high-pitched wail . . .

Dear God, what this time?

A cat ran across his path and did nothing for his nerves as he stared into a night that was suddenly full of unseen knives. He had been attacked, should lie dead but for Will Fellows intervention. What did it mean? Was this a personal vendetta or something more sinister – a secret conspiracy perhaps, directed against the Queen, who saw him as the one friend she could trust and whose loyalty was never in doubt?

Her affection had extended to leaving her justice court at Jedburgh that October, defying convention to ride to Hermitage Castle, where he lay seriously wounded and like to die after a Border brawl with one of the Elliots.

The Queen had almost died too from the folly of that wild ride. Suddenly violently ill on her return to Jedburgh, her life was despaired of, her body stiff and cold. Death seemed so imminent that her canny half-brother Moray, with an eye to bettering himself with the crown of Scotland, began to make an inventory of her jewels.

She lay at death's door for a week and it was not until the beginning of November that she was fit to travel. Wearily, she sought sanctuary, away from Edinburgh and encounters with her impossible husband, in this peaceful castle with its health-giving fresh breezes from the River Forth.

She was still frail, and at those council meetings with her nobles she was strangely silent and lifeless, as if she did not care one way or the other what happened, prepared to drift without protest into whatever future they planned for her.

The Queen was firm on one thing though. Divorce

was forbidden for a Catholic queen unless, as the lords argued, it could be granted on the grounds of consanguinity, for she and Darnley were step-first cousins and had married in haste and in passion, without awaiting the necessary papal dispensation. But, Mary said, if the Pope insisted that they were not legally married, their child, James, would lose his right to inherit the crown of Scotland.

Bothwell grimaced. The Queen's visit to Hermitage had added fuel to eager rumours that she and Bothwell were lovers. Chance would be a fine thing, he thought sourly, but that meeting, with all its scurrilous rumours and false implications, had nevertheless borne its evil seed, giving substance to a dangerous dream slowly taking shape in his own mind . . .

Chapter Two

Saturday 20 November 1566

Stumbling out of the darkness, Bothwell crossed the courtyard leading to Janet's apartments and climbed the spiral stair. He threw open the door of a room aglow with candlelight.

There, by a crackling cheerful fire, stood Janet, in a dark red velvet gown which complemented her hair. She rushed over to greet him fondly, but his response was diluted on observing that she was not alone and that he had interrupted a conversation with her new steward and factor, Tam Eildor, a tall imposing figure in a furred damask gown, unfashionably beardless like Bothwell himself.

The documents Eildor held and rustled politely hinted that estate matters were being discussed and failed to diminish Bothwell's scowl. Indifferent to his fellow men's appearance, Bothwell could not fail to be impressed by this man's latent strength and power. And these days, he thought irritably, he could always be sure to find Eildor in Janet's presence.

'What ails ye, Jamie? Jesu, you are so wet.' Janet grimaced and moved away from him, anxiously regarding the dampened sleeves of her gown.

'The rain began when I was near the postern gate.'

'Without a cloak, I see, with no thought for that velvet doublet. The silver will tarnish.'

Her admonishing tone reminded him that she had insisted on this garb. Bothwell had little taste for elegance, always being happier less formally clad in shabby but comfortable leather jack and woollen hose.

She looked towards the steward and said, with a glimmer of satisfaction, 'Tam warned that the day would end in rain. He was right, as usual.'

The man bowed and Bothwell glowered. Right as usual, was he?

'Tam kens such things. I always take his warning,' said Janet with pride, making matters steadily worse.

Bothwell's deep sigh expressed irritation and impatience. 'Madam, are we here to talk of the weather? I have just had an escape from assassination,' he added angrily.

'Jamie, dear Jamie. How on earth—' Janet's eyes widened in horror, suddenly full of concern.

'And I gave my cloak to the lad who rescued me,' said Bothwell in wounded tones.

Janet shook her head. 'Such a gift!'

'I was sorry for the lad. If I'd been slain such a cloak wouldna be much use to me. Besides, he deserved it for saving my life and getting a dagger-scratch on his arm for his pains.'

'Thank God you're safe,' said Janet. 'Sit down. Tam, bring us ale.'

'I would we could talk alone,' Bothwell whispered.

'Nay, Jamie,' she said firmly. 'Tam has great insight and knowledge. We will take his advice and he will no doubt help us find your assassin. He has provided answers for many things that have puzzled us.'

But Bothwell was hardly listening. As Eildor poured the ale, he treated the favoured servant to a cold appraisal. Granted the man was comely, strange looks but comely. Too dark for a Lowlander, over six feet tall, thirtyish – maybe his own age. He had a touch of finely polished steel about him and, according to Janet, a mind as sharp as a rapier. Small wonder the new steward was gaining the reputation of being Satan himself, conjured up by their mistress's occult powers.

Such rumours had been encouraged by his unexpected appearance at Branxholm Castle, the Borders stronghold of the Scotts of Buccleuch, who were loyal to Mary, and home to Janet, the widowed Lady Buccleuch. The household was mystified, wanting answers to the questions none dared to ask, and none were satisfied with her ladyship's vague explanations about when and why he had arrived.

As for Eildor, he had his own reasons for concern at the mention of Marie Seton and the 'Spanish lady', but with no part in the conversation now taking place between Bothwell and Janet, he was observing the lovers closely. He marvelled at colouring so similar it could have been painted by the same artist – Janet's auburn hair echoed by her lover's rough chestnut, amber eyes a foil for fox-brown. But there the likeness ended, and Eildor guessed that rough living had long ago stolen Bothwell's youth – nature's deep furrows as well as enemies' scars adding to harsh lines from nose to mouth.

Janet, however, remained untroubled by the passing years. She was as lissom as a girl, while her contemporaries were already old past man's desire and firmly laid this strange, unnatural pairing of youth and age at the door of noxious spells and revolting potions.

'Will ye not be seated, man,' said Bothwell sharply as Eildor's hovering brought further cause for offence, making him aware of the physical disadvantage of being several inches shorter.

Eildor glanced at Janet, who inclined her head in approval. Taking his seat, he stretched out long legs, so much at home that Bothwell seethed inwardly. There was nothing deferential about this servant, he thought, with new stirrings of jealousy. After all, he was not, and he knew it, the only man to occupy Janet's bed. Loving one another did not preclude more fleeting amours.

Bothwell, with a wife to love, honour and obey, was in no position to make accusations, nor was he fool enough to air his suspicions of Eildor. Any such outbursts, he knew, would be met by a gentle smile. No denial, of course, just a look that said, 'Accept my life as I accept yours, without question, and all will remain well between us.' For both knew that although physical love might not last a lifetime, they had something stronger, a bond to survive transient sexual encounters, the lust of an hour.

'What think ye, Tam?' Janet turned to the steward, her eager expression arousing yet further annoyance in her lover.

Eildor rubbed his chin thoughtfully. 'My first feeling, madam, is that the lady might well have been the intended victim, rather than my Lord Bothwell,' he said.

'What mean ye by that?' demanded Bothwell sharply.

Eildor shrugged. 'The circumstances, my Lord. He talked of her jewels.' He paused significantly before adding, 'This lad, you say, followed you from Peffermill. What business had he prowling the lanes? Did you say he was a gardener here?'

Bothwell grimaced. 'An outdoor servant of some sort.'

'Of what age?'

'A well-grown fourteen, perhaps fifteen. I didna enquire as to his age.' He paused, remembering something important. 'The lad sounded educated, perhaps some laird's by-blow.'

At this information Eildor shook his head. 'It would have served you well to find out more about him, so that we might ask him some questions.'

Bothwell coloured angrily and Janet intervened quickly, 'Ye're suggesting, Tam, that this lady, enjoying the sunset perhaps, was set upon by this youth, intent on robbing her of her jewels?'

Eildor nodded. 'Such an explanation would fit my Lord's description of the incident.'

Janet's eyes widened. 'Well, Jamie, what d'ye think of that? A distinct possibility, is it no?'

'It wouldna account for the fact that she followed me from Peffermill, knew my movements, that I walked from there each day.' Bothwell paused. That bothered him. 'Master Eildor is unaware perhaps of court matters and that she would have been unlikely to set out beyond the castle here – without her maid,' he added triumphantly, his expression scornful of such ignorance.

'Unless she had some secret assignation,' Janet replied.

Bothwell shrugged. He did not like the way the story was being twisted. There were more than enough conspiracies under this roof at present without some unknown woman wanting to thrust a knife in his back.

'We have little to go on,' said Eildor, 'and, if I may be permitted to say so, my Lord, it would have helped if you had secured the dagger that he was so reluctant to part with.'

Bothwell ignored that and appealed to Janet. 'If ye could have seen him, he was a poor specimen, pale and thin. And terrified.' He then addressed Eildor: 'I am well acquainted with cutpurses and thieves, and villains of all manner, ye've my word for that. I encounter them every day of the week, as Lieutenant of the Marches, for they appear before me in the Border assizes regularly.' Turning back to Janet again, he added, 'Ye ken I have an unfailing instinct for such cattle.' He recalled that well-bred voice. 'This lad was as different as a parish priest from a criminal.'

Janet yawned behind her hand, her unfailing gesture of boredom. She nodded in Tam's direction, indicating that he was to retire.

'Find this Will Fellows, Tam, and bring him to Lord Bothwell for further questions. As for the mysterious lady, she can bide a while,' she added softly to Bothwell, who could hardly wait until the door closed behind Eildor to take her in his arms.

Leading him towards the bedchamber, unlacing her bodice, Janet smiled. 'Rest assured, dear heart, have any been so attacked it will be cried all over the court in the morning. Now let's to bed, where we have better matters to pursue.'

When these matters had been pursued to their mutual satisfaction and bliss, they were left, as usual, with lusty appetites for less carnal fare.

Janet had made ample provision for this and as they supped wine and dismantled a roast chicken between them, she asked casually, 'How goes the divorce, Jamie?'

Bothwell looked at her and gulped: 'Divorce? God's love, sweetheart, I've just wed the wench.'

Janet laughed. 'Not your divorce, Jamie – the Queen's. How do matters stand between her and Darnley?' She paused and added innocently, 'That is what all these daily councils are about, is it not?'

'Ay, matters go well enough.' Bothwell glanced at her shrewdly, wondering how much she knew or guessed of what went on behind the closed doors of the council chamber regarding a more sinister and permanent separation than divorce. He sighed. 'She'll not consider aught that will affect her bairn's right to the throne.'

There was more, much more, to it than that simple statement. The Conspirators had agreed that reasons would be found to divorce Darnley if Her Majesty would pardon the Earl of Morton and the other royal nobles still in exile who had murdered Riccio.

'Ay, and there's the Queen's honour,' said Bothwell. 'Let us guide the matter among us and Your Grace shall see nothing but good and approval by Parliament,' he said, mimicking Secretary Maitland's formal speech. Then, with a bark of laughter, he added, 'We were all perfectly aware, the Queen as well, that Darnley, at bay, isna past hurling aspersions of bastardy in the prince's direction.'

In the small silence that followed Janet looked at him, nodded and asked softly, 'And the alternative is . . .'

'What mean ye by that?' Bothwell demanded nervously, knowing full well. As his hand tightened on the stem of the silver goblet, he remembered how the Queen, pale and unwell, had indicated her consent. As the door closed on her, Maitland hinted at 'other means' of ridding the Queen's Grace of Darnley, adding that her half-brother Lord James Stewart, Earl of Moray, would 'look through his fingers' at any such measures.

Watching Bothwell's face closely, Janet said, 'Come now, Jamie. We aren't deaf, we all know what is going on, and your noble lords have very loud voices which they don't attempt to keep low. And they have servants who have ears. I think even Lord Darnley might fear a dagger in his back.'

Bothwell was intent upon a mouthful of chicken. Janet saw by the way his eyebrows came together that he wasn't prepared to confide treasonable information, even to her. With an instinct that her suspicions were right, she turned it swiftly to her own advantage.

'I am more concerned about whose hand was on the dagger drawn on you this night.' She saw how he winced at that reminder. 'Take my advice, Jamie, talk to Tam Eildor. He'll soon solve that mystery for you.'

Bothwell climbed back into bed, looked at her sourly and said, 'I'll find out myself. I dinna need Eildor as nursemaid.' He turned on his pillow. 'What want ye with Eildor, anyway? Ye should get rid of the man.'

'Give me a reason!'

Bothwell could think of none, especially as his Borderers had failed to find out anything to the man's discredit in the Eildon Hills, where Tam was a common enough name for any Christian.

'Ye ken nothing about him, sweeting,' Bothwell implored.

'I willna do it, Jamie,' was the sleepy but firm reply.

'The man could be a spy.'

'What, another? The castle's full of them.' Janet laughed mockingly. 'So what is new!'

Chapter Three

Sunday 1 December 1566. Before dawn

Janet lay sleepless at Bothwell's side. For once it was not the healthy hearty snoring that kept her awake, but a nightmare concerning her life here in Craigmillar as wife to Sir Simon Preston. He was a cold brutal man, and despite the birth of a child, their brief unhappy marriage had ended in divorce. Created Lord Provost of Edinburgh by Queen Mary, his new wife fortunately preferred their town house near St Giles.

When the Queen had commanded her presence at court, Janet prayed earnestly each passing day that she would be spared any embarrassing encounters with her former husband. Thankfully, it was too late for her romantic and sentimental royal mistress to harbour any ideas about reconciliation.

With a sigh, Janet turned on her side and, longing for dawn, tried once again to court sleep and so obliterate thoughts of the mysterious attack on Jamie, sleeping like a noisy babe, and the vision of Tam Eildor.

The events of last night had made her uneasy. Maybe Jamie was right and Tam was a spy after all. But she didn't think so, although she remained extraordinarily vague about her first encounter with him.

There was little enough in that meeting to convince anyone of his identity, least of all herself.

Her dogs had found him in the grounds of Branxholm Castle more dead than alive one bitter March night. Not the most propitious time for a stranger to arrive, with the nerves of everyone connected to Mary stretched to breaking point by the brutal slaying of David Riccio. Cut to collops before her eyes in Holyrood with Lord Darnley's dagger well to the fore and Lord Ruthven's pistol pressed against the Queen's stomach. Seven months pregnant and like to miscarry, but thanks to Bothwell's rescue and that cruel horseback ride to Dunbar Castle, twenty-five miles away, Mary and her unborn child survived.

Now those closest to them walked softly, alert for further treachery, and none more than Janet as she had the stranger carried indoors. She was impressed and puzzled that he had somehow lulled the dogs, noted for their savagery and trained to kill or maim any intruder. Their ferocious barks, which she knew well indicated danger, had been changed into whimpers of terror.

She realized the folly of taking him into her home, but she was curious and had never been known to turn a good-looking young man away from her door. Besides, barely conscious he could do her little harm. Indeed she believed it was only her knowledge of herbs and simples, termed magic by those who feared her, that kept him alive.

Days of expert nursing followed, and the stranger eventually returned to life. When he declared himself well, Janet had remained doubtful until she looked into those strange luminous eyes under winged devil's eyebrows. She was convinced. They were not the eyes of a sick man.

'Where are you from, sir?'

He shook his head, like one who has just emerged from a long and desperate journey. His bewilderment seemed genuine. She was soon to discover that while her herbs had restored his body to health, they had failed to bring back any memory of his former life.

A shrewd woman, Janet realized such claims might not be genuine. Had he, then, some ultimate motive in remaining silent?

She often considered very thoughtfully his sole possessions. In his breeches pocket a book of sonnets with a name, his own name he thought, on the fly-leaf. As for the breeches, they were of a kind she had not encountered before and so hinted at a foreign origin.

But what puzzled and disturbed her most was that under the ragged shirt was an oval crystal stone mounted in silver. It was very old and she recognized it as a charmstone to ward off evil. A charmstone with a difference for it had no fastening. It could not be removed or pulled over his head, the fine metal chain welded around his neck like a slave's collar.

Tam made no move to leave Branxholm Castle and she had not the heart to cast him out, mindless and vulnerable, into the world beyond. Although the charmstone had little value, there were men out there who would cheerfully cut off his head for such a prize and the coins it might bring. In the same way robbers cut off fingers for silver rings from their victims left for dead.

Then, as if Tam read Janet's mind and was grateful, he proceeded to make himself indispensable. She found him amazingly competent. The details of his own past might be lost, but the skills acquired in that other life were still much in evidence.

His good looks belied him. No mincing courtier, he was extremely strong, with an air of authority that gained the other servants' respect, especially the maids, who added a few sighs and fluttering eyelids for good measure.

His accent – well, that puzzled her. It was Scots, but not as broad as hers, or Jamie's for that matter. As if he had learned it as another language.

Gradually friendship and trust grew between them. She discovered he was well bred, cultured, and his mind, although blank about his own life, was knowledgeable about the world of nature surrounding them.

When she told Jamie he scowled. 'Ye're far too trusting. Ye ken nothing about him.'

'He stays,' she said firmly, adding to herself, he has strange powers and I want to know more, I want to find out.

Tam also lay sleepless, haunted by his own demons. The odd thing was that he spoke the truth. He was as much in the dark as Janet Beaton about the events that had deposited him in the grounds of Branxholm Castle. He had no memory beyond that familiar name on the book. The crystal charmstone must, he realized, also have some part in that previous life. But what and where had he been for upwards of thirty years, since he could only guess his age by comparison with men of similar appearance?

His former life had been completely erased. And yet he knew it was there somewhere beyond his

damaged memory. Sometimes he sat beating his forehead with his hands, desperately willing the past to
return. Occasionally he was rewarded by tantalizing
fragments, a half-forgotten dream from which he would
awaken, certain he was on the brink of total recall.
Only to curse as once more it rapidly faded.

What tormented him most was his ability to see
brief flashes of future events, as if he had already been
there and witnessed them. When he tried to explain
this to Janet, she shook her head.

'Ye deal in dangerous matters, Tam.' She put a hand
on his shoulder. 'A word of caution. Best keep such
thoughts to yourself. Men and women have burnt for
foretelling the future.'

She soon discovered that he was good with figures
too, knew about accounts. Her faithful old steward,
Mark Scott, was sick and had lately taken to his bed,
and as he was unlikely ever to leave it again, there
was no one to manage the estate and household. A
successor had to be appointed and trained, a lengthy
business.

And so Janet decided to take a chance on Tam
Eildor. She was not disappointed. A few meetings at
the old man's sickbed and within days he had accounts
made up and settled, the household affairs regulated,
servants paid – much to their astonishment – and was
suggesting improvements.

Tam liked and respected Janet, the kind of woman
who, somewhere in those strange, elusive dreams, he
had been used to dealing with. A woman as much out
of her time as he felt he was out of his, this warrior
woman who had avenged her husband's death.

He was very impressed.

She had been married three times. Her first husband left her a widow with a child at twenty-three, but she freely admitted that she had already taken another husband in the sight of God.

Tam guessed at her fearsome memories of Craigmillar. With yet another child, at last released by divorce from marriage with Simon Preston, she became wife to Sir Walter Scott of Buccleuch.

A happy marriage at last, with four more children. Buccleuch, however, was unfortunate enough to meet his hereditary enemies, the Kerrs, on the High Street in Edinburgh. They left him fatally wounded, to be finished off by the daggers of their servants.

The Kerrs thereupon pleaded provocation and implored forgiveness from the Regent, the Queen's mother, Mary de Guise. The royal pardon did not satisfy Janet.

At the head of two hundred Scots, she rode to the Kirk of Lowes in Yarrow, where the Laird of Cranstoun had given Kerr sanctuary. Finding the church door barred and bolted from within, Janet took an axe and, forcing an entry, tore her victim from the altar.

'We delivered him to Border justice,' she told Tam grimly.

Looking into her eyes, Tam thought it wiser to ask no more questions. He guessed that her reputation as a witch who could stay untouched by time and use her powers to seduce men of all ages was not based on black magic but on the stardust heaven, or the devil, thought fit to sprinkle on the very few.

Mistress of none but the Earl of Bothwell, whom she loved and honoured, she took other men to her bed briefly as need or fancy dictated.

So it was with Tam Eildor. He found it an enjoyable experience, but not one he cared to repeat while he was her steward. She sensed his reactions and there was a tacit understanding that their sensual pleasure in each other's bodies was not to be a regular, or, as he considered the uncertainties of what his future might hold, even an irregular occurrence.

Bothwell was awakened by the Mass bell, which as a Protestant he could safely ignore. Asked by Janet if he had slept well, he confessed to uneasy dreams.

'Concerning women wishing your death, no doubt,' said Janet mockingly.

That was true.

At his uncomfortable expression, she laughed. 'Alas, not many are as understanding of your failings as I am.' Continuing to brush her hair, she said with a coy glance, 'At least Lady Jean doesna seem to care about what she's missing.' She frowned at him. 'I've been thinking though – God be thanked ye're rid of that wretch Anna Throndsen. Remember Anna, who ye once promised to marry, forgetting of course that we were already handfasted. And ye still wear it, married or not,' she added, her smile a sweet reproach as she stretched out and touched the silver Fede betrothal ring he wore, with its bezel forming clasped hands.

Regarding it, a little shamefaced, he said, 'It willna come off.' Then, shuffling uncomfortably, he continued briskly, 'Ye ken well the reason, sweetheart. I needed the Throndsen woman's dowry to pay my mercenaries. Black looks and whispers, dear God, a threatened mutiny on my hands. I had to find some means, any means, of paying them off. Love didna enter into it.'

Janet nodded. 'Aye, that was your idea, but ye didna reckon she'd think different and make a perfect nuisance of herself, following ye all over Europe.'

Bothwell shuddered at the memory. 'She wouldna want to kill me, that's for sure. The woman was frantic with love and lust for me. She did nothing but weep over me because I didna make love to her.'

Janet smiled sympathetically. 'Be thankful she has taken herself back to Norway.' She considered him tenderly. 'Poor Anna, mad for love of ye,' she said, repeating his words and drawing his head down to hers. 'I can well believe it. And I ken the reason why,' she whispered with a sigh.

Taking her hungrily in his arms again, Bothwell dismissed Anna Thronsden, her brief tearful presence in his life now reduced to occasional guilty thoughts of the unacknowledged son she had borne him. Five-year-old William, abandoned and living with his grandmother, Lady Morham, at her home near Haddington.

Pregnant a second time shortly after following him to Scotland, Anna was determined to be presented to the Queen as Countess of Bothwell. Equally determined to be rid of her, Bothwell packed her off home. The ship could have sailed to hell for all he cared, but Norway-bound it called at Lerwick, where by way of consolation she might visit her favourite sister, Dorothy, wed to a Shetland merchant.

He remembered her whining and weeping, imploring for the love he could not give in person, in long, tortuous letters and how that first pregnancy with William had made her more lustful than ever.

For most men that would have been an added attraction, but Bothwell was finding her increasingly repulsive. As she wailed at being left alone and afraid in their Brussels lodging, he had made for her protection a small but deadly jewelled dagger.

Vaguely recalling its design, he had a sickening idea that this might well be the very same weapon, briefly glimpsed, that Will Fellows had snatched from the mysterious woman's hand.

With so many imponderables in the Queen's future, Bothwell could do without the added anxiety of continually glancing over his shoulder for a vengeful woman's dagger, poised ready to strike. For his peace of mind, Will Fellows must be found, the dagger recovered, whatever the cost, and this mysterious woman tracked down. Even if it meant asking for Tam Eildor's assistance to have the matter speedily dealt with.

Meanwhile, he was greatly relieved to have rumour confirmed that the court was moving to Stirling Castle. By the Queen's command he was to arrange the baby prince James's baptism.

In Peffermill House, Bothwell's servant and valet 'French' Paris was considering his master's formal wardrobe in anticipation of resuming their travels. As was normal, rumour had reached the servants' ears of the move to Stirling with the speed of light, long before the court was officially acquainted with the news.

When his master had looked in last night on his way to Mistress Beaton to ask if all was well, Paris omitted to mention one trifling incident regarding a meeting with a lady in a local tavern.

True, the light was dim, but not so his hearing, nor his sense of smell, and her perfume told him this was no tavern whore but a fine lady. Impressed that she should favour him with her company, for he was a vain fellow and thought much of his own good looks, he was delighted when she responded with alacrity to his sly suggestion that they adjourn immediately to his master's rooms at Peffermill.

Alas for his hopes of romantic dalliance. Before he could even undo his doublet, he was overcome with the effects of the ale he had been drinking. He awoke next morning to a headache of mammoth proportions. Staggering into his master's bedchamber, he found that the lady had gone and the trunk which accompanied the Earl of Bothwell on all his travels had had its lock forced.

Sweating with fear, Paris was relieved to see that family papers and state documents, as well as the jewel casket, were intact. He relocked the trunk with a thankful prayer. All the thief had taken seemed to be a few letters, dismissed by Bothwell as the passionate outpourings of a tedious lady whom Paris had never met.

They would never be missed.

Chapter Four

Tam Eildor was also alerted by the Mass bell. Since he had no knowledge of whether he was Catholic or Protestant, he closed his eyes again before opening one of them apprehensively. Never quite sure what he would see when he awoke each morning, his feelings of transience were part of his present memory loss.

It was with some relief he recognized the dark raftered room two storeys above Mistress Beaton's apartments in Craigmillar Castle's west tower, its sole light afforded by a large slit, like an inverted keyhole, installed so that the unfortunate servants did not die of suffocation while they slept.

Tam was fortunate. Servants were up at five, to light fires, carry ewers of water up a series of spiral staircases and attend to the demands of royal residents and lesser but equally demanding courtiers.

And if unhappy servants had strength or imagination enough, they might congratulate themselves and thank God in his mercy that their lives evolved around a splendid building of stone and mortar instead of a thatched, smoky, windowless hovel.

Tam was sure the present discomfort bothered him only because he had known better in that life which still eluded him. He might have brief flashes of what was future, but what he really wanted to see was his recent past.

You can learn to live with anything, he told himself firmly. Survival is the key, no matter what. And doubtless some day a great rush of memory would bring it all back to him.

He shivered. God knows, there were enough draughts circulating through the loose stones. The view was magnificent from the keyhole window but was not for servants to waste time upon. Difficult enough for himself, over six foot tall, to scramble on to a rickety stool and be rewarded with a glimpse of the walled garden. Its central fishpond was a coy innovation of Simon Preston's ambitious rebuilding programme in 1549, laid out in the shape of the letter 'P', the top loop forming a tiny ornamental island.

Beyond the curtain wall, a heavily crowded wooded bank and the ruins of a long-forsaken medieval quarry from which the castles of Craigmillar and Edinburgh had been built. Winter had bleached the landscape, reflecting a sunless bitter day, a dead world, a grey lifeless corpse, but undeterred the Queen emerged from the side of the castle, Mass having been celebrated in her private chapel.

She was accompanied by her four maids-in-waiting – Livingstone, Fleming, Seton and Beaton – who had been with her since childhood, following her to France and back again to Scotland. All shared the same Christian name – Marie – and, usually inseparable, were collectively known at court as 'the Queen's Maries'.

Now they walked briskly towards the walled garden, all attired in warm fur-lined hooded capes and preceded by a dozen yapping lapdogs. The Queen was distinguished by her height. Deep in conversation with Livingstone, the first of the Maries to wed and a mother within months of her royal mistress.

Tam's heart gave a now familiar lurch as he recognized Marie Seton, the smallest and slightest of the group. She was not the most beautiful, but it was not merely looks that had drawn him to her. There was something irresistible in her smile that gave her face sudden radiance, something that warmed his heart, echoing other elusive memories.

They had first met when he had helped her recapture the Queen's favourite parrot. Marooned on the fish pond's small island, it had shrieked at them from a rose bush, frustrated that with clipped wings it could not fly.

Tam had gallantly leapt across the intervening water. The evil-tempered bird, which took delight even on a good day in nipping any mortal flesh, was near at hand. Now in a rage, he rewarded his rescuer with some angry shrieks and severe pecks about the wrist, to which the rose thorns added their contribution.

Tam, however, was quite oblivious of pain. He had looked into Marie Seton's admiring eyes, had known he was the one who was truly lost.

The Queen had hurried towards them. Dear God, how young she was, Tam had thought, too pale and frail-looking since her illness to hold a kingdom in her hands. Six foot tall, such height in a woman and a queen should have been regal and commanding, but red-gold hair and golden eyes turned beauty into the brittle fragility of Venetian glass. The Stuart eyes and a slight weakness about the chin hinted at indecision and vulnerability, suggesting a less stern calibre than her wily cousin Elizabeth of England. A mere lass, to be at the mercy of power-crazed Scottish nobles.

As Tam restored the parrot Pierrot with a deep bow, the Queen's chiding turned to tinkling laughter. Thanking him, she gave Tam her hand to kiss, a long-fingered thin white hand, flower-like, hardly adequate to wield the ruthless sceptre of state.

When he later told Janet of his encounter, she had laughed. 'All the good young men fall in love with her, ye ken. Want to advise and protect her. And she does love a well-set-up lad, as ye'd guess from Lord Darnley.'

Now, observing the little group far below, Tam came to a sudden decision. The moment was oppor-tune, it gave him a chance to question Marie Seton about the Spanish lady Will Fellows had seen walking with her in the gardens. Hastily, he threw on his cloak and ran down the spiral staircase in time to meet the ladies, as they emerged from the walled garden.

He bowed low and, to his delight, Marie curtsied, drew him aside and whispered, 'Her Grace was very pleased with you for rescuing the horrible Pierrot, Master Eildor. She wished to hear all about you, a stranger to the court. She asked did you sing, play the lute.'

When Tam replied that he did not play an instru-ment but that he thought he could sing a little, Marie was pleased.

'Her Grace hates this cold dreary weather. Will you sing for us this afternoon, Master Eildor?'

The unexpected honour and the possibilities it offered delighted Tam. He bowed, stammering, 'It will be my pleasure, Mistress Seton.'

'Come at three of the clock then. Her Grace will enjoy some entertainment. She longs for laughter these days.'

There would not be much of that about once the court reached Stirling, where her sullen lout of a husband would join them, in time for his son's christening. The Queen had tried, perhaps not very hard, to persuade him to join her at Craigmillar, but he had refused and retired to sulk in his father's Glasgow house. From all accounts, the Queen would be well rid of this disagreeable young man with, Tam had heard, a taste for pretty young boys as well as serving maids. According to Janet, he would tumble anything that came his way.

'When Darnley is hot with lust,' she said sourly, 'no one is safe from him, male or female.'

Such behaviour in royal courts was by no means new. Many monarchs and their princes were well known to have tastes considered unnatural and regrettable for humbler men – men whose idea of gratification was no more than a quick tumble, whether for lust or in the sterner duty of procreation.

Tam found it difficult to imagine the delicate-seeming Queen he had just met as a lusty bedmate and he wondered out loud if word of Darnley's peculiarities had by now reached the sharp ears of John Knox.

'It would surely give him more concern than the

Queen's Masses. Do you think she knows?' he said to Janet.

'She must by now. But at the beginning she was so in love with him. I wish you could have seen her. So radiant and happy. He is beautiful, or was – and when he wooed her, she thought herself in paradise. Then she awoke, poor lady, and found herself in hell with the devil instead,' Janet had added with a shudder.

A sudden darkening of the already grey sky indicated a storm more immediate than Darnley was heading their way. Ahead of them the Queen and her ladies had quickened their steps towards the shelter of the castle.

Tam put a delaying hand on Marie's arm. 'Stay a moment!'

She stopped, looked anxiously at her retreating companions and then turned to him, smiling. 'What is your wish, Master Eildor?'

He had no idea how to broach the subject. How do you say, 'An unknown lady, possibly Spanish, tried to murder Lord Bothwell. His rescuer, a servant, possibly a gardener called Will Fellows, saw her walking in the garden with you. Tell me what you know about her.'

'Seton – come! At once. Her Grace awaits you.' The shrill command was from Fleming.

Tam was spared. With a sigh he bowed to Marie, held her hand to his lips. 'We will talk this afternoon,' he said.

She curtsied. 'I trust so, Master Eildor.' Her smile was an invitation.

But for the moment he had another plan. Earlier he had observed, close to the fishpond, men at work repairing a stone wall. Retracing his steps, he came upon them unloading carts of malodorous night soil into what was to be a sweeter-smelling rose garden.

An old gardener busy with a spade gave him a toothless grin. 'By Her Majesty's command,' he said proudly. 'T'will please her to look down on it when she visits the castle in the summer. She keeps us all busy.'

Listening to the old man, Tam, blessed with excellent long sight, searched for someone of the youth's description under the sacking hoods the men wore. There was one who fitted well Bothwell's description of his rescuer. Tam cut short the gardener's eulogy on rose-growing and with a hasty apology darted towards the boy, who glanced across and, as if aware that he was the target of Tam's approach, vanished around a corner of the castle. Was that Will Fellows, behaving like one who wished to avoid a confrontation?

Tam shouted, 'Stop!' and the gardeners also stopped working and looked suspiciously at this upper servant from the court, running through their ranks in a less dignified manner than suited his scholar's cloak and velvet bonnet.

'What ails ye, sir?' shouted the old man.

'I thought I saw someone. Know you Will Fellows?'

'Will Fellows,' the gardener mouthed slowly. 'I ken none o' that name'

'A young lad, about fourteen or so. A handsome lad, well set up.' Tam paused hopefully.

This raised foolish grins, some coughing and meaningful glances, which brought a flush of annoyance and embarrassment to Tam's face. Obviously aware of royal pursuit by Lord Darnley, they misunderstood his interest and intention. And possibly to further protect the lad, heads were shaken all round. Heads down, work hastily resumed. The subject was closed. No one knew Will Fellows or whatever his name was.

Tam turned away briskly. One of the younger men left his companions and came after him. 'I've heard tell of a man in charge of the woodcutters, name of Ben Fellows. Over yonder.' He pointed downhill, in the direction of the wood's ruined quarry. 'Maybe the lad you seek is kin to him.'

'I thank you,' said Tam, but the man lingered meaningfully until Tam realized that a reward was expected for this information and thrust a coin into his hand.

His rapid departure was accompanied by some badly stifled mirth. He pretended not to hear the jeering comments directed at him.

Admitted to the Queen's audience chamber that afternoon, Tam was cheered by the sight of a roaring log fire. In keeping with the wintry weather outside, gone were the formal court gowns, the fashionable Spanish farthingales. These had been replaced by long-sleeved woollen kirtles and tight bodices with the neck of the shift underneath gathered into a ruff. Satin slippers had lost favour to ones made of softest deerskin and woollen stockings. The 'Sunday best' winter dress of any Edinburgh merchant's wife, it would have gladdened the heart of even John Knox, who raged at his Queen as a model of extravagance and depravity.

Today her only extravagance was her jewellery, which she loved. Many pieces she had inherited from her mother, Mary de Guise, and others she had brought with her from France. In addition to the gold crucifix, she wore her favourite Scottish Tay pearls and drop earrings.

The atmosphere was to be of friendly informality. The Queen handed Tam a piece of music and sat down in readiness at the virginal to accompany him. Shyly at first, but with growing confidence. Tam managed the song the Queen had written, much to her delight.

He was pleased find her accomplished and with a natural gift for putting words to music. As she played with ease, smiling and lost in a happier world, a romantic ballad of love lost and found again, the years as a sad widow and abused wife seemed to disappear, revealing a carefree girl awaiting her first experience of a man's love.

As their eyes met, in that languid smile Tam thought how easily a man could become besotted by this lovely frail woman, aware of the dangers seen and unseen that beset her. Many men before and after him would be overwhelmed by the desire to protect her, with their lives if necessary.

As the sounds of the music they had made together died away, their efforts were greeted by applause from the four Maries and the Queen indicated a seat where her ladies were gathered. In this newer tower of the castle, the window was larger and commanded a magnificent view towards the city of Edinburgh.

This was the sight the Queen encountered when she opened her eyes each morning, the castle on its rock, where her son was born, dominating the skyline. The great palace of Holyrood with its recent terrors hidden by the great bulk of Arthur's Seat, a long-extinct volcano, so learned men claimed, a place of sinister legends and magic.

The four Maries were laughing as they dealt out playing cards. Tam recognized primero, a game for gamblers more associated with the barrack room than the Queen's chamber on a Sunday afternoon.

He was considering how John Knox would have reacted to this latest piece of Sabbath-breaking debauchery when, aware of his interest, Marie Fleming, soon to marry William Maitland of Lethington, the Queen's Secretary of State, asked, 'Do you also tell fortunes from the cards, Master Eildor?'

He laughed and shook his head, unwilling to commit himself.

Fleming frowned across at Marie Beaton. 'You told us your aunt Janet said he might.'

'I did not,' Beaton protested, flustered and going rather red in the face, embarrassed at being caught out with Branxholm gossip about Tam Eildor.

The Queen, concious of the sudden tension, smiled. 'Beaton is trying to say what we have all been led to believe, Master Eildor.'

Tam bowed. 'And what is that, Your Grace?'

The Queen's eyebrows raised mockingly. 'Why, that you are a wizard.'

Tam bowed. 'Alas, madam, I make no such claims.'

Fleming was not to be put off. Determinedly she came forward. 'We have heard rumours that you can foretell the future,' she insisted. 'Beaton told us that you also share her aunt's gift of palmistry.' So saying she thrust her hand toward him, palm outstretched. 'Come, Master Eildor. Tell me what my marriage holds. Will I be happy? Will my husband always love me?' she asked softly.

'Alas, no one can tell you that.'

Fleming darted a tight-lipped look of reproach in Beaton's direction, while the other two Maries sighed deeply.

But Marie Seton smiled at him, albeit with a touch of anxiety in her expression, as if she was apologizing for having enjoyed and helped spread a little too much harmless gossip about him.

The Queen put a hand on his arm and said gently, 'Come, Master Eildor, satisfy my dear Maries. Tell them what you think you can see.'

Tam bowed but shook his head. As he opened his mouth to protest that this was beyond his powers, Mary looked at him sternly. 'Tell them,' she insisted. 'It is but a game we wish to indulge in.'

'Is it your command, Your Grace?' When she inclined her head, smiling, he sighed. 'Very well.' He took the hand of each in turn, while the others looked over his shoulder, eager and watchful, as if they too might interpret what he saw.

He saw marriage for Fleming, a happy marriage, but the line was short. They would not have many years together. This he did not tell her. There was marriage for Beaton. For Livingstone, now Lady Semple, a long life and many children.

For his Marie, he could predict love, yes, many men would love her.

'You see no marriage for me then?' she whispered, gazing into his eyes.

'I see you refusing many suitors,' Tam replied. 'Many men will love you. You will have a long life.'

'But no marriage.' Something in her sad voice told

him of her hopes too, that he might marry her. Said in no words: Do you not want me as I want you?

Aware of the Queen's intent gaze upon him, he was saved further confusion when she thrust out her hand. 'Now it is my turn, Master Eildor. I have been pleased to listen to these others. Now tell me what is in store.'

What was in store? He panicked as he held the delicate hand in his. A daunting prospect indeed. Men had died for less than a royal prophecy that went wrong. He gazed at her palm. The life-line was not long, but there was much suffering, much separation from those she loved. There was confinement – prison. But over all there was blood.

Blood to be shed. Death.

He had not guessed any of this.

He knew.

It was one of his terrifying leaps in the future, as if he was reading all he knew of this lovely woman in a book still to be written, where Mary would go down in history as Scotland's tragic queen.

The burden of such knowledge was intolerable. But the Queen was awaiting his reply. He had to tell her something. He touched her hand to his lips. 'History will tell better than my humble efforts, Your Grace. Your fame, your glorious name, will become a legend among men. It will last for ever. You will be revered by generations of men yet unborn whose sole regret in life is that they never knew you. Men through the ages who would have died to serve you.'

It was quite a speech and she looked at him gravely from under those pale gold eyebrows, her eyes tear-filled as she pulled her trembling hand from his.

How much, he wondered, of her future does she already know or guess?

At that moment a welcome interruption, the sound of a crying baby. Livingstone, with a glance at the Queen, rushed to the door and ushered in the wet-nurse proudly holding a shawled bundle of small yelling humanity.

As Livingstone curtsied to the Queen, who held out her arms for the baby, for a moment Tam wondered if the babe was Prince James, brought to Craigmillar from Stirling Castle. There the Queen had placed him last summer in the safekeeping of the Erskine family, with his wet-nurse Lady Reres. Present at his birth in Edinburgh Castle, she and her family were hereditary governors of Stirling, known to generations of Scottish kings as 'the royal nursery'.

This decision was against Mary's better judgement, for she was in perpetual longing for her tiny baby. But she succumbed to the advice of her council, since the prince's safety might well be in jeopardy until matters were sorted out between herself and Darnley.

Now it was the Queen's wish, confirmed by Marie Seton, that Livingstone's baby daughter was brought to her mother every afternoon at four of the clock, so that the Queen could enjoy vicariously the pleasure of a tiny child the same age as her own.

As Tam looked at her, she was transformed into tender motherhood as she rocked the infant in her arms.

'*Cela, ici votre tante, my wee lamb*,' she crooned, kissing the rosy small face into an amazing silence.

Bowing himself out with an ominous feeling of disaster, Tam was reminded of that other Mother and

Child, the Virgin Mary and her son, Jesus Christ. And neither the Queen of Heaven nor the Queen of Scots was destined to see her son in old age or hold grandsons in her arms.

Chapter Five

Wednesday 4 December 1566. Morning

Tam's search for Will Fellows had had to be set aside.
Matters concerning his role as steward of Branxholm
had him closeted hour upon hour with legal documents
Janet had brought with her. Documents relating to
estate matters long neglected by her bedridden
steward, whose failing eyesight and lack of mobility
sapped the energy to interpret the more subtle implications of life rents and legacy clauses.

Perhaps he also lacked, thought Tam wryly, the
education and knowledge of law which came quite
naturally to him, a bequest no doubt from his former
life.

Outside Janet's apartments, the court's departure
for Stirling Castle signalled frantic activity. Corridors
echoed with the noise of scurrying servants as they
balanced trunks of clothes and staggered under
favourite items of furniture that accompanied the
Queen from residence to residence. Loud voices
shrilled orders and urgent messages as if departure
was imminent and not, as was actually the case, more
than a week ahead.

Meanwhile, anxious eyes were turned towards the

weather, since a grey November had become an even colder, more miserable December. As the first gentle snowflakes fell, there was a new worry. Would their long journey to Stirling be delayed by a heavy fall, blocking narrow roads on their route? Groaning, servants considered the hazards of carts loaded with trunks and furniture, the uncertain tempers and whips of benighted courtiers.

Then one morning another flurry of activity around the Queen's apartments, with frantic scurryings and shrill voices subdued.

Whispers: 'Her Grace is indisposed.'

That was all, but it was enough. Her Grace's indispositions were wont to decline swiftly into serious illness, where her life was despaired of. She had been plagued since adolescence with recurring bouts of a strange illness with hysterial and physical symptoms, particularly severe bouts of vomiting.

Bothwell, who was a man of action, of sudden decisions and hasty exists, was frustrated, constantly interrupting Tam and Janet as they seized the lull to sort out Branxholm affairs.

'We cannot leave until the Queen is recovered, Jamie,' said Janet calmly.

'Ye ken what this means,' said Bothwell. 'The date of the christening might have to be changed.'

There was nightmare enough in that thought, since the godparents had been summoned. Soon after the prince's birth last June, messages had been sent to the King of France, who would be represented by the Count of Brienne, in whose arms Prince James would be carried to the font, the christening present of the baby's godmother, Queen Elizabeth of England, who would be represented by the Queen's Catholic half-sister Jean, Countess of Argyll, while ambassador M. du Croc stood in for the Duke of Savoy.

'Their arrangements for travel by land and sea will have been made long since and it is vital that I have time in Stirling to make sure arrangements go smoothly,' Bothwell moaned.

Janet was remarkably unmoved. By her reckoning and from long experience, crises tended to sort themselves out quite nicely if left alone. In truth, she was growing impatient with her role of ministering angel to Jamie, constantly at hand with soothing advice.

'Most of these arrangments can be left to your minions. All that is required of you is to oversee the final ceremony,' she told him sternly several times a day.

'What ails her this time? Is it serious?' Bothwell demanded.

'A disorder of the stomach, I fear.'

'Poison?' Bothwell's eyebrows shot up. Had word of the conspiracy leaked out and Darnley stolen a march on them?

'I think not,' said Janet, but she wondered too.

What about symptoms of other mysterious illnesses, never fully explained by royal physicians and beyond her own herbal remedies, in which the Queen had so much faith? The remedies were, she suspected, her sole reason for inclusion in the Queen's court, for she had achieved notable success when summoned from Branxholm to Jedburgh, where more chaotic methods of bleeding and purging almost killed the Queen.

'You might use the time to see the court tailors,

Jamie,' Janet said, looking him over dispassionately, for although he had abandoned her gift of a velvet doublet with pearl buttons after two wearings and had resorted to leather jack and woollen hose, he could hardly decline the magnificent attire of blue satin and silver the Queen had promised for the prince's christening.

'Regard this delay as a gift,' she urged. 'For preparation. You must not displease Her Grace.'

This changed a scowl from Bothwell into a smile. Janet had noted for some time now that this self-satisfied expression was his reaction to the Queen's name. God only knew, she had seen it many times before. He might well have inherited the unfortunate tendency from his late father, the 'Fair Earl', who had unsuccessfully wooed Mary's mother.

Wooing the still-married Queen of Scots was a more dangerous pastime and Janet felt certain that Jamie's feelings were being reciprocated. How the Queen melted when Bothwell was announced. How the Maries exchanged glances and sly smiles. No one in their presence could long be unaware of the spark that was ignited between the two.

And watching them together, Janet, who had been in and out of love many times, recognized the symptoms. What had been a mere spark of hero-worship in Hermitage for the wounded man who had once saved her own life showed every indication of turning into a very different flame in Craigmillar. A fierce unquenchable flame that would eat them up, destroy them both.

Perhaps Mary had had more than enough of simpering courtiers and an unconsummated child marriage to a boy Dauphin, then to a bonny but vicious pervert like Darnley. She had never forgiven him for his part in Riccio's death and that wild ride to Dunbar with their rescuer Bothwell. How, when she had complained about endangering their unborn child, Darnley had screamed at her, 'Never mind. If we lose this one, we can soon make another.'

Mary might be seeing Bothwell through a young woman's romantic eyes, but for him it was something else. As well as the charismatic charm he held for all women, ambition also drove him. The Queen presented the greatest challenge yet and would be the greatest conquest of all.

Janet groaned inwardly, wishing she could warn him of the dangers, when all her instincts cried out, not only as one whose psychic powers could sometimes penetrate the future but also from sheer common sense. 'Don't do it, Jamie, don't do it. For sweet Jesu' sake, step back before it's too late.'

For loving the Queen of Scotland was a death sentence. If the Conspirators' plot was successful and Darnley disappeared from the scene, by fair means or foul, then the powerful Scottish nobles, in need of a scapegoat to save their own skins, would most surely have Bothwell's blood, and with Mary's ambitious half-brother's blessing, they would send the Queen to hell with him.

Janet sighed. She loved Mary and owed her loyalty, not only as Queen but as kin, but she loved Jamie Hepburn more and had loved him for a very long time. She knew his sexual power even as a nineteen-year-old youth, when she first took him to her bed, aware that she was far from the first in a long line of amours.

She also knew the secret of his 'wizard's enchantment' for the Queen. He could make her laugh, and in the sadness of betrayal, how she must have welcomed some lighter moments. He talked to her in French, unlike the other Scottish nobles, for he had served in the Garde Ecossais and spoke the language well. But now and again Janet had watched him abandon his courtly speech and lapse into broad Border Scots, coarse-tongued, outrageous.

It made the Queen gasp, hoot with laughter as she said, 'Explain, my Lord Bothwell, explain.'

When he did so, she would scream with mirth, clasping her hands to her sides like a fishwife, pleading with him to stop. And that was more effective than any passionate declarations of love.

More lasting too, thought Janet grimly, for in those short hours Bothwell gave her release, helped her escape from affairs of state and from a sullen, brutish husband. Laughter more than anything else could win her love. There was no other magic like it.

And so Janet trembled for them both. The fact that the Queen had honoured Bothwell with the Prince's christening was clear indication, for those who watched and made note, that she held him in the highest regard. And jealousy was swift to revive old slights and add fuel to new rumours.

Heads were shaken wisely. There might be some truth in those hints that they were lovers after all when she rushed to his side in Hermitage. No smoke without fire!

'Ye'll be off back to Branxholm,' Bothwell said to Janet.

'Nay, I am to accompany Her Grace to Stirling.' She smiled. 'I thought that would please you.'

Bothwell nodded absently. She noted a lack of his usual arousal in her close presence, as he said lightly. 'I dare say yon Eildor will keep an eye on things in your absence.'

Janet shook her head. 'He comes with me. I need him at Stirling.'

She hoped that she did not have to explain that she felt safer these days with Eildor around. At any other time, she might have been flattered that the idea obviously displeased Bothwell, who was now frowning. Her withdrawn expression, however, said that the subject was closed and brooked no further discussion.

As for Bothwell, he had a sudden longing for his Borders homeland again, for his more modest peel towers. He was sick of royal residences, of the formality and daily regimes. He needed the freedom of a man's world again, the rough but sensible soldier's attire of shabby comfortable thigh boots, jack and morion helmet. He had little taste for velvet doublet and these damned absurdities of padded hose. I'm forever looking like a popinjay, he thought contemptuously.

Most of all he needed the company of his own undemanding clansmen, with their loud talk and coarse humour, their drinking and wenching, instead of the stifling court atmosphere. Having to watch his speech and manners, while taking good care not to step out of line by taking precedence over some other noble lords who jealously guarded such privileges.

'Ah, to hell wi' these formal bowings and scrapings.'

He sighed, looking out on the bleak landscape of East Lothian. Even in winter there was colour and a certain splendour in the wild lands and cloudscapes stretching to eternity, and majesty in the formations of geese flying to far-off places. A man could draw a deep breath beneath an empty sky and not be suffocated by the noxious odours that seemed to surround the castle indoors and out like some evil miasma.

After a month of confinement for an entire royal court of noble lords with their retinues of servants, as well as a small army of retainers, it was almost a necessity of survival to move on.

Keeping the bitter weather out – sleet and snow and fierce winds – meant airless rooms and the smells of sweat and bodily functions, stale food and worse, bearable in the country and swifter to be wafted away by sharp clean air.

Small wonder his delicate Queen had a stomach-ache.

But there was another, more pressing reason for leaving court. Meeting a known enemy head on he had never feared, used from boyhood to the feel of an oft-bloodied sword in his hand. That was his life, a situation he could deal with. However, this ever-present vulnerability in the area between his shoulder blades, the cry in the dark, was another matter.

Especially now that Janet had, without her usual tact, brought up the subject of Anna Throndsen. Maybe it wasn't all innocence on Janet's part either, he thought moodily, looking for ulterior motives. Was this her way of getting her own back, for though she had said it all with a sweet and understanding smile, he knew she had never quite forgiven him for taking up with Anna Throndsen and her dowry, still sentimental – and resentful – about their own earlier handfasting?

Aye, women, even the clever ones – or especially the clever ones – had long memories for slights, more than any man.

No doubt about it, Janet had certainly succeeded in raising his fears of Anna as the unknown assassin. He was no fool and realized now how simple it would be for a woman to mingle incognito in a castle full of female servants. Teams of them had been rounded up from the neighbouring villages for casual employment, with the domestic life of the castle under extra strain when the Queen and court were in residence. Bothwell had witnessed it all before. The clamour for places. No questions beyond a name and details of any special skills were asked, as they lined up in the courtyard, eager to serve for those few extra coins.

Twice since his narrow escape from death and Janet's painful hints about Anna he had glimpsed a woman who, although he had almost obliterated that whining face from his mind, bore a faint resemblance to Anna in her walk and height.

First, there was one who might have been her in disguise as a serving-wench. Head down, buried in a pile of bedlinen! He had rushed after her, along the castle's twisting dimly lit corridors and spiral stairs. When he called out, she ignored him at first and then, glancing over her shoulder, instead of waiting, curt-sying politely, she took to her heels. Ignoring his, 'Wait – wait, I command you!' she had bolted round the next corner and sought trembling refuge in a group of maids emerging from one of the rooms.

A closer glance told him that coarse, pitted com-plexion, those rough red hands, didn't belong to

Anna. But as the women all stared at him, remembering to curtsey, he heard one murmur, 'Ken that's the Lord Bothwell.' And as he hurried away he could imagine the girl telling her companions how he had followed her, calling on her to wait. The women would exchange glances, nodding to one another, pursing their lips, with rape in all their minds.

As for the girl, it would give her something with which to impress her family and friends. How she was once pursued in Craigmillar Castle by no lesser man than the notorious Earl of Bothwell.

His second encounter was with a more obliging maid, who immediately recognized him and curtsied: 'My Lord Bothwell.' A bold-looking girl with a sonsy figure and large brown eyes, she gave him a sidelong glance of brazen invitation. 'How may I serve you, my Lord?' she asked softly.

There was no mistaking what was in her mind as she thrust out big breasts towards him and waggled her hips provocatively. His bad reputation obviously did not worry her. He grinned, wishing he had more time to sample her charms, for she was obviously disappointed when he bowed and dashed away.

With some concern, he realized the dangers of becoming obsessed about Anna when two other, more sinister happenings aroused his fears. One evening, on his customary walk to Janet's apartments from Peffermill House, he was certain he was being followed. Hand on sword, he had turned, shouting, 'Who is there? Show yourself.' But the footsteps were merely the rustle of leaves in the sudden wind.

The next night, dark and moonless, footsteps again. This time there was no Will Fellows on hand. Again he turned, shouting, 'Halt! I see you!' The shriek not of a virago rushing down at him, dagger in hand, but of a night bird taking flight had a very unsettling effect on his nerves.

Chapter Six

Thursday 5 December 1566. Morning

Heavily embroiled in matters relating to Stirling, Bothwell should have been grateful to find that Tam had resumed his search for Will Fellows. Recalling his encounter on the previous Sunday with the gardeners, Tam set off in search of one Ben Fellows.

Down the steep slope, beyond the castle walls, the sound of sawing indicated woodcutters at work and led him directly into a clearing deep in forest litter. Logs were stacked everywhere, ready for transport up to the castle, to be consumed by fires eager to warm cold and draughty chambers.

The timber had been stripped from the nearby forest slopes, reinforced by trees from the woods at the base of Arthur's Seat. Part of the royal hunting grounds of Holyroodhouse, there were strict rules about felling so as not to disturb the deer park with wolves, game birds and wild boar, specially imported from France for the Queen's pleasure.

As Bothwell approached the clearing, a group of thatched huts showed where the woodcutters lived. One larger than the rest with windows and door suggested that this might be the home of Ben Fellows.

Work ceased at his approach. Bows, curtsies and bonnets raised greeted this unexpected visit from a man from the court on foot, with no hoofbeats to announce his arrival. Looks of suspicion were exchanged. Was he a spy trying to catch them at some unlawful activity? For he was certainly a man of some importance, as they observed from the fur-trimmed cloak and velvet bonnet.

'Will Fellows, which is he?' Tam asked.

Puzzled looks were exchanged, frowns, heads shaken.

'Ben Fellows, then. I am told he is the chief wood-cutter.'

A man came forward, bowed, twisting the cap in his hand. 'He was, my Lord.'

'Was? What happened?'

'Dead, my Lord, a week sine. He'd been in sick bed for twa weeks wi' a fever.'

'And Will Fellows?'

'I ken none o' that name.'

A woman listening intently came to the man's side. As she opened her mouth to speak, the man pushed her forward. 'My wife, my Lord, she nursed old Ben.'

The woman curtsied. 'That I did, my Lord. I nursed him till the hour he died. He was a good man and his guts were rotting away long afore our good Queen came.'

'In health,' her man put in, 'Ben was a grand worker, for all his withered leg. He never missed a day—'

The woman was not to be dismissed. 'He was a bachelor,' she interrupted, 'with none to care for him but me afore he finally took to his bed.'

'He had twa nephews used to come and help him

out betimes. Een o' they might be this Will you speak of,' said her man. 'We never kenned their first names. They were from the town – across there, ye ken.' He nodded in the direction of Edinburgh.

'What sort of lads were they?'

'Big strong lads. Kept their own counsel. But what would you expect?' The woman's sniff of disapproval indicated that they'd thought themselves a mite too grand to mix with country folk.

Tam sighed. It didn't sound much as if either would be the lad Bothwell owed his life to. However, he had better try to find out more details. They might well be kin to Will, since Fellows wasn't a common name.

'Did they come to the funeral to pay their last respects?'

'Nay, he wasna buried in the kirkyard here. That wasn't for the likes o' Ben, it seemed,' said the wood-cutter.

'What mean you?'

The man shrugged. 'The minister had been called to say a prayer over him—'

'We hadna long put him in his shroud. He'd been gone just an hour or twa when his niece came for his body,' the woman interrupted.

'Aye, and a verra grand Edinburgh lady she was,' put in the man.

'I was going to tell him that,' said his wife as he pushed her aside.

'As I was saying, a grand Edinburgh lady, she came wi' the carter to carry her uncle back to the Greyfriars kirkyard for burial in the family grave. So the minister, Mr Cauldwell, ower yonder telt us.' He indicated a church tower visible through the distant trees.

His wife smiled, preening. 'I wasna surprised. Ben wasna like the rest of the men here. He had some book-learning and I often thought that he might have known a better life, although he never talked about it.'

She was still eulogizing, speculating that Ben might have fallen on hard times and proud to have had someone who had been well born working humbly in their midst, when Tam, thanking the couple, prepared to take his departure.

A wild-goose chase indeed. It didn't sound to him as if Will Fellows had much connection with the deceased woodcutter, but he might do worse than call on Mr Cauldwell, since ministers are often privy to parishoners' confidences.

How, for instance, had Ben's niece appeared with such alacrity all the way from Edinburgh just as he died? Someone on a very fast horse must have informed her.

Or else she was already in the neighbourhood, awaiting the event. With a carter at hand. Which was very odd!

Invited to share the woodcutters' lunch of cold perch freshly caught - or, as Tam suspected, poached from the castle fishpond - he felt it would be churlish to refuse. He was hungry too and a pot of ale might not come amiss. Besides, there might be other useful information forthcoming. But he was out of luck and soon gave up. The woodcutters were either ignorant about the late Ben Fellows or had their own reasons for silence before this elegant stranger in their midst. So although Tam left with his appetite sated, the identity of Will Fellows remained as baffling as ever.

On the off-chance that there might be some women's gossip regarding Ben Fellows, Tam fell into step with the woodcutter's voluble wife, carrying her load of logs on a pony cart to Peffermill House. Flattered by his attention, she was more interested in talking about her children and grandchildren, how remarkable they were obviously in the hope that this scholarly man might have some influence at the court.

Tam left her promising to mention her clever grandsons to the master of household at the castle, and, asking in return that she report to him any further news of Ben Fellows or his niece.

She smiled but shook her head. 'I doubt we'll ever see the likes o' her again.'

'What about the carter? Did you know anything of him?'

'Aye.' Her face darkened. 'Een o' a family of thieves over Niddrie way, the Red Crozers. We steer clear o' them. They'll come to a bad end, mark my words. Rough characters they are.'

'And what manner of lad was this one?'

'Red hair like carrots. The whole breed have the same brand. Keep a watch out for them, sir.'

Tam left her thoughtfully. Could this red-haired youth be Will Fellows? He certainly didn't match Bothwell's description of a well-educated youth, even though a bonnet might have concealed red hair.

On reaching the crossroads, there was Bothwell hurrying down the woodland path from the castle. Doffing his bonnet, Tam said, 'My lord, you are the very man I wished to see. I have been continuing my search for Will Fellows.'

'Successfully, I trust?'

'Alas, no.'

As Tam told him the results of his encounter with the woodcutters, Bothwell looked increasingly glum. Once or twice he sighed loudly, shaking his head. As he failed to react to the description of the red-headed young carter, beyond indicating that this pack of local thieves were well known, Tam did not pursue any other theories and said, 'Do not give up hope, I beg you, my Lord. While you are in Stirling, I will continue my search.' Bothwell gave him a sharp glance. So the man didn't know of Janet's intention that he should accompany her.

Tam continued, 'You need have no fears. I will endeavour to solve this mystery and find Will Fellows. I am hopeful that the minister will know of any local lad who is well bred and educated.'

Bothwell grunted. 'God grant that ye're right. The sooner he is discovered the better, for, I will be honest with ye, Master Eildor, I am fearful that this woman who wants my death might also follow me to Stirling.' And nodding towards the castle, he went on, 'Has it not occurred to ye that she may well be hiding up there at this very moment, even as we speak? God knows, the place is big enough for any to get lost in it who has a mind that way.'

Tam realized the truth of that. Anyone who looked like a lady or gentleman would be safe enough. And with a sudden intuitive flash, he suspected that Bothwell's reaction indicated he knew more about the woman's identity than he was prepared to admit.

They walked together in silence. Their road passed a tavern near Bothwell's lodging, much frequented by his small army of Borderers. Pausing, Tam was about to take his leave when Bothwell said, 'If ye can spare the time, Master Eildor, will ye take a sup of ale with me?'

They entered a comfortable room with a good fire, deserted at this time of the afternoon but with the lingering ghosts of baked pies. The innkeeper bustled forward, recognizing Bothwell, and bowed low as he took their orders, returning immediately with their ale.

Bothwell downed most of his at one gulp, slammed down the pewter mug on the table and gazed across at Tam very thoughtfully. Silent for a moment, he shook his head, his manner one of considerable indecision.

Tam helped him out by saying gently, 'You have some idea, my Lord, of who this woman might be?'

'Aye, Master Eildor. Anna Throndsen. I'm almost certain it's her all right.' He breathed deeply. 'It was the matter o' that dagger Will Fellows took from her and which he wouldna part with, be damned to him. It wasna till later that I kenned why it was familiar. I'd seen it before, since I'd had one identical specially made for Mistress Throndsen when we were in Brussels. Oh, five or six years ago, but I kenned it well.' Pausing, he looked at Tam as if awaiting his comments. 'For her protection, ye ken?' he said hastily. 'She was aye fearful at being left in a strange place wi' only her maid.'

'A dagger is just a dagger, my Lord.'

'Not this one,' was the firm reply. 'Twas bejewelled. At great expense,' he added ruefully, for gifts demanded by Anna had always cost him dearly, and none more than this one, it seemed. He shook his head. 'I'd swear it was the same one the lad snatched from her in the nick o' time.' And with a heavy sigh: 'Ye have my word for it, Master Eildor. As sure as I live, I'd swear it's the bitch herself means to kill me.'

With their mugs replenished, Tam found himself listening to a story that did Bothwell little credit, although it seemed scarcely justifiable to merit murder.

It began when Bothwell stood against all the Scots noble lords in his support of Marie de Guise, Regent of Scotland, while her daughter, the future Queen of Scots, had married the boy Dauphin of France, in an alliance that had never been consummated.

The Regent trusted Bothwell and that part of the story did him most credit. She created him Lord Admiral of Scotland, and with Scottish waters harried by English pirates and Edinburgh itself under blockade, Bothwell offered to go to Denmark and enlist the aid of King Frederick's fleet.

But while Bothwell was on his journey, news reached him that the long-ailing Marie de Guise had died. In an instant the whole political scene changed, and with France and Scotland ready to sign a treaty, King Frederick could hardly be expected to undertake actions hostile to England.

'It occurred to me,' said Bothwell, 'that I could do worse than pay my respects to the widowed Queen of France before returning home.'

Tam nodded politely. He could well imagine that the event which had ended one era of Bothwell's life immediately suggested the political expediency of making himself indispensable to the new young Queen of Scots.

'A sorry day when I went to Copenhagen and was introduced into the home of Admiral Christopher

Throndsen, a high-born Norwegian with royal connections,' Bothwell continued.

Tam soon gathered that the two admirals, one old
and the other young and ambitious, got along splen-
didly. Bothwell also made himself popular with the
junior members of the Throndsen family, son Enno
and the five of the seven daughters who were unmarried and still at home.

'No easy task finding husbands for them,' sighed
Bothwell, 'these horse-faced, prim young lassies. I
dinna ken about the two who were fortunate enough
to find Scottish husbands. One married a middle-aged
widower, the other a Shetlander. And Anna never lost
an opportunity to impress upon me how much her
parents favoured Scotland, how kindly her father
would look upon another Scotsman as a son-in-law.

'I should have guessed then what she was about.
Aye, Anna was clever, I'd give her that. She spoke
several languages and wrote a good hand in French.
She'd been acting as her now ailing father's secretary.
For some while she had handled all his business affairs,
and she was cataloguing his library and papers, as well
as helping her mother rule over the household and
arrange suitable marriages for her sisters.'

He paused, biting his lower lip before continuing.
'Anna wasna the bonniest. There was little to choose
from, but there was a mention of a dowry of forty
thousand crowns which went with her. Any man would
be tempted,' he added by way of apology. 'And I was
in desperate need of money. It meant I could pay
off my debts at home, where the coffers were empty.
Besides, the men I had with me were getting restless.
A lot to entertain them roundabout, ye ken, in the way

of womanflesh and liquor, but no money to pay for it all.

'A rich marriage would solve a deal of problems, and the lady was willing – aye, more than willing.' He laughed shortly. 'Eager, even. So we were formally bethrothed – with hand, mouth and letters, as they say, I offered Anna and her parents to hold her as my lawful wife. In return I received her father's congratulations and her dowry.

'It didna last long. Not one whit as long as Anna's undying affection. She clung to me like a limpet, man, she dogged my steps, followed me everywhere – even to Scotland, and when I brought back our young Queen from France, the bitch made it plain that she was coming too, determined to present herself at the court as Countess of Bothwell.'

He made a helpless gesture. 'And what would I be doing, what sort o' a picture would I present at court wi' a pregnant wife in tow?' He laughed harshly. 'Trouble was, I had no desire to be married, and she was the last lady on earth I would have willingly chosen. She had scant charms to beguile me. She was full o' plans, for her two sisters to be brought to Edinburgh, especially her favourite, Dorothy, who lived in Shetland.'

He shook his head. 'Aye, she saw her life here as turning into one great family party, at my expense.' He paused, frowning. 'There was a bairn, ye ken. A fine wee lad, William, my heir, if I'd made yon betrothal legal. I suppose she thought that would bind me to her further. But it didna.'

Looking at Tam, he added apologetically, 'The boy

is here, ye ken. Bides wi' my mother at Morham, near Haddington.'

'You see him often?' said Tam.

Bothwell shrugged uncomfortably. 'Not all that often. I ken naught about bairns and I havena time at present to be a good father, no time to spend on a five-year-old. My mother'll see he's brought up well. She's good to him and will see his education is well taken care of.'

Glimpsing Tam's expression and guiltily sensing disapproval, he said, 'Man, ye ken how it is with me. I have a lawful wife now. And – and the Lady Buccleugh – your mistress,' he added as an afterthought.

There was a short silence before Tam summed it all up by saying, 'So you think Mistress Throndsen is here, that she's back in Scotland and trying to kill you?'

'Aye, that might well be the way of it, for I canna think o' any other woman who would do me ill.'

Tam suppressed a grim smile. The way Bothwell treated his women, he could think of quite a few, including his lawful wife, Lady Jean Gordon, who would have been his own prime suspect.

'Well, what think ye, man?' Bothwell demanded.

Tam shook his head. It sounded an unlikely story, but who was he to question the motives of vengeful women. Hell hath no fury like a woman scorned, or betrayed, or scandalously ill-used.

Grudgingly, he was forced to admit that Bothwell certainly had charm when he wanted something. He recognized in that guileless smile the boy at heart and the charmer who never gave up, allied with the sheer physical power of the man of action and its devastating effects where women were concerned. To all accounts even the Queen of Scotland was not immune.

They were interrupted by the noisy arrival of a group of Bothwell's clansmen, back-slapping, laughing, and it was plain he didn't keep all that charm for women alone. Obviously his men loved him and respected him as their leader.

Tam did not doubt that any one of them would have laid down his life for Jamie Hepburn. And in those frequent, fierce forays among the surnames that raged across the Borders, they were very often called upon to do just that.

As Tam prepared to leave, Bothwell followed him to the door. 'Do what ye can, Master Eildor. I'll be grateful and I'll make it worth your while.'

Tam bowed. 'One thing more, my Lord. What did Mistress Throndsen look like?'

Bothwell frowned, squinting heavenward. He bit his lip in an effort to remember. 'Black hair. I dinna rightly recall her eyes, but I think they were dark too. She liked to pretend she looked like a Spanish lady, fond o' dressing like one.'

Perhaps Bothwell deserved all he got, Tam thought, for the tale about his wooing of Anna did him little credit and worse was his neglect of his son in Morham.

His mind returned to Will Fellows, the only witness who had encountered the woman who might be Anna. Bothwell's description tallied with the lad's that she was 'foreign-looking'. Little enough, but something to go on. If only he could track down Will Fellows.

Tam decided that his best hope for information regarding the woodcutter who had seen better days and had been buried by rich relatives in Greyfriars kirkyard, lay with the local minister. But he would wait until tomorrow to call on him. It was already growing dark and the fine drizzle of a short while ago had turned into hail needle-sharp against his face.

Chapter Seven

Friday 6 December 1566. Morning

Tam skirted the woods to where the woodcutters had indicated Mr Cauldwell's church was situated. Last night's weather had worsened and melting snow did not improve the muddy tracks.

The church looked dismal indeed, framed against the bare branches, with a piercing wind blowing sleet showers. Only the raucous cries of corbies as glum as himself greeted him as they flew over the vast array of tumbled gravestones. Ancient and modern, crooked and straight, skull-and-crossbones, a melancholy reminder of the pestilence, with many indications that few children survived beyond infancy.

The church was old and ruinous, probably built in the time of the Templars, who had sought refuge in Edinburgh after the Battle of Jerusalem. Persecuted, they had been offered the protection of King Robert the Bruce and there were many connections with this band of warrior knights in the area.

He pushed open a door which creaked ominously, the sound echoing through the dark interior, its stone walls with niches now empty of holy water and statues of saints, all destroyed by Reformation zeal.

Tam stood in front of the altar. There was no feeling of holy presence or sense of awe inspired by the oak table, and not even a cross to denote that this was a place of Christian worship.

He shivered, for the atmosphere was cold and forbidding, hardly an encouragement for Sunday worship. Its darkness told of older gods, arousing thoughts of pagan worship still secretly practised in remote country areas.

He grinned. His lack of reverence suggested that he was unlikely to have been a priest in that other world he had lost. Just one more category to strike off a growing list.

In the tiny vestry the only sign of a minister was the cassock hanging behind the door. Walking back through the church on his way out, the door opened before him and a dark shadow standing against the light asked, 'Can I help you, sir, or is it your wish to meditate?'

Into the light, the minister emerged as a rotund, cheery-faced man and, observing the tonsured head before him, one more sign of Popery, Tam chuckled inwardly. Despite the black gown and Geneva bands, this man of God seemed at variance with his gloomy surroundings. More Friar Tuck than John Knox.

His hopes, raised by Mr Cauldwell's information that he had been minister here for the past ten years, were once more to be dashed.

'Will Fellows?' Mr Cauldwell shook his head. 'I knew Ben Fellows, of course, a fine Christian, but I was never acquainted with any of his kin. Two nephews, they told you.' He looked puzzled. 'I never met them.'

'What about Fellows' niece?'

'Ah, yes, the lady from Edinburgh. I met her briefly.' The minister brightened, for he had obviously been impressed. 'She was taking her uncle back to Greyfriars kirkyard. A very proper thing for a dutiful niece.' He shook his head. 'That is all I know. I only had speech with the lady as she was leaving.'

'What was she like? Her appearance, I mean.'

Cauldwell thought about that, rubbing his chin. 'She was in mourning, a veiled hood, but I would say comely, young by her voice and well educated. I had an impression of dark hair and eyes, but I couldn't be sure.'

'She was alone when she called on you?'

'Yes – apart from the carter, that is. He was waiting outside.' The minister made a grimace of distaste. 'A very low fellow. It goes against one's Christian duty to be uncharitable, but he is of a family known to be habitual wrongdoers and, alas, somewhat notorious in this parish.' He frowned. 'I did wonder about warning the lady. In fact I hinted that she should take care. But she merely laughed, said she had the matter in hand and was able to look after herself.' He sighed. 'One can only presume she was paying the young rogue well for his services.'

'What do you know of the deceased, Ben Fellows, sir?'

Cauldwell seemed surprised by this request. 'Very little. He was an incomer to the district. I believe from Dunbar, but I might be mistaken. Most likely it was Edinburgh, and you will doubtless see his grave at Greyfriars. The sexton will have kept a written account regarding his niece's instructions.'

As Tam was leaving, the minister asked, 'Pardon

my curiosity, sir, but why is it that you seek this lad Will Fellows?'

'It is none of my own business, sir. A matter concerning a member of the Queen's court.'

As Tam returned to the castle he was very thoughtful. The documents he was preparing for his mistress's signature needed all his concentration, but drifting forcefully to mind were those discrepancies concerning the behaviour of Ben Fellows' devoted niece. The minister's account had suggested this was no ordinary fine lady, but a woman of strong character and determination who could bargain with a known rogue and thief.

The logical reason for her deep mourning was that she was recently bereaved – but not of her uncle. How she could have received information and made arrangements for his burial at Greyfriars and bribed a dubious character like the carter to transport her, within hours of the old man's death was beyond him.

Later that afternoon, Tam went in search of Lord Bothwell and was told he was walking in the gardens. Head down, still brooding on the minister's information, or lack of it, he turned a corner and narrowly missed colliding with the royal party.

Bothwell with Mary, leaning on his arm. This was her first day abroad since her illness and she looked pale and frail and so very trusting as she stared intently into his face, smiling, inclining her head, for she was half a head taller. But what Bothwell lacked in inches he more than made up for in power and masculinity. In truth, he gave the illusion of being a tall man, until

you stood up alongside him, Tam thought, as he bowed
low.

With one glance Bothwell quickly resumed his
urgent whispered conversation with the Queen. This
indication that he was not to be interrupted left Tam
no option but to follow at a discreet distance in the
hope that an opportunity for a private word would
present itself.

As he stood undecided, the four Maries
approached. Seton detached herself and came to his
side. Her excuse, if she needed one, was something he
did not overhear, but arch looks from the other three,
their smothered mirth and Marie Seton's rosy face,
suggested that all were aware that Tam Eildor had
found favour with her.

The thought was encouraging as they walked
together behind the little group, until he noticed that
Marie was somewhat distracted, hardly listening to his
conversation. All her attention was directed towards
her royal mistress and Bothwell. At one time it seemed
that she was quickening her steps in the hope of
catching up with them.

Tam put a delaying hand on her arm. 'Stay, Mistress
Seton, or we will be on their heels.'

Marie frowned and, with a despairing glance at the
two ahead, she slackened her pace. Her obvious
anxiety confirmed Tam's suspicions that rumours concerning the Queen's growing affection and dependence
on the Earl of Bothwell were common knowledge in
the court.

Quite suddenly, Marie put it into words for him. 'I
believe I can trust you, Master Eildor. Beaton's aunt
has told us that we can rely on you.' She gave him a

sideways smile. 'You have an honest look about you and, God knows, there are few but enemies surrounding us here.'

Tam bowed. 'What is it that troubles you, Mistress Seton?'

Again she smiled. 'I would that you call me Marie,' she said softly.

'Gladly I will. And your trouble?'

Marie took a deep breath. 'It is not my trouble – Tam.' She added his name in a whisper, acknowledging it with a brief curtsey, which pleased him. 'I fear for my lady, for Her Grace.' She nodded towards the couple in front so absorbed in each other. 'There is no other man close to her who can exert a good influence. No husband, alas, and as for her half-brother Lord Moray, she will hear no ill of him. She believes that he loves her, has her welfare at heart – alas.' She shook her head sadly.

Tam knew from Janet Beaton that Lord James Stewart, foiled in his many unscrupulous and nefarious attempts to gain the throne, had resorted to trying to prove that King James V was not his true father. That way, as Mary was not his sister, he could wed her and win the Crown Matrimonial.

'The man is a scoundrel of the first order,' had been Janet's caustic comment, he remembered, as Marie continued. 'Her Grace sees my Lord Bothwell as the one man she can trust. When they are apart for even a few days, she writes to him. Such long letters, which she thinks of as innocent outpourings of her heart to her dearest friend, her most loyal subject.' Marie sighed. 'She often reads them to us, anxious to know if she has said too much – or, more often, too little.

For he never replies, not my Lord Bothwell,' she added bitterly.

And Tam thought about those innocent outpourings and the dire consequences should they fall into the wrong hands as, with another sorrowful glance at the two ahead, Marie went on. 'I fear that she already loves him deeply, even if she does not know it or refuses to admit such feelings. For it is like a candle lit behind her eyes for him whenever he enters her presence. Poor lady, we have known her since childhood. It is hard to conceal secrets from such close companions . . .' She paused before adding, 'Or from her enemies here in the court and the spies of the Queen of England who covets her throne.' She sighed again and looked up at him. 'Love is a dangerous game, Tam.'

Her blush confirmed what he already knew, the truth behind her friends' teasing. It made his heart leap with longing for her. Suddenly he didn't care about Bothwell, or Will Fellows. All he knew was his desire for this woman, his yearning to seize her in his arms, kiss her, drag her into those trees, strip off all those garments, hold her . . .

' . . . not see it too?'

She was waiting for comment and he realized he hadn't heard a word she was saying. She looked down at his hand, tightly clenched over hers.

'Tam,' she said softly. 'Oh, Tam.'

He stared at her tear-filled eyes, knowing that all her heart too was in that single word as she spoke his name. And in that moment a sense of bleak despair came over him, for a future that could never be, for a love doomed to be lost for ever.

Leaning down, he kissed her cheek and gently released his hand. But she seized his hand again, raised it to her face and held it, trembling. A tear splashed. He touched it with his tongue and tasted salt.

Dear God, this could not, must not, happen. He must not let it happen.

With considerable effort, he moved away from her. 'What were we talking about, Marie? Her Grace, was it not?'

And with an effort equal to his own, she sighed once more. 'Two marriages, yet she has never known a real man.' Aware of that dangerous ground between herself and Tam again, she whispered, 'Until now.' And with a hasty change of subject, 'Rumours abound that she and my Lord Bothwell were lovers when she visited him in Hermitage.'

'A wounded man, lying at death's door,' said Tam wryly. 'So I have heard.'

'Talk of divorce from Lord Darnley will add fuel to that fire,' Marie continued anxiously. 'Especially when she does not trouble to conceal that my Lord Bothwell has replaced poor Davy Riccio, who was always her devoted friend.'

Pausing, she looked up into Tam's face, held his gaze intently. 'We who sleep in her chamber can vouch he was never more than that. None but Lord Darnley ever shared her bed. She would never have believed tales of his depravity, his chasing whores in Edinburgh. Whores and worse – young pages from the court.' She nodded towards the distant figures of the three Maries, and well ahead, laughing and talking together, Bothwell and Mary. 'Do you wonder that we tremble for them both, though truth to tell I must confess that

I have never held my Lord Bothwell in high regard.'
She smiled wistfully at Tam. 'I have never desired to
throw myself into his arms as other females do. I can
resist him because I know my limitations—'

'Your limitations?' Tam interrupted softly. 'Surely
you are mistaken. You have a mirror . . .'

'Nay, Tam. He would use me and soon tire. And I
have no wish to be one of a string of mistresses.' With
a shrug she added firmly, 'I want to love and be loved
by one man alone. And for ever.'

Even as she said the words, Tam felt the agony of
knowing he could not be that man. After all, what if
returning memory presented him with a wife – and
children too. And God only knew what other commit-
ments. What if he was or had been a criminal on the
run? Certainly he had been the victim of some violence
and that would account for why he had turned up,
mindless and wounded, in Janet Beaton's gardens at
Branxholm. And it would account for his nightmares,
which were sinister and violent enough for anything
to be possible. Even murder.

With difficulty he brought himself back to the
present. This woman had chosen him to love. He was
sick for love of her too. But he must never make the
fatal move that might destroy her happiness, her
future, for ever.

Far ahead now, the Queen and Bothwell had
reached the courtyard and disappeared into the royal
apartments. The three Maries trooped after them and
his Marie, with a brief curtsey and her heart in her
eyes, touched his hand.

'I must go, Tam.'

'A moment, if you please. Know you a lady by the name of Anna Throndsen?'

'Anna Throndsen.' Marie frowned. 'Why yes, she and my Lord Bothwell were betrothed – some years ago – in Denmark. She was in hot pursuit of him when he returned from France escorting Her Grace to Scotland.' She shrugged. 'Poor lady. She must have gone home long ago, abandoned all hope of marriage now that my Lord Bothwell is wed. Why do you wish to know about Mistress Throndsen?' she asked with a puzzled glance.

Ignoring the question, Tam said, 'I gather then that she has not been in the royal court for some time.'

Marie shook her head. 'She was never in the royal court, or allowed access to the Queen's circle. There was an incident – once—'

'So you have met the lady?'

'Once only. On that occasion. She made a great fuss, insisted on her rights to be recognized as Countess of Bothwell.' Marie smiled. 'Much to my lord's embarrassment.'

'So you would recognize her again, if you met?'

'I believe so. She was not a lady one would easily forget.'

'In what manner?'

'A very vivid creature. Why do you ask, Tam?' she repeated.

'She has not been in your company recently?' Tam persisted.

'No.'

'Seton! Come!' Fleming and Beaton were beckoning frantically from the castle doorway.

'At once, Seton. Her Grace awaits you.'

With a brief curtsey, and looking somewhat bewildered, Marie rushed towards her companions.

The door closed and Tam was making his way back to the west tower when he was hailed by Bothwell, hurrying towards him.

He bowed. 'My Lord, I wished to see you.'

'I guessed that, but, as you would note, I couldna leave the Queen right then. Well, what news have ye for me?'

Tam told him of his visit to the minister and of Ben Fellows' niece and of the advice to see the sexton at Greyfriars for further information.

'I intend visiting the sexton tomorrow.'

'Aye, and I will go with you,' said Bothwell. 'Her Grace is feeling low at present and there is an apothecary in the High Street who makes a grand collation of herbs – Lady Buccleuch's recommendation, ye might guess. I have other matters to attend to in Edinburgh on the Queen's behalf, so we will kill twa birds with ane stone, as they say. You call upon Fellows' niece, see what she can tell ye about young Will.'

'I talked to Marie Seton, my Lord.'

'Aye, your dalliance was noted, Master Eildor.' Bothwell gave him a leering glance and a knowing nudge.

Tam ignored that. 'I was asking about the Spanish lady Will Fellows said he saw walking with her in the garden.'

Bothwell swung round. 'And?' he demanded sharply.

'Alas, my Lord, she did not recall any such occasion or a Spanish lady. However, she did remember Mistress

Throndsen and said she would have recognized her again.'

As Bothwell bit his lip, Tam said, 'I thought this information might be a relief to you, my Lord.'

'Well, well.'

'It seems that the lad was mistaken.'

'He must be found. He must be somewhere around here. Someone must know him. And I need that dagger.' He nodded eagerly. 'Man, I am quite hopeful we are going to find him and that soon.'

As Tam left, he wished he shared Bothwell's optimism. It had been a long, bitter day and as he made his way to Janet's apartments he hoped that her summons to a simple supper together was all she had in mind. Since Bothwell's obvious infatuation with the Queen, Janet had been eyeing him in a predatory manner and he guessed she needed a substitute lover, if for nothing else then to arouse Bothwell's jealousy. In his own present need, he realized he might succumb to her advances and that was more than likely to end with Bothwell's dagger in his back.

Truth to tell, he was in no mood this night to make love to any woman. Except, perhaps, Marie Seton. For in human nature, he knew, the unobtainable is always the most desirable.

Chapter Eight

Edinburgh. Saturday 7 December 1566. Morning

Tam, riding one of Janet's horses, set off with Bothwell and his valet, 'French' Paris.

Paris was not his real name. He was a sharp-featured lad with a knowing look whom Bothwell had acquired on his travels abroad and trusted implicitly. Paris' imagination never failed him. He could come up with an alibi for a pursuing husband or a convincing lie for a pursuing debtor, all without change of expression.

They trotted smartly down the hill from the castle past Peffermill House, the crossroads where one way led south to Dalkeith and Bothwell's Borderlands, the other towards the city, dominated by Edinburgh Castle on its high rock.

Bothwell and Paris occasionally exchanged surprised looks, clearly taken aback at Tam's lack of horsemanship, which he was unable to conceal.

'God's sake, man, ye ride like a sack o' Newcastle coals,' laughed Bothwell. 'What ails ye? Is it some bodily condition?' he added with a mocking glance at Tam's behind.

'It is not,' said Tam acidly. 'I care little for horses,

that is all.' Did his wariness and lack of expertise indicate that horses had played no part in that other life?

Bothwell's eyebrows rose in horror and he shook his head sadly. What kind of well-educated man was this? Only peasants without the price of a beast did not ride. On the Borders, bairns were put on horseback as soon as they could stand and all lads and lasses rode like centaurs. Man and his hobby (as the small tough Border breed was known) were inseparable and often the means of saving a man's life.

Through the muddy lanes and snow-covered fields of the Pleasance they rode, towards the Flodden Gate, entering the town at the Netherbow Port.

Pointing to the steep High Street, Bothwell said, 'Ken it as a herring's spine, wi' all the closes and wynds the wee bones, topped and tailed by the royal residences of the castle and Holyrood, wi' those o' the nobility in between.'

At the central area around St Giles lay the heart of Edinburgh's commerce, occupied by luckenbooths – locked booths from which the merchant guilds conducted their business. On either side, walled gardens, the townhouses of noble lords separated by narrow closes or wynds where the bourgeoisie, the rich merchants, lived. Steep three-storeyed wooden houses, with balconies a hands'-grasp from those opposite, thereby increasing the hazard of fire.

With roofs straw- or heather-thatched, huddled cheek by jowl, a fire in one house would soon set the whole street ablaze. The lower half of the windows were wooden-shuttered, with round decorated holes large enough to enable occupants to thrust heads through to greet each other or take note of passers-by.

The shrill vendors and the noxious smells grew more oppressive and Tam was thankful for one blessing on this chill winter's day. A brisk wind cleared the air more efficiently than the heavy drowsy heat of summer, when flesh and fish became less fresh and more offensive as the day progressed.

Here they were to part, Bothwell to the apothecary and Tam to Greyfriars. As they reined in to appoint their next meeting place, a window above them opened for an instant. Neither took much notice of a face that stared down at them, hastily withdrawn, but Bothwell was never nearer death in that second before Tam rode away.

Leaving his horse tethered to the railings, Tam wandered round Greyfriars kirkyard. Once the Franciscan priory but sacked by Reformation riots in the days of her mother's regency, four years ago the Queen had permitted the grounds to serve as a common burial place, replacing the congested 'kirk-heugh' of St Giles.

The sexton was nowhere to be seen so Tam began searching for Ben Fellows' newly dug grave. There were three that seemed of recent date by their freshly turned earth, but he had no way of identifiying their occupants.

One infant's mutilated grave drew his attention: 'Magdala, beloved daughter of—and sister—'. The names had been savagely obliterated. How cruel, he thought, for the bereaved parents.

Footsteps announced the sexton, who wished him good-day. Informed of Tam's mission, he shook his head.

'Fellows, you say. Ben Fellows, sir. Alas, I cannot

83

help you there. None of that name has been laid to rest in my time. And I have been here since the first burial four years since. I would have remembered a family vault of that name. I fear your information is mistaken. However, if you would care to look at my register . . .'

Tam followed him into the crypt attached to the church. As he suspected, the sexton was right. He had drawn yet another blank in his search. There was one other possibility.

'Since there is no Fellows grave, the reason might be that the man I search for was unmarried. Perhaps he was interred with his niece's family, under her married name.'

'That is true,' said the sexton. 'But the last three interments do not fit the description of an old man. There were two women. One died in childbed and one was a middle-aged wife of a lawyer. The third was an infant two years old.'

Thanking him, Tam returned defeated to the noisy tavern at the Netherbow Port where Bothwell and Paris awaited him.

When he heard about the failure of Tam's mission Bothwell was puzzled, but then Tam said, 'The error could have arisen with the woodcutters. Perhaps they got the name wrong. Or the name of the kirkyard.'

However, with no information to carry the search further, mere speculation was a waste of time and Tam could hardly examine every kirkyard in Edinburgh.

Food and ale were served to them before they set off back to Craigmillar, their return route by Holyrood-house, as Bothwell had papers to collect for the Queen.

Taking Paris with him, he promised to delay no more than a few moments and Tam sat on the wall in the courtyard to enjoy the warm sunshine in a sheltered spot.

Lacking the court it was strangely peaceful. No sound of horses issued from the deer park, no dogs barking or flurry of birds rising. Once the Forest of Drumsheugh, with the lofty head of Arthur's Seat visible from its slopes, the Queen's favourite hunting ground had severe anti-poaching laws to preserve it for royal use. Four years ago she had added an artificial loch at Hunter's Bog for her courtiers' pleasure.

As well as deer there were wild boar imported from France. They were dangerous creatures to encounter, but the Queen was a fearless rider who loved the excitement of the chase, her favourite hawk hooded on her wrist, at her side the great Irish wolfhounds who could bring down a stag with one leap to the throat.

Tam watched Bothwell leave the palace and head in his direction. He was strangely silent and preoccupied. Perhaps because of the papers he carried or, Tam wondered, was he seeing in his mind's eye the murder of Riccio, his body buried somewhere nearby in an unmarked grave. The terrible night last March when the Queen had escaped those who wanted her death too, remembering how he had rescued her with Darnley trembling at her side. And how when they had passed by Riccio's grave she had said, 'In another year, I swear, another head will lie as low as his.'

Was that how this pretence at divorce and separation was to end – with the planned death of Darnley and Bothwell's own elevation to the side of the Queen who loved him? Would they rule Scotland together, wisely and well?

Was that his dream? Tam wondered, as Bothwell indicated the faster route back to Craigmillar by way of Duddingston village.

A low-lying sunset glistened redly on the loch and at the water's edge, bending over something lying there, a small crowd gathered. At their approach, a fisherman shouted, running towards them.

Bothwell reined in. 'What's the trouble, man?'

'Sir, it is a body washed up, drowned in the loch, I fear.'

'Indeed, that is unfortunate.'

With little interest in the matter, Bothwell prepared to ride on, but the man said, 'Sir, I fear it was foul play, for he was tight wrapped in a cloak, a gentleman's cloak.'

Bothwell dismounted with a sigh. 'I will take a look.' And to Tam: 'Bear with me, I am Sheriff of Edinburgh too, for my pains, so duty calls.' He turned to Paris. 'You may need to summon the Town Constable.'

With a strange feeling of foreboding, Tam rode down the slope with them. The body was indeed wrapped in a cloak and Bothwell swore, changing colour as he gripped Tam's arm.

'Don't you see. For God's sake, man, that cloak. It's mine. Look at the insignia on it. It's the one I gave to the lad Will Fellows. That bitch must have killed him too.' Then, to the waiting fishermen he said, 'Let us see his face, if you please.'

The hood was pulled aside, and Bothwell's explosion of tightly held breath told Tam what he wanted to know. The corpse was most certainly not that of Will Fellows, unless he had aged fifty years in a week.

The face they beheld was that of an old man, white-bearded and, Tam was beginning to suspect, a corpse before he was immersed in the water of the loch.

Bothwell stepped back and swore. 'Who can this be? What treachery is this, that he's wearing my cloak.'

Tam said, 'May I examine him, my Lord?'

'Do what you please,' said Bothwell angrily, 'if you think that will tell ye who stole my cloak from the lad to wrap up a corpse.'

Tam looked at the old man's body. He was particularly interested in the thin veined legs. The left one was slightly withered, the foot twisted. He remembered the woodcutter saying, 'He had one leg shorter than the other, lame from birth, poor man, but he was strong apart from that.' Tam knew he need look no further. He drew Bothwell aside. 'I think, my lord, our search for Ben Fellows' grave is at an end. This is his body.'

'The old woodcutter?' Bothwell stared at him. 'But you said his niece had taken him to Edinburgh for burial.'

'He never got there. I said what I was told, what they believed had happened to him.'

'So you think there was an accident – that the carriage overturned and the niece too is drowned?' Bothwell paused, staring at the grey waters. 'And what of the carter, the red-headed lad?' And remembering that history of thieving and villainy, he whispered, 'Dear God, did he murder her too?'

'Maybe so,' said Tam.

To the fishermen who were staring at them and

awaiting instructions, he said, 'There is no need to summon the Town Constable. This is an old man from Craigmillar way. He died a few days ago and his body was to be taken into Edinburgh. He must have rolled off the cart and into the loch.'

The men shook their heads and looked at Bothwell, who seized the opportunity. 'I am Sheriff of Edinburgh. This is my order, that the corpse be returned for burial at Peffermill. See to it.'

The fishermen bowed, recognizing authority and relieved to be out of an unpleasant situation with a hangman's rope at the end of it. If it was murder and no likelier suspect could be found than the men who had found the body, then in the interests of a speedy solution by the authorities they might find themselves arrested and accused.

'The man died of natural causes according to this gentleman, who is the Queen's physician,' said Bothwell, pointing to Tam. 'As he said, the man was dead before he fell into the loch. The matter will soon be sorted out. An accident with the cart, I fear.'

Tam stared at him. It sounded very lame to him and he was taken aback at this new description of himself and how easily he saw himself fitting into the role. Was this a link in his missing memory? With a sudden rush of excitement, he wondered if he had been a physician. Was that it?

Bothwell rode beside him down the twisting road. 'So, Eildor, we have our answer. The red-headed Crozer murdered the woodcutter's niece, robbed her and tipped her with the old man's corpse into the loch.'

Eildor shook his head, but said nothing.

Bothwell frowned and demanded, 'So what do you think happened?'

'I can only tell you what I suspect, my Lord.'

'And that is?' said Bothwell impatiently.

'The dutiful niece who came for Ben Fellows' body was no kin to him. She was already in mourning. That puzzled me at the time.'

'That surely is natural.'

'Not if he had only been dead a few hours. How could she have received that news in Edinburgh and acquired mourning veils and hired a carter – from Niddrie – to come out and collect his body? It just isn't possible.' He paused a moment before adding, 'This lady, this dutiful niece, is, I suspect, none other than the one who attacked you on the road to the castle.'

Bothwell paled visibly then he gave a great shout of laughter. 'God's sake, Eildor, if the carter murdered that bitch, then I owe him a debt of gratitude for ridding me of her.'

Eildor shook his head. 'Alas, my Lord, I can appreciate your feelings, but I fear it is not as simple as that. Think of the cloak. A corpse wrapped in a valuable cloak, my Lord? That does not make sense.'

'And why not?'

'Because, my Lord, your cloak would be of considerable value to the carter. Men have been murdered for much less, for a few coins, in these hard times. If our carter had murdered the old man's niece, then he would most certainly have stripped both of them of all their valuables – including their clothes – before throwing them into the loch.'

Bothwell heaved a sigh of disappointment. 'So how do you account for all this?'

'Somehow this woman acquired the cloak you gave to Will Fellows. She wrapped it round the old man and bribed the carter to tip him into the loch.'

'But why on earth, in God's name, should she want an old man's corpse?'

'Because, my Lord, she thought and hoped that it would sink to the bottom of the loch. When and if his body was recovered, the fish would have got at it. It would be beyond recognition.'

'But why the cloak, God's sake – my cloak?'

'Don't you see, my Lord, the cloak with your insignia might hopefully be identified and returned to one of your servants. When you heard about it you would believe that, having given it to young Will, it was his body in the loch.'

He paused to let that also sink in. And as its full significance reached Bothwell, he changed colour.

'You mean – you mean,' he whispered, 'that this bitch wanted rid of Will Fellows too.'

Tam nodded, but he thought, No, not quite. She wanted Bothwell to believe that Will Fellows was dead. Somewhere the lad was still alive and somehow he had to find him, for he and the missing dagger that belonged to Anna Throndsen, were the keys to this mystery.

As for the red-headed carter, he did not greatly fancy tracking him down. One of a cutthroat fraternity who accepted bribes to rob or kill without question, he was unlikely to know the real identity of the old woodcutter's wealthy Edinburgh niece.

Tam realized the necessity of caution. Too many questions and he was likely to end up with his own throat cut. He would consider things carefully tomorrow.

Earlier that day in Edinburgh . . .

Walter Pax, advocate and spy in the pay of Lord Thomas Randolph, English secret agent, observed one of his apprentices pause in his labours. The youth was watching my Lord Bothwell, his servant and an unknown man of imposing appearance pass under the window.

Pax too had a special interest in Lord Bothwell, whose every movement, as well as those of Mary of Scotland, was of great interest and concern to the Queen's cousin, Elizabeth of England.

Turning, he looked with great satisfaction at the scene in the room behind him, where his little band of scribes were at work industriously and most carefully copying documents to be forwarded to his master and thence to England.

There were several young lads, mostly apprentices to the guilds, eager to earn a few extra coins for their work. But for security's sake, none was allowed to read or copy a complete document. Pages were withdrawn, and many were coded, given at random to each, so that the vitally important matters remained secret.

This new lad, Ned, who stood by the window was different, brighter than the rest, with a remarkable hand. His writing and copying far outshone all the others.

Pax had the satisfaction of recognizing an expert forger in the making and one who could copy any text presented to him so perfectly that even the Queen herself would not notice the difference.

Ned would go far, for he was quiet and sober and of good family. His father had been a lawyer in Musselburgh, lately deceased, and the lad cared most dutifully for his sick mother and several younger siblings. When he had threatened to leave his employment because of this commitment, to take some work on a farm nearer home, as Pax confided to Lord Randolph, he was immediately offered the use of one of Pax's fine horses so that he might visit his family regularly.

Clever natural forgers were hard to come by and Pax did not want to lose this valuable asset, sure that Lord Randolph and his royal mistress might have a future for young Ned. Which would be greatly to his own advancement should Elizabeth's painstaking efforts to depose her rival queen succeed.

The 'Spanish lady' had looked down on Bothwell as he paused beneath her window. She realized at that moment her power. She could have killed Bothwell then and there. With a pistol at close range she could have blown his head to Kingdom Come.

But that was not her way. She had decided on a long, lingering end, the more painful the better, a stab wound that would keep him awake at night as the agony of his rejection had kept her.

She was in no hurry, and anyway killing him right here would not have been wise. With the hue and cry that would have ensued once my Lord Bothwell was dead beneath the window, escape from the scene would have been difficult with only one door to the street. And she did not greatly fancy being burned. So she would wait patiently and plan with exceeding care, for other chances would certainly occur.

She would follow her quarry to Stirling, to where he fondly imagined he would be safe. The idea made her laugh out loud and gleefully rub her fine hands together.

Bliss to know that she had such power, the power of life and sudden death over this man who had ruined her life.

Chapter Nine

Sunday 8 December 1566. Morning

Awakened once again by the Mass bell, Tam's attempts at recapturing oblivion were in vain. Below his tower room the castle was bristling with activity, its various functions noisy enough for a small town rather than a royal residence, he thought irritably.

More bells – damnation! Then he remembered. Today was the Queen's twenty-fourth birthday, celebrated by special but discreet Catholic masses, Protestant prayers in St Giles and throughout the day humbler celebrations in Edinburgh which the Queen would decline to attend on the grounds of poor health. For those closest to her, however, there would be a banquet this evening, a masque with all the pageantry warranted by such occasions.

A happy thought for six o'clock on a still-black unyielding morning with the usual bitter wind whistling through loose cracks in the masonry, aided and abetted by the draughty keyhole window.

Tam turned over, cocooned in his rough blanket, and sought a more comfortable place on the lumpy straw paliasse. He closed his eyes firmly, no longer afraid of what the instant of reawakening might reveal.

He was growing accustomed to his present circumstances, losing his fears that each time he opened his eyes, it would be to find himself reinstated in one of those unpleasant scenes familiar in vivid dreams which eluded him on waking.

Last night his slumbers had been disturbed by a re-enactment of the events at Duddingston Loch, considering possible and impossible explanations regarding the carter lad's mysterious disappearance. All his theories which seemed plausible he now discarded as baseless, the product of early morning, when nightmares seem considerably more real than reality itself. His mind had scurried back and forth like a rat trapped in a cage, reliving over and over the scene by the water.

The old man's corpse and the significance of Bothwell's cloak as shroud. The missing cart which obstinately refused to fit any pattern of logic. Unlikely that it had plunged into the water, taking the two live occupants to their deaths. Had there been an accident such as a loose wheel? The carter was young and the woman's prompt actions over her departed 'uncle' did not suggest infirmity. Surely both could have leapt clear. And if they had done so, where was the wreckage of the shattered cart?

Supposing, then, that the woman had bribed the lad and had even given him a helping hand to dispose of the old man? That was the most promising explanation, the one Tam always came back to, taking into account the dubious character of the red-headed carter, as related by the woodcutters. As for the 'fine lady', evidence from yesterday's visit to Greyfriars kirkyard proved for Tam, beyond any doubt, that she was not the old man's niece, but most probably Bothwell's would-be assassin.

He might be doing her an injustice, a victim of the carter's greed, her body still in the waters of the loch, trapped by weeds. But he did not think so. He had an intuitive feeling that she was alive and well and somewhere dangerously close at hand.

But for what reason? And what of Fellows himself? He had vaguely indicated to Bothwell that he worked at Craigmillar. He was unknown to the gardeners and woodcutters. However, Tam reckoned there were many areas near to the castle, such as Niddrie, where Fellows was quite possibly not an unusual name but enquiries from well-spoken persons from the court were unwelcome. Persons like himself, regarded with suspicion by ordinary folk, had ranks closed firmly against them.

Aware that there were now two missing persons vital to his fine theory – Will Fellows and the Red Crozer lad – whatever his personal fears regarding further investigation of the latter, he felt obliged to return without delay to the woodcutters. Armed with instructions about the whereabouts of the notorious thieving family, he would pay them a visit, no doubt taking his life in his hands by doing so.

If the fine lady had resorted to bribery, then so too could he, using the lure of Bothwell's purse, and if that failed, the threat of the powerful Earl's wrath should prove irresistible.

As the noise below increased in volume, reducing any hopes of further sleep, he left his bed wearily, only moderately consoled by the fact that the Queen's birthday celebrations might offer the chance of a little dalliance with Marie Seton. This appealing prospect quite overcame any sense of urgency about tracking down the Red Crozers.

That, he decided firmly, could be safely set aside until the morrow, for as he descended the stair, the arrow-slits rewarded him with the promise of a surprisingly pleasant day.

The blackness of pre-dawn had given way to a dramatic sunrise over the landscape, yielding to cloudless blue skies. Edinburgh had decided to show its best possible face for a Queen who deserved some kindness. No easy matter for the celestial weatherman in December to present a day mild as springtime.

There was warmth in the wintry sun and, viewed from high in the castle, the melting snow on Arthur's Seat glistened like sugar on a celebration cake fit for Her Grace's birthday.

Waiting tactfully until he heard Bothwell emerge from Janet Beaton's apartment, Tam looked in to receive his mistress's orders for the day.

Janet yawned wearily, regarded him heavy-eyed with no doubt satisfying reasons of her own lack of sleep.

'Her Grace is feeling much better, we are told, and she will ride on Arthur's Seat, to her favourite place at Hunter's Bog.'

An hour later a little troop assembled in the courtyard and rode out of the castle, taking the road through Duddingston, by the place where yesterday Tam and Bothwell had encountered the fishermen with their mysterious corpse. All was quiet. There had been no more gruesome discoveries.

The Queen was in merry mood and Bothwell rode at her side. Often they reined in and exchanged a few words, which was noted by others than Tam. How close they seemed, how pleasant a sound their laughter made, floating back to the rest of the court.

This moment of joy in the Queen's life was one to be treasured, a time when she could forget her youthful disillusion with a disastrous marriage and fall in love again, know the passion of surrender for one fine perfect hour.

Let no one deny her that right, he thought, for such was true happiness, never to look ahead, to enjoy and cherish each happy moment the fates allowed us in this brief mortal life.

At his side, Janet was not enjoying a happy moment. Her conversation was somewhat more acid than usual, her patience thinner. For the first time Tam saw beyond the façade and recognized that her youthfulness was on the wane. Was it realization that she was losing her power over the young Earl or some deeper sorrow?

Suddenly she turned to him, looked into his eyes, a penetrating gaze of undisguised despair. He turned away hastily, but too late.

She laughed bitterly. 'I ken what you are thinking, Tam.' And, cutting short his polite protests, 'You are right. I am growing old. I've never admitted it to anyone, but I don't mind you knowing or seeing me as I am.' With a shrewd glance, she added, 'Time and ageing are beyond your control too, Tam. We are out of the same mould. I have long been aware of that.' She shook her head. 'My concern is not at losing Jamie Hepburn. God knows, I've lost him to many women before, younger than me, bonnier by far, but he has always come back.'

Like last night, thought Tam, and he said lightly, 'Surely the Wizard Lady of Branxholm has spells for such matters.'

She shook her head. 'I have lost my powers, Tam. I learned long ago that there is no magic against love. Besides, I cannot rival a Queen. So this time, alas, he will not come back to me – ever.' And Tam felt a chill of foreboding as she added in a whisper, 'This time his love will destroy him. He cannot win and he will take the Queen with him to her death.'

The weather seemed to agree with her gloomy forecast. The azure sky had darkened and heavy storm clouds gathered overhead. A distant rumble of thunder in the air.

The word was given: 'Enough. The Queen commands that we return.'

The bright day is over and we are for the dark. Words he had read in someone else's tragedy, Tam thought, as the gates of the castle closed upon them.

Tam was looking forward to the planned events of the evening, knowing that the cooks had been preparing the birthday banquet for several days – and nights. There had been no chance to talk with Marie Seton, since the morning's ride to Hunter's Bog had seen her well to the fore with the Maries, all of them remaining at a discreet distance from the Queen and Bothwell, an effective barrier against the rest of the party.

Frustrated by having no legitimate reason to catch up with her, without causing undue anger by breaking the rules of precedence, which were strictly adhered to both indoors and out, Tam could but hope that he would have more success that evening.

On the tables set in the great hall, gone was the everyday fare of pigeons from the garden dovecote, roasted or boiled, and from the fishpond, trout and perch. Home-brewed ale gave place to French brandy and wines as Mary and her court sat down to Lorraine soup, a French soup invented for the Queen, veal-based and rich in almonds, eggs, cream and delicate herbs. This was followed by venison *à la reine*, her mother's favourite, a haunch of meat soaked in claret for six hours before cooking. Veal or salmon flory, and for those whose lusty appetites could accommodate sweetmeats, caramelized and candied fruits, fruits *en chemise*, chantilly and caramel baskets.

Tam thought the Queen had never looked lovelier. Gone too was the informality of winter dress. She wore white satin, richly jewelled with pearls and diamonds on her gown and in her hair, elaborately dressed by Marie Seton, who excelled in that art which she had learned in France.

The meal over, the Queen was escorted to her canopy of state, where she sat with Bothwell on the raised dais at her feet. He was leaning on one elbow talking to her, thoroughly at home. Both were oblivious of the shocked court, who regarded this familiarity with revulsion. None but members of the royal family were permitted to sit in the Queen's presence on such occasions.

Tam also noticed that the Queen's magnificent attire failed to conceal her nervous hands. They were never still, plucking at her gown, toying with her strands of pearls.

Sometimes her head drooped, a beautiful flower too heavy for its slender stalk. Food and wine were taking their toll. Exhausted, dazed with weariness, she was beyond caring for the court's ritual.

Tam felt compassion for this still-sick, frail woman whose day of intense activity had been rather too much for her. At her side, Tam observed, Bothwell spoke low, tender, protective and rather anxious, as one would be about a wife. Such behaviour was noted by the onlookers either with nudges and sentimental smiles or with scowls of resentment, depending on where the two sat in their emotions and ambitions.

At last the signal was given for the evening's entertainment to begin. Those who could be aroused from the effects of the banquet and were not fighting off sleep were amused by a touching birthday masque performed by the Maries, attired in costumes appropriate to the four seasons.

Tam was enchanted by Seton's Spring, the smallest and youngest of the four as they recited poems to the Queen, addressing her as Diana the huntress, for her love of sport, and Venus, goddess of love, celebrating her beauty, the assuredness of a long and happy reign.

The Queen, laughing now, applauded louder than anyone as the four shyly curtsied and withdrew from the dais, hustled away by her female fools, who took the stage and made even greater fools of themselves in front of everyone, their blistering comments to the audience's delight.

Like the Maries, they had been with the Queen in France. Excellent mimics, their behaviour was outrageous, but no one seemed to mind, least of all those whom they were impersonating.

As the performance ended Seton came to Tam's side. Soon the Queen would retire, but he was hopeful that Marie might be allowed to stay, especially as the wine he was drinking was having an effect on him. And looking at Marie he longed again to hold her in his arms and kiss her. Without a word, he took her hand and led her out of the hall towards where he knew there was a quiet room sometimes used by the queen's courtiers awaiting an audience.

His heart was hammering but, alas, it was not to be.

'Marie!'

They turned and Marie curtsied to the elderly courtier who had followed them. 'Uncle.'

As he was introduced by Marie, Tam had no difficulty in recognizing her uncle, Sir Anthony Pieris, scowling at him ominously.

Averting his eyes, as if the sight of Tam offended him, Pieris said, 'I am aware that Master Eildor is Lady Buccleuch's servant.' Laying stress upon the word, he added, 'What business has he with you, niece?'

Marie shook her head. 'Why, none at all, Uncle.'

'Let it be so,' Pieris said sternly, taking hold of her arm without a glance in Tam's direction. 'Come with me.'

Meekly Marie obeyed, curtsying to Tam. He watched them leave and saw her look back quickly in his direction with an apologetic, despairing glance.

He also heard Pieris, who was rather deaf and therefore spoke loudly to everyone, say, 'You are aware, are you not, niece, that no man is permitted to be alone with the Queen's Maries unless he is married? Her Grace will look very gravely upon this . . .'

And then they were out of earshot. But doubtless Tam was meant to hear and doubtless Pieris would be reporting the incident to Marie's brother, Lord Seton, who would not welcome the remotest possibility of one of his illustrious family having her reputation sullied by associating with a servant.

For that was Tam's lowly position, however much he was favoured by the Wizard Lady of Branxholm. In the eyes of the court, he was still and would remain a menial. And what was worse in his own eyes, one who had no past by which he might lay claim to breeding, and no hope of betterment.

Sounds of riotous mirth issued from the hall, drinking and carousing that would go on until the small hours, until those who were able crept away to bed, while others dropped their heads on the table or slept where they fell.

Tam envied them their oblivion. Sobered by the meeting with Sir Anthony Pieris and his chastisement of Marie, he was in no mood to join the festivities. Making his way through the castle towards the tower and trying to avoid tripping over, or being cursed by more fortunate lovers seeking privacy in dark corners, he consoled himself that Pieris's arrival had been fortuitous.

Had he come upon them moments later behind closed doors, with his young niece in a compromising situation, he would have had even more to report to Lord Seton.

That would have signalled the end of Tam's career and his freedom. Servants have rotted in prison and died for less, he thought. And climbing the stairs to his bleak and lonely bed, he wondered where the Queen and Bothwell were at this moment.

As he walked softly past Janet Beaton's apartment,

her door flew open. 'Ah, there you are, Tam. Come in.'
She thrust a sheaf of documents into his hand. 'You
are to make all haste to Branxholm tomorrow. Matters
there seriously need your attention and, I suspect, all
your skills. I would go myself if the Queen permitted.'
Her manner softened and she sighed. 'I know I can
rely on you, Tam. I had not thought to be away from
home this long. Would that I did not have to go to
Stirling, but the Queen – and my Lord Bothwell – insist
that I attend the Prince's christening. They feel that
my presence will bring him luck. I cannot think why,'
she added with a weary sigh. 'The Queen makes no
move these days without my Lord Bothwell and he
makes no move – or so he says – without me.'

'Shall I await you at Branxholm when my work is
complete?'

'Nay, Tam, you are to come to Stirling.' She smiled
at his glum expression. 'This is a great royal occasion.
A once in a lifetime experience. We rarely see more
than one future king of Scotland being baptized in a
normal mortal's life. A time to remember.'

Tam bowed. 'I will leave in the morning. I had
intended looking into some matters concerning my
Lord Bothwell's safety . . .' He paused, wondering how
much Bothwell had told her.

Reading his expression, she nodded. 'Aye, the carter
and the corpse wrapped in his cloak. My Lord Bothwell
spared me no details. Indeed, he kept us both awake
with some wild imaginings.' She shook her head. 'But
I am sure there is a perfectly logical explanation and
that none of this has anything to do with that supposed
attack, by some woman or other. I can tell you, I rue
the day I reminded him of Anna Throndsen!' She

laughed bitterly. 'You need not concern yourself any more, Tam. I try to console him that once he reaches Stirling, it is unlikely that this silly woman his guilty conscience has invented will follow him there. He is making a great drama out of it, but whatever his ideas about her identity, I suspect it is merely some woman he has tumbled in the hay, taken her for a servant without realizing her identity, and she is seeking revenge. Doubtless by now her blood has cooled and she will have thought better of the enterprise.' And, with a shrug, 'Or met some more reliable lover.'

Tam wished he could believe her, but thought better than to argue. He could put forward convincing evidence that she was wrong, certain that the woman who wanted Bothwell dead did not remotely resemble the description Janet was prepared to accept.

'You will need to leave early, but not too early, Tam.' She smiled. 'For I have some cheering news for you. Before leaving for Stirling, Seton is going with Fleming to Haddington to visit an elderly aunt, a relative of Maitland's. They will need an escort and perhaps this will not be too onerous a duty for you.' She gave him an arch glance. 'Just a small diversion on the way to Branxholm. The two Maries always look in on my Lord Bothwell's mother at Morham, as it is quite nearby. The Dowager Countess has had a difficult life, with much to put up with – a disagreeable husband who chose to woo the Queen's mother, left her with Jamie and a sister, Janet, who married Her Grace's half-brother, Lord John Stewart. They live at another of the Bothwell strongholds, Crichton Castle.

'The "Fair Earl", as he was called, on account of his complexion rather than his character, gave Morham and its estates to his wife as compensation, and she has lived there ever since. Her son visits her all too rarely. Her health is poor and she is almost blind, but her mind is as sharp as ever. And she now has the companionship of a small grandson. A lovely child,' she added wistfully, 'and she's devoted to him.'

Chapter Ten

Monday 9 December 1566. Morning

Tam was diverted and delighted at the prospect of spending a few hours in Marie's company, but he had not bargained for the small army who made up the escort: Bothwell's 'servants', steel-helmeted, stern-faced and keeping their own counsel. Allied to the watchful looks of mosstroopers, they carried an impressive armoury of weapons, suitable for all occasions, from fierce foray to ambush.

Tam eyed them nervously, wondering if they were expecting trouble on this particular outing or if this was normal when they escorted Bothwell or those under his care.

The need for caution became evident, however, once they left the safety of Craigmillar and the city of Edinburgh behind them. Their progress was through a wild land made more dangerous by their halting progress on inaccessible winter roads. Bothwell's mosstroopers were a daunting prospect and only by moving in the protection of armed men could travellers be safe from wolves in winter.

And there were greater dangers as they rode past

isolated camps inhabited by the broken men, thieves and cutthroats as predatory as any of the wild animals.

The road, where it existed as other than a muddy track, seemed peaceful enough, but Tam was disappointed and frustrated at seeing little prospect of speaking to Marie alone.

Instead he found himself riding by the side of the lovely Fleming, the subject of much scurrilous whispering for agreeing to marry a middle-aged man like the Queen's ambitious Secretary of State, Maitland of Lethington, who was devoted to her. Regardless of rumours circulating about their behaviour, particularly from the direction of John Knox, who had a very dirty mind, Fleming seemed equally entranced by her lover, even though he was old enough to be her father.

Tam soon discovered he had an ally in Fleming. Watching him looking so hopefully in Seton's direction, and either unaware of or disregarding rules and regulations expressed by Sir Anthony Pieris, she rode ahead on several occasions and remained out of earshot, with her own maid as well as Seton's, leaving the two together.

Tam and Seton exchanged smiling glances as Fleming looked back and kissed her fingers to them. Happy, with her own future assured, she was sentimental and romantic, prepared to be kindly disposed to others not so fortunate who, she fancied, shared her blissful state of being in love.

But however Seton's reckless inclinations towards Tam might be interpreted by her companions, her future was not assured. She was ill-advised, blind to the folly of linking her dreams with a servant. Her brother's anger and disapproval would make it perfectly plain that under no circumstances whatever could their particular romance have a happy ending. Even if Tam had been able to offer a reliable future. Or any sort of future at all.

Older and wiser, sadder too, Tam was aware that he brought no licence for compromise from his former life. Whatever his change in circumstances, his personality and moral outlook were unaffected.

As for Marie, the only way loving him would end was in misery, and shame. A hastily arranged marriage with someone of her brother's choosing and God only knew what horrors for himself, for his audacity.

And yet time mocked them, for this was a day for love. The trees cathedral-like above their heads were a fine woven tracery against a cloudless sky. Great birds, corbies and ravens, circled the ancient prehistoric mound of Tarprain Law and on the road far below them another of Bothwell's strongholds, Hailes Castle, the one-time scene of his father's wooing of Mary de Guise.

At Tam's side Marie, as if aware of his preoccupation, enquired anxiously about his loss of memory, which concerned her deeply. But as he had no past beyond a bewildering labyrinth of dream places, he could offer no consolation of the kind she no doubt wished to hear.

Glad to change the subject, he encouraged her to talk of her home at Seton, on the East Lothian coastline, a short distance from Craigmillar.

'Fleming, Livingtone and I all lost grandfathers who fell at Flodden at the side of Her Grace's grandfather King James.' She sighed. 'Such a disaster for Scotland, the flower of our noble lords died on the field that day.

My family were fortunate to have heirs to carry on the name, for the Setons have always had close connections with the throne. One of my ancestors married the sister of Robert the Bruce,' she added proudly. 'Seton House is a favourite retreat of Her Grace. She and Lord Darnley spent their honeymoon with us.' She smiled sadly remembering those joyful days before the Queen's happy world collapsed and, turning to Tam, she whispered, 'I hope some day soon I will be able to show you Seton. I want you to see all the lovely things there that I treasure.'

Tam murmured his thanks, without any hopes at all that such a privilege would ever come his way, at least not while her brother, Lord Seton, was in residence.

A shout ahead at a distant prospect of Haddington.

'Morham is just a short distance now,' said Marie.

'Our ways part there, Marie.'

'Must you leave us so soon?'

'I fear so. The weather is with us and I hope to make Branxholm before nightfall.'

Remote and barely visible until they left the steep hill twisting down and away from the drover's road, a tiny village clustered around Morham, a modest peel tower hardly to be classed as a castle after the grandeur of Craigmillar.

As Tam prepared to leave the group at the gates, Fleming smiled, 'Surely you need not leave us immediately, Master Eildor. Will you not stay and make the acquaintance of the Lady Morham?'

'Please do, Master Eildor.' This eagerly from Seton,

her eyes suddenly hopeful. 'She sees few people and yearns for company.'

'Indeed, she is especially fond of Lady Buccleuch. She will be eager to have news of her,' said Fleming.

'Before she turned lame, Lady Morham often visited Branxholm,' added Seton breathlessly.

Tam smiled. Such an invitation was irresistible and he followed them into the courtyard, where Bothwell's men, who seemed to know their way about, headed wordlessly in the direction of the kitchens.

The two Maries led the way through a walled garden, informing Tam that Lady Morham had been a keen gardener before her eyesight and her legs threatened to fail her.

Through a tiny door leading along a narrow corridor to wide spiral stairs, they emerged in the main hall. Stone-flagged and raftered, it had a well-used, comfortable feeling. Chairs upholstered in Spanish leather, rugs and animal skins on the floor, tapestries hiding rough stone walls, a large table and armoire and, best of all, a roaring fire in the vast fireplace.

Seton smiled. 'Winter and summer, it is ever thus. Lady Morham feels the cold somewhat these days.'

From a high-backed chair, Bothwell's mother turned to greet them. She clapped her hands and a servant appeared. Food and ale were ordered.

Obviously the two Maries were great favourites and welcome guests. Acknowledging Tam briefly, she indicated that he was dismissed.

Seton leaned forward. 'Master Eildor is Lady Buccleuch's steward, madam. She thinks highly of him.'

'A most valued servant,' prompted Fleming. 'He was trusted to see us safely on our journey.'

Lady Morham seemed impressed by the two girls' enthusiasm and this glowing reference. Studying Tam – whom she could not distinguish all that well, though she was at pains to conceal this disability – she nodded and said, 'I trust Lady Buccleuch is well.'

Tam bowed. 'Exceeding well, madam.'

Lady Morham's polite nod indicated dismissal as she turned eagerly to talk of preparations for Fleming's forthcoming wedding, to be celebrated on Twelfth Night in the Chapel Royal at Stirling Castle. The discussion led to suitable gowns and disappointment that Livingstone's baby girl was too young to attend as maid to the bride.

With no part in this women's gossip, his presence by the door ignored apart from an occasional apologetic glance from Marie to indicate that he still existed, Tam wondered how soon he could take a polite departure once he had a bite to eat and drink.

'And when are we to find you a husband, dear child?' Lady Morham asked Seton, who blushed prettily.

'I hope some day, madam,' she murmured.

Lady Morham patted her hand. 'Make it soon, my dear. It is time you were wed. I shall have a word with your brother. Get him to see to it.'

Marie darted a despairing look in Tam's direction. A look that made his heart beat the faster. But alas, his dear Seton was proving to be a poor actress, one who wore her heart not on her sleeve but in her eyes, for all the world to see.

Was she so infatuated that she was stubbornly

oblivious of the dangers of her family's disappoval for them both? The hopelessness of the situation between herself, the daughter of a powerful family of nobles and companion to the Queen of Scots, and the Branxholm Castle steward, a man of mystery whom no one knew anything about. A man who owed his present role solely to Janet Beaton's interest in him and her influence at court.

And thinking of Janet, he turned his attention to Bothwell's mother, who, although her contemporary, looked considerably older. In youth her resemblance to her son had been marked by russet hair and fox-brown eyes. Tam knew from Janet that as Agnes Sinclair, she had married her cousin the 'Fair Earl', Patrick Hepburn, both orphaned by the Battle of Flodden. When his burning ambition led to a violent and almost insane pursuit of the Queen's mother, Mary de Guise, and an insistence that she had agreed to marry him, in readiness he divorced Agnes on the grounds of consanguinity, a useful excuse.

Perhaps it was in the blood, thought Tam wryly. If Patrick had survived death from consumption at forty-four, would he have cheered on his son and heir, who had inherited a similar taste for a Scottish Queen?

A door opened at the far end of the hall and a small figure appeared dressed for outdoors in a furred robe and bonnet, clutching a serving-man's hand.

'William – is that you? Come here, dearest.'

The boy ran to her, hitched on to her knee and looked round the company as he was solemnly introduced as her beloved grandson. Five years old, unmistakably Bothwell's son, thought Tam, for he had inherited the hair colour, the wide mouth that already held something of his father's expression.

Only the eyes did not belong to that pattern. They were large, so grey that they looked black. Huge tragic eyes, too large for the small face, and too sad by far for a child.

Lady Morham hugged him to her, kissed him, stroked back his hair. As the two Maries went forward and knelt beside the chair, adding their caresses, Lady Morham nodded over their heads in Tam's direction.

'William is the sunlight in my life. He has been with me almost since his birth.'

'When did he lose his parents, madam?' asked Tam, who knew the answer quite well.

'Alas, his mother found it necessary to return to her own land when my son was forced into a political marriage,' she replied, sighing.

So that was the story Lady Morham had been told, or pretended to believe, thought Tam, as she continued. 'His father does come to see him when he can be spared, but court duties make it difficult.' She smiled into space.

Poor lady, but poorer child, Tam thought. He was angry for them both, aware of Bothwell's self-confessed indifference, with Morham but an hour's ride from Edinburgh.

Kissing the top of William's head, Lady Morham, whispered 'But we have each other, have we not, dearest?'

The child looked up at her, nodded solemnly, put his arms around her neck and hugged her. It was a touching moment.

'Yes, grandmother, we have each other,' he repeated, like an oft-learned lesson.

As he slid from her knee, she said, 'Off you go now, dear boy, it is time for your ride.'

'Yes, grandmother.' He kissed her hand, bowed to her gravely and once more for the Maries, then with all dignity swept aside he scampered across the floor, shouting for the servant who waited by the door.

'What a lovely child he is,' said Seton wistfully.

'I swear he grows each time we visit,' Fleming laughed. 'You must be so proud of him, madam.'

All this pleased his grandmother, who sighed. 'He is a dear sweet child and, alas, sore neglected all his life but for my attention.' She brightened. 'But I have to tell you all that will end soon.' At their enquiring looks, she said, 'Have you not heard, my dears, his dear aunt Dorothy, his mother's eldest – and, she tells me, her favourite – sister is here on a visit from the Shetland Isles. She at least wishes to see more of her little nephew.' She paused. 'Such a tragic story. Poor Dorothy married a Shetlander, a merchant named John Sinclair, a man of means who traded with Norway and Denmark. He was introduced to the Throndsen family while the admiral was living in Copenhagen. And there he met his future wife.' She frowned. 'That would be ten years ago – or more. There was only one child to the marriage, a son who died in infancy. Two years ago, Master Sinclair was drowned when his ship was attacked by English pirates patrolling the Scottish coast.'

There were sympathetic murmurs before she continued: 'Dorothy was desolate and I understand that Shetland is a very bleak and lonely place, especially in winter. She has long had a fancy to see Edinburgh, for Anna told her much about it when she visited Shetland on her return journeys from Scotland. And being childless, poor Dorothy has long wished to see her little nephew.' She took Seton's hand. 'You would love her, my dear. You could not wish to meet a sweeter or more gentle lady. I am quite captivated by her and, as for William, the dear child recognizes goodness and they took to each other immediately.' She smiled sadly. 'I believe there is quite another reason for this visit to Edinburgh which is that it is in his aunt's mind to persuade her sister that she should adopt little William. Indeed, that would be the happiest future for the child and it suits us both well.' With a shake of her head, she added; 'Alas, my infirmities will not improve with time. And Dorothy has no intention of taking my little darling away from me. With naught to keep her in Shetland, she wishes to settle in Scotland.' She sighed. 'My health is indifferent and I am indeed relieved and comforted to know that when I am gone William will have his aunt to love and care for him. As his parents have failed to do.' She ended on this hollow note, speaking as if to herself, staring bleakly into the fire.

For a while no one spoke. Then, suddenly aware of them again, Lady Morham gave a start and apologized. 'It is wrong of me to make judgements, but his mother abandoned him when she finally returned home and left him, a mere infant, in my care, hoping that my son Jamie would be a true father and provide for him, give him an education and in due course a place at court.' She looked at them almost tearfully and pointed towards the door through which William had departed. 'That child has been used, used all his life. I believe Anna never thought of him other than as a means to further her own ambition. With William as heir to the Earldom of Bothwell, she fondly believed this would put pressure on Jamie to legalize their marriage.' She laughed harshly. 'She did not know my son! What cares he for his own flesh and blood. He rarely comes to Morham. Looks in on us for an hour or so, pats the child's head, throws him a coin and is gone again. I am not unaware that he has important matters to attend to at court, that he is well thought of by the Queen and is in charge of the Prince's christening at Stirling. But surely, surely – ' she spread her hands wide – 'no matter can be more important than his only son – his only child so far,' she added significantly, 'who could be his heir.'

'As for his mother, 'tis years since she saw her son, occasional letters are all that come from Norway. You know she returned there when her father, the Admiral, died, to devote herself to caring for her widowed mother who was in poor health. One might reasonably have thought some consideration would be given to the child she was leaving in Scotland,' she added bitterly.

Fleming broke the small unhappy silence with a practical question: 'Has Mistress Sinclair reason to believe her sister will support her plans for adopting William?'

'I fancy she will be glad to have him off her hands, for all the devotion she has ever shown.' She nodded eagerly. 'Indeed, Dorothy is quite confident that this is so. Especially as her sister can no longer entertain the faintest hopes of using William for her original purpose, now that he is wed to Lady Jean Gordon. Happily, I hope,' she added somewhat forlornly.

As if suddenly aware of their solemn faces around her, she straightened her shoulders and said, 'But I do go on. Let us say I have great faith in Dorothy's intentions for little William.'

Heads were shaken sympathetically, murmurs of agreement, and then, to everyone's relief, food and ale appeared at last, were consumed, and then it was time to depart.

As they rose to leave, Lady Morham embraced Seton and Fleming: ''Tis pity you have to go to Stirling so soon. In fact, had you come a day later, you would have met dear Dorothy who has gone to Edinburgh to engage lawyers about various matters concerning the matter of her property in Shetland and, of course, legal documents concerning William's adoption, which must be sent to Norway for her sister's approval.' She shook her head. 'Such matters take some time.'

As they kissed her goodbye, the two Maries adding their good wishes for a speedy settlement, Tam remembered how Bothwell had told him that Dorothy was Anna Throndsen's favourite sister, and once established as Countess of Bothwell, wished to see her family elevated to some position of importance.

Described by Lady Morham as a sweet and gentle caring woman, widowed and childless and eager to adopt Anna's neglected child, Tam also regretted that Mistress Sinclair had not been present. He would have liked to hear more about her sister and, bowing over Lady Morham's hand, he resolved to call in again at Morham on his return journey from Branxholm, with just such a prospect and a valid excuse in mind.

With neither time nor opportunity among the gawping faces of servants to do more than bow and wish godspeed to Seton and Fleming, Tam and four of Bothwell's mosstroopers turned their horses' heads towards Branxholm, the remaining escort continuing to Haddington with the two Maries.

As they rode away, Tam mused on the information he had received. If, as Lady Morham stated, Anna had long been settled in Norway, keeping her invalid mother company, she presumably had not set foot in Scotland in recent times. In that case, then, they were nowhere nearer discovering the identity of the mysterious Spanish lady who wanted Bothwell's death.

Chapter Eleven

Morham. Friday 13 December 1566. Noon

Dawn had settled into the promise of a bright cold day as Tam started off on his thirty-mile ride from Branxholm back to Craigmillar hoping to join the last of the baggage train leaving for Stirling Castle. He felt it imperative to visit Morham again and make the acquaintance of Mistress Sinclair, on the off chance that she would have knowledge of her sister's whereabouts. Or at least confirm that she was still in Norway, taking care of her widowed mother.

He had not intended spending so long at Branxholm, but his plans had been frustrated by bad weather that, though it might have been expected at this time of year, had not been foreseen by Janet Beaton, despite her legendary powers in other matters concerning the future.

Worsening conditions had put paid to activities both in and out of the castle. Being slowed down by places and tenants made inaccessible after a heavy fall of snow was one thing, but considerable effort was also needed to re-establish order within a household rapidly descending into chaos in the continued absence of Lady Buccleuch or an active steward on the premises.

Tam spent his time overseeing repairs to the roof – buckets and pans were in constant demand to keep the rooms dry – having larders replenished from dove-cotes, shooting wild game and hares on the estate. He was fortunate in the knowledge that the icehouse could be relied upon.

Because of the transience of his visit, in desperation Tam sought the advice and assistance of the old steward, Mark Scott, concerning tenancy life-rents, documents relating to a contested legacy from one of Lady Buccleuch's uncles and further complications offered by the opposed dowry from the second marriage of her eldest daughter.

At Mark Scott's bedside sat his grandson Jacob, working as a carpenter on the estate. An intelligent young man, last of a family who had served Branxholm for generations, Jacob had benefited from his grand-father's teaching and had inherited his way with words and figures.

His eagerness to be helpful brought Tam to a decision to appoint the twenty-year-old as temporary steward. Jacob was delighted, proud to take on the responsibility. Any passing doubts Tam might have had, were assuaged by the knowledge that his grand-father could advise from his sick-bed and, in an emergency, supply the requisite knowledge.

Also in his favour, as far as Tam was concerned, was the fact that Jacob was on amiable terms with other members of the household, most of whom had known him since childhood and, newly married, his young wife held a position of authority in the kitchens.

It was the best Tam could do in the circumstances, until Lady Buccleuch's return from Stirling, and he hoped she would approve of his decision. Jacob Scott was such an obvious choice and while wondering why it had not occurred to his grandfather to put forward his name as his successor, Tam also recognized this as a matter of some urgency, similar to the preparation of a last will and testament.

Of one thing he was certain: his time here was limited and he would not remain the Branxholm steward indefinitely. One day memory of his past existence must return, to unleash its disruptive elements on his present life.

Involved with his thoughts he almost missed the road down to Morham, but it was almost as if his horse knew the way. No horseman, Tam was learning respect for Janet's fine bay, Ajax. With time at his disposal, he might even come to regard riding as a pleasure, rather than a gruelling and uncomfortable necessity, since horses were the swiftest means of travel available.

Even the Queen and her Maries rode everywhere, whenever possible. Litters and unwieldy carriages were only for sick women and the elderly.

As he approached the courtyard at Morham, he saw that the iron gates were firmly closed. Waiting for a servant to answer the clanging bell's noisy summons, he remembered fondly that other arrival just a few days earlier with the two Maries, familiar visitors who arrived informally by way of the walled garden and who would now be comfortably installed at Stirling with their royal mistress.

He tried not to dwell on the long weary ride ahead of him and concentrate instead on the pleasant prospect at the end of it. The joy of seeing Marie Seton again.

Meanwhile, he was growing impatient, as no servant had appeared. The courtyard beyond the gate looked ominously deserted and, with an unhappy feeling that his journey was in vain, he rang the bell vigorously once again – this time with more success. A liveried footman appeared and peered at him resentfully through the iron bars.

Without any attempt at opening the gate, the man demanded his business. On being told that Master Tam Eildor wished to see Lady Morham, he answered, 'Lady Morham is away from home.'

'When do you expect her to return?'

The man shrugged and gave Tam a superior look. 'I have no instructions regarding Her Ladyship's return.'

'Have you no idea? Today – tomorrow?' said Tam desperately.

'I believe we might expect her in a few days.'

Turning to leave, Tam remembered the real reason for his visit. 'Mistress Sinclair? Perhaps she will see me.'

'No,' was the firm reply.

'She is not at home?'

The man shrugged. 'I believe she is at present with Lady Morham.'

'Would you know their destination?' Tam asked. 'I am a friend of Lord Bothwell, I visited Lady Morham last week with Lady Seton and Lady Fleming.'

Where all else had failed, mention of his illustrious friends worked wonders. The man's grim expression softened. 'Ah, sir, yes of course, I do recall your visit. I understand there is a birthday party at Traquair. Master

William has been invited and it is a rare thing for the lad to have the chance of the company of other bairns,'

Perhaps aware he was saying too much of what was common gossip in the kitchens, he paused, cleared his throat and added, 'However, sir, if your business is urgent . . .'

Tam thanked him and left. Wishing he could think up some valid excuse to appear, uninvited, at Traquair, deep in thought he headed back towards the Edinburgh road.

An hour later, when he should have been within sight of Craigmillar, Tam wondered seriously if he had lost the way. The sun was slipping towards the horizon and the sky had darkened ominously. Often now as he paused and looked over his shoulder, a prickling sensation at the back of his neck told him that he was being followed.

Urging Ajax on, he realized he had completely ignored the perils of travelling alone in this wild area. He had not given it much consideration leaving Branxholm, as the area was very much under Bothwell's surveillance and jurisdiction. His safety had been assured with the mosstroopers, who departed at Branxholm without any questions relating to his return to Craigmillar. Presumably it had been expected of him to arrange such matters, instead of setting off without a thought to the dangers that might beset a lone traveller.

Too late now.

Even as he panicked, the bushes around him erupted into several men who rushed forward and seized his bridle. Using his whip, he fought them off, determined to leave his mark if this was to be his fate. He kicked out with his feet too, but only succeeded in unseating himself. As he fell to the ground, they were on him, punching and kicking.

'The horse, get it,' someone yelled, but Ajax was away, racing through the wood.

'Come along, you,' another cried.

They dragged him to his feet.

So they weren't about to rob and kill him on the spot, that was a relief. They led him through the trees and into a small encampment, with a very smoky fire and the smell of unappetizing cooking.

His eyes smarted and, when the mists cleared, he saw he was surrounded by a group of rough-looking customers, distinguished by heads of varying shades of red hair.

He groaned inwardly. He had fallen foul of the Red Crozers. Struggling in vain as they bound him hand and foot to the nearest tree, his mind worked rapidly, only to reach the conclusion that whatever their purpose in taking him prisoner, he need entertain little hope of escape. Especially when one of the men came forward and pressed a murderous-looking knife point against his throat.

'Where's Archie?' he demanded.

'Archie,' gasped Tam. 'I don't know any Archie.'

There was a growl of disbelief as the man turned to others who had moved closer.

An exceedingly pretty, very young, very pregnant girl with long red hair pushed her way to the front. 'Let me have that knife, faither. I'll soon mak him talk.'

Tam gulped. He had no doubt that she would. She looked even fiercer than her father, at that moment having the knife wrested from his grasp.

'Hold on,' said Tam desperately. 'Hold on. Who is this Archie? I don't think I've had the pleasure—'

Angry derision greeted this denial and shouts of 'Kill him, kill him!' The girl stepped forward in an unmistakably menacing fashion, urged on – if she needed urging – by the more bloodthirsty members of her family.

'You are making a terrible mistake,' said Tam frantically as she stood on tiptoe and the knife point, inexpertly held, drew blood. He felt it trickle down his neck.

'It's yersel makin the mistake, takin' Archie.'

Tam moved his head back as far as possible, but the tree was in the way. The knife hovered. The girl was enjoying herself.

'Is Archie your husband?' he demanded.

She stared up into his face and her lip quivered. 'Tell him, faither, tell him afore I slit his throat.'

'There, there, lass.' The violent man showed some tenderness, putting his arm around her.

The action suggested there might be sense here at last, and Tam appealed to him, in what could be his last chance. 'For God's sake, man. Who is Archie – is he your son?'

'Nay. His father's gone long sine. We've had the caring for Jenny since she was a wee lass and they were to have been wed twa' days sine. We had all prepared, the minister brought – and Archie never came.'

'He never came!' screamed the jilted bride. 'Bastard!'

Tam had a moment's fleeting hope. 'The minister – Mr Cauldwell – can explain. It is him?'

'Aye, who else?'

'He can tell you what happened.'

'Can he now?' A mirthless grin. 'He's ower there. He's been here a wee while now, persuaded to wait for Archie.'

And Tam's relief was short-lived as the group stood aside and he beheld an unhappy-looking Mr Cauldwell seated uncomfortably on the edge of a large boulder. His hands behind his back, doubtless firmly tied, he himself, was as much a prisoner as Tam.

'Jenny wanted it all proper, ye ken, wi' the bairn an' all. There's money in it,' said her father, his eyes gleaming. 'Frae an' auld granny. Born on the wrong side o' the blanket was Jenny and she has tae be married afore her eighteenth birthday. That's today.'

'Haud yer whisht, faither!' This from Jenny, pushing him aside and flourishing the knife in Tam's face. 'We're wastin' time, let me get at him.'

Light was beginning to glimmer through the darkness for Tam. He glanced across the clearing towards the minister, who shook his head sadly. His heavenward glance indicated that prayers were in order and that there was no other help to be expected from their captors.

'Wait, I tell you!' Tam shouted. His voice still had enough authority to halt the girl's hand. 'Did Mr Cauldwell tell you that Archie had been last seen taking a cart carrying a corpse towards Edinburgh?'

'Aye, he did that.' And Archie's father took Jenny's arm, held it fast. 'Ben Fellows' corpse. He telt us that a scholar-like man from the castle had been unco' interested in Archie. The woodcutters had the same tale, so that's why you're here.'

Further incensed by this dramatic story, the girl shook off the restraining hand and lunged towards Tam.

'Tell me, tell me what have you done wi' Archie – and what's to become o' me wi' a fatherless bairn.'

'Give over, Jenny,' said her father, trying without success to remove the knife from her grasp. 'Ye'll no be the first lass left wi' a bairn. We'll tak care o' ye, like we always have.'

By standing on tiptoe, Jenny brought her face close to Tam's. In happier circumstances, he would not have found such a pretty face unappealing. However, as she tickled his throat with the knife, he decided Archie's disappearance had been occasioned by second thoughts. If that was the case, then Archie had done well to escape while he could from what promised to be a trying married life.

Jenny was still staring up into his face. 'A handsome well-set-up cheil, ye are, mister,' she said, her voice suddenly soft and feminine. 'An' I have a fancy for a husband.' Turning to her father, she said sharply, 'He'll do. I'll marry him.'

'What about Archie?' her father asked. Hardly surprising, he sounded scandalized at this sudden decision.

'What about ma legacy? Tae hell wi' Archie, faither. He's let me down, again. Promised marriage months sine.' Again she regarded Tam, narrowly looking him over as Her Grace the Queen might have considered an enticing addition to her riding stables. 'I need a man – this day. This fine cheil will do just grand.' And pointing to the minister, 'Have him to do the necessary, make the document for me to put my mark, so I can claim ma legacy,' she added imperiously.

'Wait a moment!' Tam began to protest and the knife drew blood.

'Ye wanted to say something, fine mannie? De ye no fancy me as wife to ye? I'm grand in the bed, so I'm told,' she purred.

With the proof of such activity clear before him, Tam had little doubt about that.

'She can skin a hare too. And bake fine bread,' put in the anxious father, eager to be helpful. And fine pleased with such a peaceful solution, he rubbed his hands gleefully. 'Aye, young sir, and I give my consent. What d'ye say?'

With a knife held at his throat by his now promised bride Tam was speechless.

'Ye have the look of an honest man,' his prospective father-in-law continued in a wheedling tone. 'We dinna see a deal o' them aboot, so if we give you yer life back, will ye take Jenny?'

Getting his life back was an attractive prospect, but the price of a marriage alliance with the Crozers was a little more than he was prepared to pay. The matter needed careful consideration and an escape clause. He decided to play for time.

He smiled down at Jenny. 'First of all, if you'll please stay calm and put that knife away, I'll tell you all I know about Archie.'

He wondered if this was a wise move, that telling them about Ben Fellows' devoted niece and the reappearing corpse in the waters of Duddingston Loch might spell his own doom, for it hardly sounded believable even to himself. And by the way Jenny was looking him over, in anticipation of forthcoming ownership, he had a suspicion she was rapidly going off the idea of waiting for Archie.

But not quite. Mention of the cart and the fine Edinburgh lady brought forth a shrill scream of anger. 'I telt ye, faither. Archie was always one to be led away by a sniff o' the gentry. He'll be in her bed right now,' she added with a stifled sob. 'The bastard!'

'Hush, Jenny lass. Hear the, er, gentleman out.'

But by the time he had reached the end of the story, the Crozers, and particularly Jenny, had lost interest. There were roars of, 'Get on wi' the weddin', Jenny lass!'

They don't even know my name, thought Tam, but that was soon to be remedied. A young man who might well be Jenny's brother had led Mr Cauldwell from the boulder. The minister's hands, now untied, were clutching a prayer book, which trembled a lot as he was pushed forward.

Tam realized this was also his last chance. Once released from his bonds, he would put up a brave but useless fight that would no doubt end with his death.

But he was to be denied even that privilege. A reluctant bridegroom, as a matter of caution he was to remain where he was, tied to a tree. And once the ceremony was ended, he decided grimly, Jenny would probably kill him anyway if he attempted to desert her.

Now she stood at his side. The Crozers gathered. Mr Cauldwell, urged on by a knife at his back, opened the prayer book.

'Dearly beloved brethren,' he spluttered inappropriately, for fewer men in his parish had ever been less dearly beloved, or less brethren. 'We are gathered here together . . .'

This couldn't be happening, thought Tam. For dear God's sake, and he began to struggle again. He was ignored.

' . . . to witness the joining in marriage of this man and this woman.' He paused. 'I do not recall your name, sir.' He looked towards Tam.

As Tam considered giving a false name that would at least make the marriage invalid, the air was suddenly split by a piercing whistle. To his astonishment, and that of Mr Cauldwell, his congregation melted away. Where there had been a bride and two dozen hopeful wedding guests, there were now only a smoky fire, an unhappy minister and a reluctant bridegroom tied to a tree.

'Wait,' Tam shouted, and to Mr Cauldwell, 'For God's sake, untie me.' With trembling hands, the minister fumbled with the stout ropes in a way that suggested he had never untied even a piece of string in his entire existence.

'Make haste!' pleaded Tam.

Whoever had caused the instant flight of the Crozers must be an even fiercer foe. He didn't think he could face another such ordeal. Then the silence around them was broken by the distant drumbeat of horses' hooves growing steadily nearer. Still trussed up like a chicken, Tam struggled to free himself, but managed only to make Mr Cauldwell's efforts more ineffectual.

It was no use. 'Go, man – run,' he said. 'Save yourself.'

Mr Cauldwell moved indecisively from one foot to the other.

'Go, I tell you. Save yourself while there's time.'

As the minister obstinately shook his head and squared his shoulders bravely, Tam tried not to think of the fresh horrors that were rapidly heading their way.

A rival surname, stronger, better-armed than the Crozers. He groaned. That was it. No chance of dying bravely now.

But only four horsemen rode into the clearing. Steel-helmeted, jacked, armed. Bothwell's moss-troopers. And Ajax on a leading rein.

'Thank God,' was the minister's answer to his prayer.

'Would you please release me?' said Tam, weak with relief as one of the men approached and, with a sharp knife, proceeded to loosen the ropes. Another sauntered over, chatting amiably to Mr Cauldwell, who was only too eager to give a graphic account of what had happened.

The man came back, joined his companions and grinned at Tam's discomfort. 'Uncle Davy sez ye nearly got your gizzard cut that time, Master Eildor. And got yourself a wife and bairn into the bargain.'

All four chortled, seemed to think this a splendid jest, as Tam stepped out of the last of the ropes that had bound him with as much dignity as was left to him. There seemed little point in outraged indignation. He was, at that moment, getting used to the bliss of still being alive.

He dabbed at the trickle of blood from his throat. 'You were just in time. Thank you.'

The man laughed. 'Dinna thank us, Master Eildor. 'Twas yon horse of yours, riding about the countryside. A valuable beast, and riderless, telt us that ye were in trouble. We were on the road to Craigmillar, so we backtracked wi' him and – here we are.'

Mr Cauldwell left them at the crossroads, escorted home by his nephew, after bidding farewell to Jock Hepburn, as he addressed the leader of the moss-troopers. His leavetaking of Tam was dignified, just a trifle stiff and reproachful, as if Tam were responsible for the indignities that had befallen them. As for Tam, he whispered words of gratitude to Ajax, who snorted down his neck.

'Ye should have telt us when you meant to leave Branxholm and we would have collected ye,' said Jock Hepburn sternly. 'Onyways, we'll see ye delivered safe back to Craigmillar. If ye're no too hurt to ride. We have orders to head for Stirling at daybreak.'

'I don't wish to put you to any inconvenience,' said Tam, rather put out by being treated like a helpless infant. 'If you set me on the right road, I will manage the rest of the way back.'

Jock shook his head. 'Ye canna ride this territory single-handed and unarmed, man. That's begging for trouble – trouble like the Crozers.'

'Ye're a stranger here,' put in his second companion. 'Ye need protection.'

'Or a sword,' said the third.

The mosstroopers had never been so voluble.

So Tam remounted Ajax, conscious of his usual lack of skill, to some shaking of heads and restrained mirth from his escort. But the horse was patient and understanding, having obviously sized him up and made due allowance for this poor specimen of humankind.

As they made their way back to the castle, Bothwell's men once more relapsed into their customary silence. Occasionally they reined in and looked back to see that Tam was following them, making him feel like a child out on its first pony. Had he not been grateful to them for his survival, such behaviour would have raised his indignation, but today he was too weary to care a fig for their damned opinions. He would have been a lesser man indeed had he not been aware of a very narrow escape from oblivion. Mr Cauldwell would have approved of him counting his blessings. Alive and breathing, unharmed, and without a wife and an imminent babe to add to his problems.

As Craigmillar Castle came in sight, he was already looking forward to a peaceful interlude at last. The much vaunted intuition that he had relied on failed completely to warn him otherwise.

Part Two
Stirling Castle

'I know for certain that this Queen repenteth her marriage, that she hateth Darnley and all his kin. I know there are practices in hand contrived between father and son to come by the crown against her will. Many things grievouser and worse [than the murder of Rizzio] are brought to my ears, yea, of things intended against her person.'

– Thomas Randolph, English spy, to the Earl of Leicester

Chapter Twelve

Saturday 14 December 1566. Evening

As Tam with Bothwell and his mosstroopers crossed the bogland and approached Stirling, the light of many torches on the castle's high rock heralded their approach. A sight to gladden the hearts of the travellers, not least the last of the royal baggage train, with the few remaining servants from Craigmillar, all exhausted by the rigours of the journey.

As they rode wearily up the steep twisting hill to the castle, through a babel of shrill voices, they could scarcely negotiate the narrow streets blocked by whole retinues of important foreign personages. Invited for the Prince's christening, all were desperately and voiferously demanding lodgings.

Late-comers were included in the throng, of many strange hues and in many exotic liveries, adding to the turmoil by seizing local passers-by despairingly in one last hope for a bed anywhere. But heads were shaken dolefully, since none understood them and they understood none.

For this particular christening, there was no room at any inn.

Tam groaned. His head ached and his backside was

raw, as if the bones were coming through the skin after two days' hard riding through every kind of weather God invented over drove roads that had ceased to exist, washed away by rain or vanished under seas of mud.

Such conditions were not for the inexpert horseman. He had to admit that, although he had no love of horses, he was changing his mind, grateful as an understanding grew between the exhausted rider who often fell asleep in the saddle and the patient, long-suffering Ajax.

When at last they reached the castle forecourt, Tam's irritation at being stopped and challenged fell narrowly short of abuse. To that particular officious sentry, he felt their destination and reason for arriving must have been painfully obvious. Finally allowed access, they dismounted and were led to where the royal apartments formed three sides of a quadrangle.

The central courtyard was known as the Lion's Den, in honour of its ancient occupant, a king of the jungle of uncertain years and unreliable disposition. The pet of Mary's grandfather King James IV, it had been presented to him as a playful and engaging cub, the gift of some long-forgotten foreign potentate or ambassador. The King refused to part with this lovable creature, ignoring ferocious maturity when it demolished, and subsequently relished, the occasional servant unfortunate enough to wander into its domain.

Thus the lion earned itself territorial rights of the central courtyard. The King, beseeched to provide a secure iron cage, refused to listen, not from sentiment but because, as he pointed out, in such anxious times a king might sleep peacefully at night guarded by such a fierce deterrent beneath his windows whose occasional roars of frustration rocked the entire building.

As Tam and the riders trooped round the high walls of the enclosure, the jungle smell from within persuaded Tam that even in its declining years, the King's lion was not an adversary he would have cared to meet in a rapid descent from the royal apartments above them.

Now from those regal windows came noises of a different and less threatening nature. Snatches of lute music (being practised somewhat inexpertly) and raised voices in speeches (being prepared somewhat frantically) drifted down to them, as well as assorted shrill screams and curses accompanying the moving of furniture in preparation for Tuesday's great event.

Tam's head ached. He longed to rest it on a soft pillow, to close his eyes, he didn't much care where. Any place, he decided, would be better than the abominable lodgings *en route*, the cold wet tavern floor, with a single blanket against the freezing draughts that had been his last inhospitable sojourn.

All of Scotland was, it seemed, on the move, heading in the direction of Stirling. The high price extracted by the innkeeper had been the final insult, told that sir was luckier than some persons of influence who had to sleep in the barn with their horses.

At the door of the royal apartments he was again challenged. Assuring the guard that he was Lady Buccleuch's steward, he saw Ajax led to the stables and was pointed in the direction of a turnpike stair, at the top of which were the servants' quarters, he was told.

'How far is it?' Tam asked wearily.

The cheerful response was just to keep going, he'd

get there eventually and be thankful, when he remembered the crowds outside who would envy him.

Such a warning didn't seem promising and, fearing the worst, he had climbed about forty steps when a door opened and Janet Beaton poked her head out.

'God's name, Tam, where have you been?' She ushered him inside. 'What kept you? You should have been here days ago. Is all well at Branxholm? What about the roof?' she demanded anxiously.

He leaned against the wall for support, trying to answer coherently her barrage of questions one at a time.

She stopped speaking. He looked dreadful and she put a warm hand on his arm. 'Poor Tam, I see ye're weary. Never mind the details, come and sit by the fire.'

Tam was delighted, past words of gratitude, to see a roaring fire once more and he stood by it, letting its heat flow over his aching bones.

'Drink this.' Janet thrust a posset of some fiery herbal liquid of her own invention into his hands.

It burned his throat on the way down, but by some magic made him feel considerably better. Remarkable, he thought, as she indicated a chair.

'Take off those boots, Tam.'

Thanking her, he did so gladly, as she said, 'Now, tell me all.'

Disposing of domestic matters concerning Branxholm, he was pleased that she offered no objections to his appointing Jacob Scott as temporary steward without her consent.

'I had him in mind before you arrived,' she said to Tam's relief. 'He will do fine till we return.' And refilling his goblet with more of the fiery liquid, she asked, 'When did you leave?'

He told her and when he reached his ambush by the Crozers, she listened sympathetically, with occasional exclamations of horror.

'My Lord Bothwell will be interested. I expect his lads will pass on the news.' She paused and shook her head sadly. 'I have seen little of him of late. He is much involved in preparations for the christening, as ye ken, and hardly ever leaves the Queen's side. Much to Lord Darnley's disgust, I am told, since he was hoping to have his conjugal rights restored – and with some enthusiasm. It has been several weeks since they went their separate ways – the Queen to Craigmillar and himself to his father's house in Glasgow. He laments that his wife now refuses to grace his bed.'

Tam said nothing and she took his hand, held it tight. 'I like not this situation between them. I fear for the future, Tam.' And with a shake of her head, 'It is in my bones, something I cannot shake off, something I dread. I wish we were back safe in Branxholm. I am so sick of living at court, sick of intrigue, of plot and counterplot.' She threw her arms wide. 'I long for good clean air to breathe, for simple fare – and a simple life as it was before all this.' Then, regarding him through narrowed eyes, she whispered, 'I am lonely, Tam, that's the truth of it.'

How could anyone be lonely in the midst of such activity? Tam thought. After the discomforts, the miseries of never being alone day or night, during the last hectic days of travel, loneliness, a solitary state, was infinitely to be desired. One he would have welcomed, as she went on.

'I feel deserted, abandoned, as I have never done in my life before.' She paused and looked at him. 'Where do you sleep tonight?'

When he told her she raised her eyebrows in horror. 'God's name, not in that draughty hellhole, full of fleas and stinking humanity. They're crowding twenty or thirty servants to a room. Nay, Tam, I willna have that for ye. I wouldna put a dog o' mine up there.' She smiled and said softly, 'You shall sleep here tonight.'

Tam bowed. 'As you wish, madam.'

She grinned. 'Not madam, Tam, just Janet. We are friends – and more, remember?' she whispered with an arch glance, and Tam knew there was no mistaking her meaning.

The fiery liquid had restored him quite amazingly, but he was doubtful whether his performance as a lover would be equal to the occasion. In all honesty, given a choice, he would have opted for a less exhausting role and a good night's sleep.

But the offer of sharing that warm, inviting bed at the far side of the room, with fine linen sheets and soft feather pillows, was irresistible. His only prayer was that Lord Bothwell would not be feeling lonely too and have a sudden amorous urge to surprise his mistress. He would not be the only one surprised, thought Tam grimly, deciding he had no wish to pay for his comfortable night's lodging and pleasuring of Janet Beaton with an irate lover's dagger in his ribs.

He awoke in darkness. He had been dreaming that he was in bed with Marie Seton at his side. He had been making love to her. The sound of gentle breathing stirred him, but it was Janet's head on the pillow beside him. Her arms were tight around him and he could not move without disturbing her.

He closed his eyes and drifted back into sleep again.

Chapter Thirteen

Sunday 15 December 1566. Morning

Janet awoke him with a posset of ale and some bread. 'Break your fast, Tam, quick as you like. The Queen has summoned you.'

'The Queen?' asked Tam dazedly.

'Aye. News of your arrival has reached her. That is all I know. You are to attend her at noon.' She paused a moment before adding, 'Her Grace is very upset. One of her pet dogs died last night. I think it was poisoned,' she added grimly.

'Poisoned? Who would do that? Are you certain?'

'Aye.' Janet nodded. 'This is just between us, Tam, and I am at pains to keep it from Her Grace, but I believe the poison was meant for my Lord Bothwell. They were having supper together – alone – and a dish of sweetmeats had been brought in after the main dishes had been cleared.' She shook her head grimly. 'Some of them were undoubtedly poisoned.'

Tam took another gulp of ale. He didn't feel so hungry any more. Poison in the royal apartment opened up a number of alarming and sinister possibilities.

'The Queen?'

'Her Grace knows nothing of this. You were unconscious – you sleep like the dead, Tam – when I was
sent for. Her fat little spaniel Ado – short for Adonis –
had been very sick.'

'Odd that she should send for you in the middle of
the night.'

'Not at all. I frequently take care of her sick pets.
She has great faith in my herbs for animals as well as
humans. My powers, as a worker of miraculous cures,
are at her disposal any hour of the day or night. That
is why I am invited to accompany her, Tam.' She
sighed. 'By the time I got there, the poor beast was
beyond my help. He was dead.'

'My Lord Bothwell was present?' Tam asked.

She shook her head and smiled. 'Nay. He had left
earlier, discreetly and before any of this happened –
fortunately. Her Grace was in floods of tears, inconsol-
able, the Maries comforting her. I examined the dog,
and by the smell of the vomit I knew it had been
poisoned. I took my niece Beaton aside asked what
had happened.

' "Poor little Ado was greedy," she told me. "He can
smell sweetmeats and no one can stop him stealing
them. He gobbled down that whole dish of marchpane
while our backs were turned, in less than the time it
has taken me to tell you." Janet sighed. 'I guessed the
poisoning had been deliberate but I wanted to spare
Her Grace, so I said it looked as if he had eaten too
much and choked on his vomit. I pointed out tactfully
that he was an old dog. I didna mention that he was
overfed and too fat.' She looked at Tam intently. 'Ye get
the drift of this, nae doubt, Tam?'

He nodded and she went on. 'I didna care to

145

confide my true thoughts. This is a very serious matter, one that goes far beyond poisoning her pet dog.'

'You're telling me someone tried to poison the Queen, is that it?' Tam demanded sharply.

'Nay, Tam. Not the Queen. All who are responsible for her food ken that she rarely eats sweetmeats and she hates marchpane. But marchpane just happens to be Lord Bothwell's favourite.' She sighed. 'Everyone who has eaten at a banquet with him knows that.'

'So it was meant for him.'

'Aye.'

'He must have had a lucky escape – to say nothing of the Maries,' he added as the appalling thought struck him. Did Seton have a taste for marchpane sweet-meats?

Janet nodded. 'Whoever put poison in them was clever, kenned fine that Her Grace wouldna touch them and kens that none of the Maries are greedy. They have their tight bodices and their whalebones to contend with. One or two wouldna hurt them or any grown person, beyond feeling a mite sick. But that would be more than enough to poison a small dog.' Her voice trembled. 'And a whole dish would have been fatal for Lord Bothwell.'

While making good use of Janet's portable bathtub and a razor, which he presumed to be the property of Lord Bothwell, Tam considered Janet's words. It was evident that Bothwell had been the target and from someone who was well acquainted with his habits and the Queen's. Someone very close who hated them both.

But who? A body servant, bribed by the Queen's half-brother Lord James? A jealous angry wife, Lady

Jean Gordon, who was present for the christening but occupied her own apartments? Lord Darnley, the estranged husband? Tam weighed up the possibilities as he presented himself at the Queen's apartments.

Marie Seton was awaiting him in the anteroom with Jean Gordon, at that moment leaving the royal presence. And smiling for once, she said, 'I have now settled the question of gowns with Her Grace, Seton. The decision was hers and fortunately it is my own favourite, the one she gave me for my own wedding last year.'

As a bowing Tam held open the door for her, she acknowledged his action with an icy glance and turned again to Marie. 'And how is my maid? Is she serving you well?'

'She is, my lady. I am grateful to you.' Watching the door close on Lady Jean, Tam considered that the introduction of a new maid into the royal apartments, allegedly to serve Marie Seton, might be a matter worth investigating. Who had better opportunity to be the purveyor of poisoned sweetmeats? And who knew better the weakness of Lady Jean's husband for march-pane than her maid?

Kissing Marie's hand, he tried to push aside his anxiety and not feel guilty that he had been unfaithful to his dream. For such was Marie's role in his life. A dream, where Janet Beaton was the only solid part of his existence. Loving Janet could not destroy her, as it could Marie.

She was saying, 'Her Grace will be so glad to learn that you have arrived safely. She is most taken with your singing and has asked for you constantly,' she added proudly. 'She wishes you to practise some ballads with her. Perhaps you will be invited to take part in the entertainment after the christening.'

Tam was somewhat taken aback by this suggestion as he followed her into the royal presence, where, bowing low over the Queen's delicate hand, he thought how frail she looked, so thin, her skin almost transparent. As if still haunted by the illness and the stresses she had suffered at Craigmillar.

When Seton was dismissed to join the three Maries by the window, Tam felt honoured and in awe, but any awkwardness was soon dispelled by the Queen's informality towards him.

The songs she offered him were in French. She did so almost apologetically and was glad to hear that he had a tolerable knowledge of the language, without telling her that it must also form some small part of his forgotten former life. She sat at the virginal and played a few chords.

'Do your best with the songs, Master Eildor, they were written specially for me by my dear friend, David Riccio,' she said sadly.

Tam had struggled through a few bars when the door was flung open without announcement. A man who could be no other than the Queen's husband strode in. A tall golden youth, his outstanding good looks marred by a weak wet mouth, a sullen expression. His character, Tam decided, was written in his face for all to read. The beauty of angels shattered like some unholy mirror by the sickness of evil.

He rushed over and, ignoring the Queen's hands on the keys, closed the instrument sharply. 'Madam, a word with you.'

'Later, my Lord. As you will observe—'

'I observe nothing, Madam, except that you choose to waste your time on matters concerning music, of which you know nothing.'

There was a faint gasp of protest, quickly stifled, from the Maries.

'I have my own trained musicians in the court, as you are well aware. They are here to provide entertainment. It is on other matters I wish to speak.'

He made an impatient gesture of dismissal to Tam, who bowed and joined the Maries. Pretending not to hear Darnley's angry voice, they stared down into the courtyard.

'I have precedence above all others and when I wish to speak to Monsieur du Croc, it is a royal command. Do not you forget that. You will see to it, Madam, at once! That is my command.'

The Queen murmured something inaudible to the listeners, in a cold but conciliatory tone.

'I will not have it, Madam. Do you hear? He has refused to see me – three times, Madam. Three times on some paltry excuse. And that is your doing. You have turned his face against me.'

'If you will tell me what is your business with the ambassador, then I will attend to it,' the Queen said stiffly.

'My business, Madam,' he said flatly. 'That is none of yours. Just see to it that I am heard.'

As he looked towards the window, four of the five heads quickly turned away, but Tam merely bowed. Seeing this, Darnley scowled and, striding over to the virginal, he snatched up the music Tam had been singing from.

To the Queen he shouted; 'French songs, madam! Is that not an ill choice?'

'I think not,' she said coldly. 'Master Riccio was my good friend and servant. My conscience is clear of his death.'

'Good friend and servant, is that so?' And turning to Tam, 'Come here.'

Tam drew nearer, bowed.

'And what have we here, another good friend and loyal servant? A well-set-up lad, prettier by far than yon poxy Italian.'

He moved closer, a hand on Tam's arm, staring into his face. As they were of an equal height, this gesture put him at a disadvantage, for he was used to looking down on those he considered menials. With a forefinger, he jabbed Tam's chest. 'Take care, if you are disposed to be a good and loyal friend and servant to Her Grace. Let it go no further, and mark well that Her Grace's secretaries often come to an unhappy, nay, even a bloody and violent end.' His voice held an unmistakable warning as he added; 'Take heed, make certain that you follow not their example.'

Turning on his heel, he swept out of the room, the four Maries only just remembering to curtsey as their mistress stood with one hand on the virginal, motionless, staring after him.

It seemed, as the door closed, that all of them, simultaneously expelled the breaths they were holding.

The Queen's eyes were not tearful, not afraid, merely cold and angry. The Royal Stuart look that had condemned men and women, guilty and innocent, to the scaffold.

She summoned a smile for Tam, held out a hand. 'Come again later, Master Eildor. We will continue our practice then.' She nodded in the direction of Seton, who curtsied and escorted him to the door.

As it closed behind them, Seton whispered, 'You see how impossible Lord Darnley is. He brought with him from England a band of Yorkshire musicians, five brothers – the Hudsons. He is angry and resentful that they have not been put in charge of the musical entertainment for the royal christening and that the Queen put such matters in the hands of Sebastian Pagez, her valet, who has a talent for organizing masques.' She made an angry gesture. 'The King treats her so vilely, we all hate him for it. We wish he – he – was . . .' She left the word unsaid and went on sadly, 'What will become of her if this divorce does not prosper, we dare not think.'

Tam said nothing, for he was nursing his own unhappy thoughts regarding the Queen's angry husband and a dish of poisoned sweetmeats.

'Will you walk with me a little?' asked Marie. 'I am going to visit my dear maid, who has been with me for ten years or more and has never suffered a day's illness until now. I am concerned deeply for her since we came to Stirling. Not even the Queen's apothecary can find a cure for her sickness.'

'A cure? What ails her?' asked Tam, his thoughts full of sinister possibilities about a new maid recommended by Lady Jean Gordon.

'Pains. A bloody flux. Aunt Beaton has promised to take care of her. I trust it is not something in the air here,' she added gloomily. 'This is a difficult time for a new maid, since she will not have the least idea of my needs and the constant care Her Grace requires. She can hardly bear to let any of us out of sound and sight.'

Remembering the Queen's pallor, Tam asked, 'I trust Her Grace is in good health?'

'Reasonably so, but alas, not in spirits. It was here she came to nurse Lord Darnley when they first met. He had fallen ill with measles – and she fell in love with him. An ill-fated day that turned out to be, and for all of us.' With a sigh, she added, 'Stirling has never been a happy place for Her Grace. It was firmly fixed in her mind with disaster. Her mother brought her here as a small child to escape the attentions of the English King, Henry, who was trying to capture her as a bride for his young son, Edward. The rough wooing, they called it.

'And once, on a short visit, her bed curtains caught fire mysteriously and she almost smothered. Since then she insists that one of us shares her chamber.'

Tam thought about that too. From what he had just seen, the Queen's vigilance was in order. He would not put it past Darnley to be abroad at night with a lit candle, ready to further his advancement to the throne of Scotland by setting fire to his wife's bed.

As they walked round the high walls of the courtyard, Marie pointed to the sky. 'See – up there.'

Above the castle battlements, the wheeling black shapes of birds, hovering, silent and watchful.

'Corbies, Tam. You have not had time to notice yet, but there are many corbies gathering here.' She shivered. 'Birds of ill omen. I trust that Her Grace has not observed them, for she is much taken with omens, alas. She was very upset as we were leaving Edinburgh, just as we were riding past the Nor' Loch, there was a body being pulled out of the water, a young man. Lord Bothwell rode down and returned to report a drowning accident. Poor lady, we knew she regarded this as an ill omen for the outset of our journey. My Lord Bothwell had difficulty in persuading her that time did not permit us all to troop back to Craigmillar and depart again on the morrow. She had to settle for Masses being said when we reached Stirling. For the safety of all of us.' Pausing, she looked up at Tam wistfully. 'Now you must tell me of your adventures since last we talked together.'

As Tam spoke of his visit to Branxholm, omitting mention of Morham and of his abduction by the Crozers, his mind was elsewhere. The sudden unexplained sickness of Marie's maid was no light matter. The hint of some mysterious sickness could spread like wildfire, catastrophic with so many foreign visitors, ambassadors, princes and retainers, sparing none as it swept through a town.

Or had the sickness also been induced by poison? Had her maid a secret taste for marchpane, a ruse by which a new maid might be introduced into the Queen's apartments?

Marie left him staring down into the Lion's Den, wondering how he could interview the maid without arousing her suspicions or her young mistress's curiosity. It was at this point that a messenger approached, saluted and said, 'Lord Bothwell requires your presence. You are to attend him within the hour.'

Bothwell's apartments were only a degree less splendid than the Queen's. A little more defensive, they provided an excellent and watchful view over the approaches to the castle.

But at that moment Bothwell was surrounded by tailors, armed with swatches of material, wrestling with documents for every available space on floor and table. An atmosphere of feverish activity prevailed and he was not in a good mood.

Tam wondered nervously if the kindness bestowed on him by Janet Beaton on his arrival last night was the cause of the deep frown that creased Bothwell's forehead.

Bothwell swung round to face him, thumped down the document he had been studying and said, 'So ye're back, are ye?' He led Tam over to the window embrasure. 'And ye have news for me – good, I hope.'

'What sort of news, my Lord?'

'Ye ken fine. About the bitch – have ye found her yet?'

Poison attempts in the Queen's apartment had swept aside Bothwell's other problem and in confusion Tam's thoughts drifted to canines. Were there some in the kennels at Branxholm that he was supposed to mind?

He stared at Bothwell, who demanded, 'Ye ken fine who I mean. Mistress Throndsen. Did yon sister o' hers tell you aught about her that would help?'

Tam shook his head and explained that Mistress Dorothy had been absent from Morham when he had called a second time, but that he had understood from my Lord's mother on their first visit that she was in touch with her sister Anna, at present in Norway. Bothwell scowled as Tam added, 'I understand that

Mistress Sinclair is at Traquair at present. With William, my Lord.'

It was Bothwell's turn to stare. For a moment, Tam realized, he had not the slightest idea who William might be. Then he recovered. 'Oh aye, the wee lad. Trust he's in good health,' he added heartily, to which Tam could only respond that it was so, as far as he was aware.

Bothwell hrrumphed and nodded vaguely. 'Grand wee lad, right enough. But naught about yon other matter?'

Taking this to refer to the still-pressing matter of the now distant attempt on Bothwell's life and the disappearance of Will Fellows, Tam launched into the story of his ambush by the Crozers.

Bothwell's laughter cut him short. 'Aye, aye – the lads told me how they rescued you from an unco' violent end. Trussed like a chicken, they said.'

Much to Tam's discomfort, he could hardly restrain his mirth. His lads had obviously found the incident a cause for considerable merriment, worth relating with, he did not doubt, fitting embellishments.

Composing his face with difficulty, Bothwell said, 'Aye, and a lass much in need of a husband, we gather. A mighty narrow escape, Master Eildor.' He tut-tutted and shook his head. 'Well, well. It explains why the lad disappeared right enough, wi' such a young harridan to deal with. We need not concern ourselves any further about him. Doubtless he'll have returned and made an honest woman of her and father to her bairn by the time we get back to Edinburgh.' His face took on a brooding look. 'At least I'll be safe enough here from yon bitch,' he said slowly.

Tam hoped he was right and that his prickling sense of disaster was wrong. For had he been a gambling man, he would not have sunk many coins on Bothwell's bet that he was rid of whoever wanted to kill him.

From the evidence at Morham, Anna was in Norway. Danger from that source was non-existent, except in Bothwell's guilty conscience, but the poisoned marchpane indicated that someone – here in Stirling, as well as at Craigmillar – wanted him dead.

And if, as he suspected, that person was masquerading as one of the mass of servants in the royal train, nothing could have been simpler for her – or him – to follow and remain hidden in the castle. Searching out a killer would be as difficult as looking for any proverbial needle in the haystack.

Bothwell was surveying the scene of activity in the room behind them, studiously avoiding eye contact with a tailor frantically bowing in his direction. 'Ye see how it is with me – ' He made a hopeless gesture. 'All this . . .'

Tam immediately offered his services. 'If I can help in any way, my Lord.'

'Aye, if I think o' something ye might do, and if Mistress Beaton can spare ye. Did she mention that Her Grace had a wee bit o' an upset as we set out from Edinburgh?'

Tam realized this must refer to the drowning incident, as Bothwell went on, 'Aye, most unfortunate at that particular moment. Just as we rode past, there'd been a young lad fished out o' the Nor' Loch. As Sheriff of Edinburgh, I rode down, but they'd sent for the Town Guard. I was told it was likely a suicide. Her

Grace wanted to know what had happened, but I spared her finer feelings, said it was an unfortunate accident, a boat overturned.' He shook his head, his face grim. 'No matter, she turned to omens and the like, as females will.' He then repeated what Tam had been told by Marie: 'If time had allowed, she would have had us all trail back to Craigmillar and sit on our arses until the morrow.'

'What was this suicide like?' Tam asked.

Bothwell shrugged. 'They said he was young. I didna care to inspect. The matter was in hand, it was none o' my business.'

Tam said nothing, but he went away very thoughtfully, wishing Bothwell had been a little more interested and a little less in a hurry to notice if the drowned lad had red hair, and was the missing carter Archie Crozer, a 'suicide' that might be murder.

Chapter Fourteen

Tuesday 17 December 1566. Five in the evening

Grateful for Lady Buccleuch's influence at court, Tam had a seat beside her in the gallery of the Chapel Royal, an excellent viewpoint overlooking the altar.

For the past hour they had been seated, waiting for the christening to begin. They were not impatient, since there was much to observe and comment on, although the heat from several hundred candles was already almost overpowering, the atmosphere heavy with smoke and the smell of hot wax.

Inside the chapel, and from every church throughout the town since dawn, carillions of bells had been joyfully and sometimes tunelessly, proclaiming this royal pageant, as crowds assembled and townsfolk lined the route that would be taken by the great and famous. Necks were craned hopefully for a glimpse of the wicked Queen Elizabeth of England, godmother to the Prince James.

Disappointed that she was not after all to appear in person, they had to make do with her envoy the Duke of Bedford. Despite the pomp of an escort of eighty horsemen, as a Protestant, the noble Duke would feel obliged to remain outside the chapel during the ceremony.

His retinue also included the magnificent Sir Christopher Hatton, the famous 'frisking' dancing partner of the English Queen, and there was considerable interest in this part of the procession. As it slowly wound its way through the steep, narrow streets towards the castle, the waiting crowds' tired eyes and aching legs were also rewarded by the splendid sight of the royal horses, caparisoned in cloth of gold adorned with silver fringes.

Surging forward for a closer view, the spectactors made the streets even more inaccessible for the important townsfolk, baillies and constables. All jostled impatiently for precedence over foreign diplomats, and fists were seen to be raised, blows exchanged and angry challenges issued on more than one occasion, while unseen inside the castle frantic last-minute preparations had also raised tempers and grievances among servants and courtiers.

Now the great moment had arrived, the sound of trumpets announced that the Queen was about to appear.

Tam and Janet had an uninterrupted view of the ceremony over the baptismal Cloth of Estate of crimson velvet, edged with gold. The massive gold font gleaming with precious stones was Elizabeth of England's christening gift to her royal godson.

'That must have cost a fortune,' whispered Tam.

'Aye, and from a monarch not known for her generosity, whose motto is '"Tis more blessed to receive than to give",' murmured Janet. Considering the splendour all around them – the silks and satins and glittering jewels of the congregation – she added, ''Tis a very different scene from Her Grace's own coronation in this very chapel, in forty-three. Nine months old, she was.' Janet shook her head. 'A very drab and parsimonious affair, and accounts of it made her all the more determined that her son's christening should be an occasion to be remembered by the whole of Europe. Let them see that a Scottish Queen who is also the Dowager Queen of France can light up this cold and barren land, scorned by many. Through her endeavours they will take back with them a vision of Scotland as a great country, a power to be reckoned with, and herself as glorious as any other monarch in Europe.'

Tam refrained from mentioning the rumours he had heard that twelve thousand pounds Scots was being raised by taxation in Edinburgh to pay for the christening.

Janet continued, 'See her noble lords, all those in splendid new garments especially created for today, and at her own expense. Take a good look, Tam. Some are in cloth of silver, others in gold, and by her command each man rather above than under his degree,' she added.

Tam caught a glimpse of Lord James Stewart, Earl of Moray, the Queen's crafty half-brother, magnificent in green and gold, Argyll in red and silver, Bothwell in blue satin and silver.

They stood by the door, their splendour entirely lost on the congregation. Since strict adherence to the Protestant faith made it an offence in their eyes to attend a Catholic ceremony, all intended to remain outside.

A fanfare of trumpets, closer now, echoed through the chapel. A choir at first unseen, heard as an angelic chorus only, made its way slowly down the aisle to the altar, where an archbishop, several bishops, priors, deans and archdeacons had taken their places to await the procession.

A stir in the congregation, a craning of heads, and the baby appeared, carried by the French ambassador from his room to the Chapel Royal between two rows of barons and gentlemen holding wax candles and adding to the already unbearable heat inside.

The Catholic nobility of Scotland followed, bearing the great serge, the salt, the cloth, basin and ewer.

Tam had a glimpse of a dark gnomish face shrouded in a magnificent baptismal robe, ten yards of figured silver as the prince was handed across the golden font into the arms of Jean, Countess of Argyll, the Queen's Catholic half-sister, acting as proxy godmother for the English Queen.

The ceremony began with all the pomp and ritual of the Roman Church. Tam and Janet were among the fortunate who could see and hear what was happening through the smoke of the huge candles.

As the primate began, 'I baptize thee James Charles,' the Queen stepped forward.

Breaths were held at this interruption. Those close enough heard her whisper, there was to be no use of the primate's spittle for this particular royal babe – later reported as 'she deemed it a filthy and apish trick rather in scorn than imitation of Christ. Her very own words were that she would not have a pocky priest to spit in her child's mouth.'

At Tam's side, Janet whispered, 'Mark it well, since

the disease for which the primate has been treated by a doctor in Milan cost him at a fee of eighteen hundred gold crowns, Her Grace's decision is more practical than symbolic.'

Again the trumpets sounded, the heralds proclaimed James Charles three times, with the long list of his titles. More triumphant singing from the choir and the babe was carried back out of the chapel.

'A very royal and dignified infant,' said Tam approvingly. 'Not a whimper out of him.'

'And not a sign of his noble father either,' said Janet, as the congregation, duly blessed, bowed or curtsied to the departing royal party. 'No one has seen him all day. Though no doubt he will appear for the banquet.'

A magnificent feast of fish and fowl, of meat and venison, of sweetmeats and elaborate desserts had been prepared all day and set out in the great hall of the castle. The long tables now lay in disarray, the contents consumed and wine drunk in accordance with the desires and capacity of several hundred guests.

The Queen sat at a small table with the English and French ambassadors on either side of her, and opposite the ambassador from Savoy. Her husband was not at her side, as had been expected, but it was solemnly noted that she did not appear in the least distressed by his absence.

Those who knew her well whispered that she must have been relieved not to have been embarrassed by Lord Darnley's loutish behaviour when he drank too much.

It was observed that she looked happy, laughed a

great deal and was more at ease than at any time since her arrival in Stirling. Doubtless the tension was over and she could afford to be very pleased with the diplomatic results of her extravaganza.

From one of the long trestles for the upper servants, Tam kept a jealous watch on a large table where the four Maries were seated, carefully placed beside the important dignitaries and representatives from the European monarchs.

Each time he looked in Marie Seton's direction, which was often, she was in animated conversation with an exceedingly good-looking young man with the same attractive fair colouring as herself. As they were leaving the hall, Marie hurried to his side, eager to introduce him to Adam Drummond.

'We are old friends.' said Drummond. 'Marie and I have not met since we were little more than children.'

As he spoke, he regarded her fondly, obviously pleased with what the passing years had produced. She smiled up at him, taking his arm in a friendly and understanding gesture.

Tam knew a moment's jealousy. Then it faded, to be replaced with relief. Intuition told him this was the right partner for Seton, someone with whom she could share a happy life.

As for himself, he could not seriously regard this young man with his frank and engaging manner, his open countenance, as a rival. He loved her but could offer her nothing; indeed, his presence in her life was a danger to her future. But if she fell in love with this young man, the burden of her hopeless infatuation would be lifted from him.

The three Maries approached and greeted Drummond affectionately. Obviously he was a favourite with them too and Tam bowed his way out, his departure almost unobserved.

In the hall, the meal over, the trestles cleared, the Queen returned and took her seat under the Canopy of State. The entertainment began with galliards and stately pavans in which she was partnered by the foreign ambassadors, and once by Sir Christopher Hatton himself, their performance closely watched by the court. They need not have feared, for their Queen acquitted herself well with this famous dancing master. She had learned it all long before in the French court.

Tam was relieved he had not been asked to take part in the singing that followed, led by the absent Darnley's Yorkshire musicians.

At last the royal party withdrew and, for Tam, there was nothing left but to secure a place on the crowded attic floor while there was still space available. He did not expect to get much slumber, if any, by the time the servants arrived, now at liberty to indulge their appetites on the remains of the banquet's food and rich wines.

As he was making his way across the courtyard, he heard his name called. Turning, he saw his four deliverers from the Crozers, Bothwell's mosstroopers, led by Jock Hepburn.

In jolly, hearty mood, they suggested that if he had nothing better to do, he could explore the town with them, including its many taverns, which were doing a roaring business, as were the town whores. If they got there soon, he was told, they still might be able to pick and choose.

It seemed like an interesting way of seeing Stirling

and Tam went along with them. The noise, the wine, the screeching of pipes, the women who sat on his knee and kissed him – he saw only a sea of painted faces before his wits failed him.

Chapter Fifteen

Wednesday 18 December 1566. Morning

The condition of Tam's head allowed scant remembrance of the night's wild carousing. When he awoke in a strange bed at the side of a young girl who could not have been more than thirteen, his first thoughts were of a lucky escape. With one so young and new to the game, he had less chance of catching the pox, as he remembered with a shudder the ravaged faces of the older whores.

In sleep, the young girl looked almost childlike. He had no memory of lovemaking and, since they were both fully clothed, he decided on a hasty departure. Pleased to discover that his purse was intact, he left most of his remaining coins for her and crept down the stair.

A door opened and a woman looked out at him.

'Sleep well, my Lord?' She grinned.

'I did indeed.' Tam wondered if she wanted money for the night's lodging with the girl he had left.

'You were gone to the world when Jock and Davy put you into the bed,' she chuckled.

Tam suppressed a grateful sigh. He need no longer

feel guilty about that child, for so she was, asleep upstairs.

As if the woman read his thoughts, she said, 'Flora's my daughter. I was glad it was you she was left with and not the Hepburn lads. Nice enough, ye ken, and generous, but devils wi' women. Just like their master.'

'How old is Flora?' asked Tam, with rising feelings of indignation.

The woman, who on closer terms was even younger than himself, shrugged. 'Twelve,' then, at the expression on his face, she said defiantly, 'Going on thirteen.'

Tam tried to find the right words. 'Surely she is a little young.'

'Young!' the woman laughed. 'As soon as we're old enough isn't too young. What else is there for a woman to keep from starving?' She nodded towards the closed door. 'I have three more weans in there, twa lasses and a laddie. Their father ran off wi' another slut, so how am I to feed them, my fine sir? This is the only trade I ken.'

Tam knew it was true. Again his thoughts went to Flora, asleep so innocently. 'Can she cook or sew?'

The woman grinned broadly. 'Aye, she's a good broiderer. She can sew a fine seam.'

Tam came to a sudden decision. 'Then send her to Lady Buccleuch, at the castle. She's to say Tam Eildor sent her and she wants employment as a seamstress.'

He cut short the woman's gratitude, her awe that this was a real gentleman who had come into their humble home. 'Just do as I say.' Then he walked out into the chilly brightness of the cold December morning towards the castle far above him.

At the sound of horns and voices, he leaned over a wall to watch a party of riders, with pennants flying, heading towards the forest that marked the royal hunting park. This was their sport for today, wild bulls and anything else that fled from their approach and suggested a likely target.

The Queen was well ahead of them, Bothwell at her side.

Tam was thankful he had not been called upon to accompany Janet, relieved to miss another day riding Ajax. Since he knew nothing about archery and, out of joint with the time in which he found himself, was averse to killing animals for pleasure, he was glad he was not being asked to enthuse about the day's activities.

Returning through narrow streets of the town where signs of last night's debauch were evident, he fought his way into a smoky tavern, bought ale, bread and cheese and, emerging into cold fresh air again, walked down the hill towards Stirling Bridge.

On this very spot William Wallace's heroic battle had saved Scotland. King Edward I, triumphant from the defeats of Berwick and Dunbar, with John Balliol as prisoner, had made a triumphal tour of Scotland, collecting the Stone of Destiny from Scone on his way home to England. Expecting an easy victory over the troublesome outlaw William Wallace, the English army massed on the south bank of the River Forth to take Stirling Castle, was watched by Wallace and his troops from their vantage point on top of Abbey Craig, some two miles distant. Early on the morning of 11 September 1297, Lord Cressingham led the English vanguard over the narrow bridge. It was a disastrous move, for when they were halfway across Wallace and the Scots rode down and met them.

The English, unable to move forward on the bridge or retreat, were massacred, their piled-up bodies preventing Lord Surrey and the remaining forces from joining the affray. Cressingham fell and Surrey fled, leaving the victory to Wallace and Scotland's future secure.

Tam leaned on the bridge, savouring that moment of past glory. In no hurry to return, he needed time to think about his own future. Presuming that he had a future to think about, instead of a past he could not remember. And a present that included pressing matters from Branxholm awaiting his attention in Janet Beaton's apartment.

Remembering the scene he had witnessed earlier of the Queen and Bothwell at the head of the hunting party, he looked up at the royal apartments far above his head. Where was the king? Was that the thought in everyone's mind, as he had not been seen since before his son's christening.

The thought came unbidden then. Was he even still alive?

Tam's wrestling with Branxholm documents was interrupted by commotion in the courtyard below. The royal hunt had returned.

He heard Janet and her attendants come up the stairs and the door close. A short while later, Janet, now clad less formally but considerably more comfortably in a loose-fitting gown, came in, looked over his shoulder and sat at the table opposite him.

'This is not my Lord Bothwell's day,' she said. 'He had a narrow escape this morning.'

'Another?'

'Aye. During the hunt an arrow misfired and hit the tree beside him. An inch closer – ' she paused, shuddered – ' and he would have lost an eye, or worse.'

'You say the arrow misfired, an unfortunate accident.'

Janet looked at him and slowly shook her head.

'You think it might have been deliberate? The poisoner at work again?' Janet shrugged. 'I dinna ken. But the hand o' coincidence is well to the fore.'

Tam thought about that. 'You mean that having failed once, he lost no time in making a second attempt. Do you get a feeling of urgency in the air?'

'You said "he", Tam.'

'I doubt if his mysterious Spanish lady, whoever she is, could have been behind this one.'

Janet leaned forward, her elbows on the table. 'And what makes ye think that, Tam? Ladies o' the court go along to the hunt. It is expected of us, and archery is not restricted to men. Some women take part, but most just sit on their horses and watch. Like Lady Jean Gordon,' she added significantly. 'The kill, however, is for trained archers. It's not a game any longer. Hunters get very excited at the kill and ye ken what bows and arrows could be like in the hands of folk who dinna heed the dangers.'

'Who else was there?' Tam asked.

Janet gave him a shrewd look. 'I presume ye mean those who might consider doing Lord Bothwell a mischief. The king didna put in an appearance. No one expected him. And neither on this occasion did Her Grace's loving half-brother—'

A tap on the door, a maidservant appeared, and before he could be announced Bothwell pushed past her into the room.

As Janet rose and curtsied politely, Bothwell gestured her away. 'Aye, Janet. It's not you. I want a wee word wi' Eildor. If ye'll leave us.'

As the door closed, Bothwell took the seat she had vacated. 'Did ye hear that there was almost a nasty wee accident during the hunt?'

When Tam said Janet had mentioned it, Bothwell leaned forward. 'She did, did she? And what d'ye think?'

'You said it was almost an accident, my Lord.' Tam chose his words carefully. 'Am I to understand that you think it might have been deliberate?'

Bothwell nodded vigorously. 'Aye, that I do. Especially when the question was raised and no one admitted to letting loose that particular arrow.'

'I take it they have no personal or distinguishing marks?'

Bothwell shook his head. 'Nay, for the royal hunt they're just issued piecemeal.'

Tam thought if it had been his arrow that had narrowly missed killing the Earl of Bothwell and no one noticed, he would have been tempted to keep quiet too. Especially if he had considered what would then be the fate of some minor court official. Prison, and perhaps some trumped-up murder charge, since members of the court were particularly nervous of the tense atmosphere here at Stirling.

'Well?' demanded Bothwell impatiently.

'You have someone in mind, my Lord?'

Bothwell's brow darkened. 'It couldna have been my first choice – Yon bitch we've spoken of.' He laughed harshly. 'She couldna handle a bow and arrow to save herself.'

Tam remembered Janet's words on archery for court ladies. And in the years since Bothwell and Anna had last met, with nothing better to do, she could have become proficient in a sport which was becoming increasingly popular among fashionable rich women. An elegant and daring pastime if they could find an attractive master in the art, since it offered close physical contact between tutor and pupil.

'She knew about daggers, my Lord.'

'Aye, but that's a different matter. Come, man, ye can do better than that. I'm relying on ye to put some sense into it.'

'Let us consider the Spanish lady, sir, whose identity is still unknown to us. She could have bribed someone to attack you. We can guess she paid Archie Crozer well to drive the cart with her and throw Ben Fellows' corpse into the loch.'

The door opened. Lady Buccleuch was awaiting him.

Bothwell stood up, clearly disappointed. 'I dinna agree. Ye'll ha' to do better than that, Eildor.'

Tam's feelings were mixed indeed. The thought that the Spanish lady was in the court somewhere and had followed them to Stirling, although perfectly feasible, was not popular with Bothwell, who wanted to believe he was safe from her murderous attentions.

Tam wasn't prepared to argue. What would Bothwell's reactions have been had Janet confided in him that the dish of sweetmeats – marchpane that he was known to find irresistible – contained a poison that would be fatal if consumed in large quantities?

That was unlikely to be the work of a woman who was still in Edinburgh, and he considered his growing list of those who might have reason to be Bothwell's secret enemies here in Stirling.

Heading the list was that man of subtlety Lord James Stewart. Poisoned sweetmeats did not readily fit his character, but an accident with a misfired arrow, arranged while he was not in the vicinity of the royal hunt, was a distinct possibility.

Second was Bothwell's wife. A more obvious choice, who now loomed large and far from secret by her presence during the hunt, who had greater reason to hate Bothwell for his infidelities. Humiliated at seeing him riding at the head of the hunt with the Queen, was she overcome by another murderous impulse now the poisoned marchpane – which had a distinct woman's touch – had failed? The sudden unexplained sickness of Marie Seton's maid and Lady Jean's gallant substitution of one of her own servants smacked more of contrivance than coincidence. And again Tam realized the urgency of a meeting with Seton's new maid.

Third was Darnley, one of the key players, conspicuously absent from his son's christening and from the royal hunt. An excellent reason, if nervously disinclined to incur his Queen's wrath by being present at the scene when Bothwell fell to a fatal arrow wound.

Tam made a shrewd guess that the King was unlikely to make the same mistake as he had at David Riccio's murder. This time he would have no trouble at all in bribing one of his less scrupulous minions to 'accidentally' kill his rival to the Queen's affections.

Tam's only glimpse of him had been when he stormed into the Queen's apartment and, among other unpleasant topics, threatened him with a fate similar to that of David Riccio.

He had not been seen again.

Tam stared up at the windows of his royal apartment. Stirling, known as the royal nursery for its guardianship of infant monarchs, had not a healthy happy reputation for kings.

James I had executed the Dukes of Albany and Lennox, Darnley's forebears, here in 1425. James II had murdered the 8th Earl of Douglas, another Darnley kinsman, and thrown him out of the window in 1452. His son James III had been murdered nearby after the Battle of Sauchieburn. James IV had died at Flodden and Mary's father, James V, had died, so men said, of a broken heart after the Battle of Solway Moss.

Once again, Tam asked himself whether Darnley was still alive. If he too had fallen victim to someone's scheming, what move could be expected next?

Chapter Sixteen

Wednesday 18 December 1566. Evening

The Queen was hosting another great banquet for the visiting ambassadors and her nobles, with a masque organized by Sebastian 'Bastian' Pagez, her favourite valet from Auvergne, who was expert in such matters.

A platform decorated with laurel holding six singing naiads piled high with the first course of the banquet was pulled into the great hall by dancing rustic gods and twelve satyrs carrying torches.

At the round table where the Queen sat with her thirty chosen guests, the satyrs handed their torches to bystanders. Taking the dishes from the naiads, they proceeded to serve the Queen's guests, while nymphs sang appropriate ballads. Overcome by their success as waiters, the satyrs put their hands behind them to wag their tails.

The English guests were shocked and sorely affronted by this vulgar display, sensitive to an inaccurate but widely held belief in Europe that Kentish men were born with tails, in token of divine disapproval of the murder of Thomas à Becket.

Some stood up in protest and, bowing briefly but politely to the Queen, deliberately turned their backs on the scene. Her Grace, unaware of the legend, was in turn bewildered and put out of countenance.

Speedily the Duke of Bedford explained. Dignified apologies were made and accepted, order restored and the satyrs, ignorant of a possible international incident just averted, were somewhat bemused as they bowed themselves out.

For the remaining courses of the banquet, the platform reappeared, once as a rocky hill – Parnassus with a fountain, the Castalian spring – and later as a globe from which a child emerged, symbolism to compliment the infant Prince; sadly this finale caused the platform to collapse.

Anxious glances were cast in the Queen's direction. Would she consider this another dark omen regarding the Prince's future? To everyone's relief, she joined in the laughter and applauded the servants' scramble to restore the platform's equilibrium.

Without further disasters, the company passed into the moonlight and hard frost of the December night, where, under a clear sky shining with the brightness of a thousand stars, a wooden fortress had been constructed near the churchyard of the Holy Rude.

Ice like diamonds gleamed on the castle's ancient walls as the royal party took their places on a raised platform beneath a sheltering canopy, where brazier fires added to their comfort. From this vantage point they were to be entertained by a mock battle, the fortress under siege by real soldiers from the castle guards, assaulted by a weird assortment of mythical creatures. The attackers were kept at bay by 'fire-balls, fire-spears and all other things pleasant for the sight of man'. This pyrotechnic display had taken forty days to prepare and set back the treasury by nearly two hundred pounds.

As the last gleams faded from the demolished fortress, signalling the end of the christening celebrations and the imminent departure of ambassadors and their retinues, Tam gave a sigh of relief. He had looked frequently and anxiously towards Bothwell, seated at the Queen's side during the noisy mock-war explosions. Was he still in danger, despite his certainty that he had nothing to fear from the 'Spanish lady' here in Stirling?

And for Tam there was the still-unsolved mystery of Archie Crozer's disappearance. Was his the body in the Nor'Loch? If that was so, Tam felt suicide was a very unlikely cause.

While it would be more comfortable to believe that Jenny's lover had lost his taste for marriage and in a last-minute bid for freedom had simply deserted her and their unborn child, having met that close-knit, vengeful family, Tam had now decided this was unlikely. He had a strong feeling he had not heard the last of the red-headed carter.

Even as Tam made his way up to his attic floor, Henry Darnley, the Queen's consort, sat in his room, which he had seldom left since Mary's arrival in Stirling. During that time he had suffered sundry imaginary grievances and plotted revenge as he ached with disease brought about by his own folly, which he pretended to ignore but which, if he lived long enough, would claim his life and his sanity.

Meanwhile, he resolved to show them who was king. He thought angrily of M. du Croc, who had refused to listen to his complaints and spiteful allegations against the Queen, as well as the plots he was certain were being fomented against him.

The ambassador's excuse had infuriated him. Since Lord Darnley was 'not now in good correspondence with the Queen', the French King had instructed du Croc to 'enter into no dealings on his behalf'.

Darnley swore he would have his revenge. Let them continue to wonder why he had not appeared for his son's christening. He hoped it would embarrass Mary for playing up to the English Queen. He suspected that Elizabeth had always been against the marriage and had instructed Bedford as her proxy not to accord him the privileges due to the King of Scotland. He had decided that he would not give Bedford and the English the satisfaction of seeing how far he had fallen, how low was his prestige in the Scottish court.

All he wanted was some support from France, such as a fleet kept in readiness off the Clyde, near enough to Glasgow and his father's home, so that if one of his most earnest plans came to fruition, he could successfully abduct the infant Prince James from the royal nursery here at Stirling and rule Scotland as his guardian.

Such was also, he knew, the secret hope and plan of Mary's half-brother Moray and of Elizabeth's ambassador Cecil, to dethrone Mary and put an end to her as a rival queen.

A pretty intrigue, but du Croc had refused to listen. And when Darnley insisted, he had pointed out that as there were two doors to the suite of rooms, should the King as he called himself, enter by one, then he, du Croc, would speedily leave by the other.

If only Mary had behaved like a queen, forgetting and forgiving. After all, Riccio was just a damned servant and a foreigner too. If only the Scottish nobles had not forced him to go with them to the supper room in Holyrood that night and then used his own dagger on the wretch.

And not for the first time his mind turned to ridding himself of Mary Stuart, who had failed to fulfil her early promise of granting him full recognition and powers of kingship. Worst of all, she had turned from a passionate lover into a cold, calculating woman.

Disposing of her had always been at the heart of all the schemes of his father, who had dinned into him since childhood that as he, a Lennox Stuart, and Mary were cousins, they had equal rights to the throne. His father had whispered into his ear frequently enough that he could see the vision glorious: his son as king.

If only Prince James had not been born. If only Mary had miscarried, or died on the night of Riccio's murder. For her death had been the unspoken intention of the Scottish lords, of Ruthven with his pistol hard pressed against her stomach.

Darnley had realized almost too late his own danger by implication in the plot, but Mary had helped him escape the consequences of that night's dread deed. She had shown great strength and courage, for, against all the odds, she, a frail and heavily pregnant woman, and their unborn child had survived.

He tried to console himself that Mary was not immortal. She was frequently ill with mysterious symptoms. Should she die suddenly, he was hopeful that there would not be too many awkward questions asked about a queen who had been sickly since childhood.

Then with himself as regent, at last in a position of power, for a babe could not deny the plans or policies of his father and guardian, he would seize the opportunity to speedily dispose of his enemies, putting all those who had opposed or slighted him under the executioner's axe.

He could, he would, make it happen. There were others in the court who plotted in secret, who would stand by him. He would put his faith in some accident that might be arranged for Mary and thus rid himself of this burdensome wife who was Queen.

He took another goblet of wine, held it high in a toast: To the King of Scotland.

All was silent outside the windows, the absurd fireworks seemingly at an end. And suddenly he needed company, for he felt sorry for himself, lonely and rejected, with a wife who hated him, was cold, refused his bed and picked quarrels with him.

He had to confide in someone. Strange how thoughts of murder always aroused his lust. He summoned his valet, whispered instructions, sat back in his chair and waited. He felt almost cheerful at last.

For tonight he had a new lover at hand, eagerly awaiting his summons in the antechamber. A lover. At least he hoped that was how the night would end, although there had been only hints at the consummation he desperately needed.

That made him angry, unused to being thwarted, his merest whim obeyed. Boys and women leapt into his bed, obedient to his command. He was King, after all, impatient and not to be satisfied with a few caresses, an almost chaste kiss or two, he thought, as the door opened and a handsome youth in black velvet was ushered into his presence. He bowed low.

'Come!' And Darnley stepped forward to greet him, kissed his cheek. There was no resistance, a shy smile. Eager to please. 'You may remove your bonnet.'

The youth had outstanding good looks, wearing his hair longer than was fashionable in court. Slightly built, but with good legs. He liked his boys and young men to be smaller than himself and beardless.

'You will take some wine with me. First.'

The youth's eyebrows raised a little, a flicker of interest slipped across his face. 'As you please, sire.'

Darnley smiled. 'Indeed, there is something you can do to please me exceedingly.'

The youth bowed. 'As you wish, sire.'

Darnley regarded him through narrowed eyes. 'You mentioned that you have a sister in court.'

'Aye, Your Grace. A twin sister.'

'And where is she this night?'

'She is maid to Lady Seton.'

Darnley nodded. 'A twin sister, you said.'

'Aye, Your Grace. We are like as two peas in a pod.'

Darnley nodded again, this time eagerly. Twins, a boy and a girl, both young and comely. He licked his lips. That would be a new and novel experience. Female whores, male pages, servants, he had them in plenty, at the snap of his fingers. But twins, a brother and a sister, alike as two peas. He thought of lying between them, perhaps one on top, one below, the very thought of so many different positions sent the blood rushing to his loins.

'This is what I wish.'

The youth looked at him, smiling.

'Fetch your sister. It is my command. I need to have you both – in bed to comfort me, this night.'

The youth departed and Lord Darnley waited. From outside there was more noise, shouts and a burst of red light. A loud bang, the very last of the fireworks.

He looked out of the window and saw that the artifical fort had been completely demolished, vanished under a pile of rubble.

Gunpowder. In larger quantities, there would be enough to blow up a quite substantial house, leaving no trace, no survivors to bear witness. To talk and betray. He rubbed his hands together, a gesture of almost childlike glee.

Aye, gunpowder. The very thing.

Chapter Seventeen

Inchmahome Priory.
Thursday 19 December 1566. Morning

Tam slept in the antechamber, where a trestle bed had been provided for him by Janet Beaton's command. He was grateful, her excuse that should any ask, he had much work on her behalf and she did not wish him to sleep on the overcrowded attic floors, carrying fleas and God only knew what other vermin on his person.

His slumbers were peaceful and undisturbed by troublesome dreams, till he opened his eyes to the wavering light of a candle, with Janet's face hovering above him.

'Wake up, Tam. The Queen commands that you accompany her to Inchmahome Priory.'

Tam blinked at the window, still bright with stars of a frosty night. 'When do we leave?'

'Now – immediately! And it is not "we", Tam. It is you! Her Grace knows better than to expect someone of my antique years on her wild revels. My Lord Bothwell and you are the chosen ones.'

Wild revels at this hour? 'It is still dark,' Tam protested, pointing out the obvious.

'No matter. She wishes to see the sunrise over the Lake of Menteith. So hurry up. I shall return to my bed,' she added with a happy yawn. Watching him pull on doublet and hose, she said, 'Her Grace loves the old priory on the island. She was only four years old when her mother, the Regent, took her there for safety from Stirling Castle after the Battle of Pinkie and the possibility of her being taken hostage by the English King. Inchmahome was a natural choice, not only as an island sanctuary but because its commendator was Her Grace's guardian, Lord Erskine's son. It has fond memories for Her Grace and for the Maries, who were with her.'

As Tam pulled on his boots, she added, 'You'll need a warm cloak. It is freezing outside.'

Half an hour later, Tam had collected Ajax from the stables and joined a group of riders in the courtyard: five young men and six pages bearing torches. Janet's warning about the bitter dawn had been right and all were huddled in cloaks against the chill air that seemed to eat through to their bones.

'Are we awaiting Her Grace?' he asked the tallest of the young riders next to him, clad in black doublet and hose, a black bonnet with a huge feather pulled well down over his eyes.

'Her Grace is here beside you, Master Eildor,' was the whispered reply, and the Queen's laughing face turned towards him.

Taken aback, he bowed, swept off his bonnet. 'Your Grace,' he stammered.

She chuckled. 'Hush!' And, pointing to the other

four young men, 'There are our companions, Master Eildor.'

Hearing her laughter, four faces turned towards them and Tam recognized the smallest and slightest of the quartet as Marie Seton. She raised a hand in salute.

A horseman approached. 'Ah, here is Lord Bothwell.'

Bothwell rode alongside, also dressed in black, swathed in a dark cloak.

'We are ready to leave, my Lord,' the Queen said, and to Tam, 'You two gentlemen are to be our escorts.'

The order was given and, as they rode down through the castle gates, Bothwell leaned across and thrust a pistol into Tam's hands.

'I presume ye can use one o'these?'

'Yes, my Lord,' said Tam, looking at the weapon with distaste.

'It's already primed, so take care,' warned Bothwell.

'Do you expect danger?' Tam asked.

Bothwell shrugged. 'I dinna suppose ye'll need to fire it, but one never kens what lies ahead.' And, looking over his shoulder as the troops gathered to ride down through the still-sleeping town and into the dawn, he grinned. 'As ye should ken well from recent experience, Master Eildor, to ride unarmed is to court disaster.' Pausing to let that painful reminder sink in, he nodded in the Queen's direction. 'A man would be a fool indeed not to be well prepared for every emergency wi' such a precious cargo.'

Leaving the town behind, they rode swiftly along the flat approach road, the boggy mire Tam remembered from his arrival now transformed into rock-hard ice. As they galloped, the first gleam of sunrise touched the hills of the Campsie Fells, rose pink under the breaking clouds of a new day. Their breaths hung upon the icy air, their horses' hooves striking diamonds of light from the hard ground.

They had ridden more than two miles when a horseman raced towards them. The Queen's troop halted and Tam recognized Sebastian Pagez.

Bothwell rode forward, they spoke for a few moments and the Queen's excited laugh drifted back to Tam. He heard her bid the rider Godspeed back to Stirling and turned to the waiting group.

'Pagez reports that the loch remains frozen hard and has been so for two weeks now. The canons at the priory told him that from their certain knowledge there is no possibility of a sudden thaw and if we take the route they have indicated, we can ride safely across the ice to the priory.' At the suppressed expressions of alarm, she continued, 'Rest assured, we are in no danger, *mes amis*, so be of good cheer. The canons have orders to await us with hot possets. We will break our fast with them.'

That at least sounded like good news to Tam.

'Are you enjoying our little adventure?' He turned to see that Marie Seton had positioned her horse alongside Ajax.

He smiled. 'I will answer that question when we are safely on dry land.'

As they moved off, she said, 'We must allow Her Grace some indulgence, for she has had an anxious time of late. She has been upset by Lord Darnley's unpredictable behaviour and still grieves for her darling little Ado, her favourite pet, greatly treasured as the last gift from her late husband, the King of

France.' Marie shook her head. 'As I told you, Stirling is not a happy place for her and she wishes to visit Inchmahome, where she was truly happy in the past, to take away the sour taste of the present.' She paused and looked across at Tam. 'That is not so hard to understand, surely?'

'Not at all. But what is surprising is to masquerade in boy's clothes.'

'Do you not approve, Tam?' she asked coyly.

'From what I can see of you and your companions, I have no complaints.'

Beaton and Fleming made convincing boys, but Livingstone would never have deceived anyone.

Following his gaze, Marie laughed. 'The cloaks are useful for those of us with ampler curves.'

'Are those pages your servants also, in boys' clothes?'

Marie laughed. 'Nay, Tam, they are the stable boys. Our maids would never ride so well.'

This was Tam's chance and he took it. 'And your new maid? How does she?'

Marie shot him a curious look before replying. 'Bess is over her malaise and will go to Drummond with me. As for the other maid Lady Bothwell gave me . . .' She shrugged. 'I had nothing against her, but I did not care for catching her reading my private letters. Not dishonest, merely curious, I expect. Anyway, I'm glad to be rid of her and have my dear Bess back with me.'

'Where did your other maid go?'

Marie stared at him. 'Abigail, you mean? I have not the slightest idea. I knew nothing about her and I was not very interested, Tam.' She hesitated. 'Why do you ask? Is Aunt Beaton in need of another maid?'

Tam smiled. 'No, I was just curious.'

Marie's glance suggested she found his curiosity about a servant odd.

The Queen's laughter drifted back to them once more. Bothwell was close at her side and she seemed happy.

'Her Grace makes an excellent boy, do you not think so?' And when Tam agreed Marie went on, 'Sometimes I think she regrets that she was not born a prince instead of a princess. Scotland, she feels, would have been a safer place with a king. Her Grace has always enjoyed dressing as a boy and taking us along with her.' She laughed. 'One gets used to it. In happier times, with Lord Darnley,' she added sadly, 'she often roamed the streets and taverns of Edinburgh disguised as a boy. Once when he was awarded the Order of St Michael, Her Grace dressed in men's clothing to present the French ambassador with a dagger.'

Now that Tam was getting used to the intense cold, grateful for the warm heat rising from Ajax, he was enjoying this new experience. The sunrise was magnificent and it was good to have Marie at his side in such a romantic setting, sharing as she did the Queen's happy childhood memories of the priory.

'It was founded for a community of Augustinian canons by Walter Comyn, Earl of Menteith, in the thirteenth century, hoping to ensure by their perpetual prayers the salvation of his soul and the preservation of his dynasty. Such a religious endowment close by one of his principal residences at Inchtalla also provided a family burial place.'

They had reached the lochside, the frozen water a wide stretch of amethyst in the early light.

'See, over there. Inchmahome and the island to the right.' She pointed to a dark tower visible amid a tracery of winter trees. 'That is Inchtalla.'

As the party gathered on the lochside, Bothwell instructed Tam to lead with the pages, followed by the Queen and her Maries, with himself bringing up the rear. Viewing with trepidation the wide expanse of ice before them, Tam had very mixed feelings about the crossing. Presumably Bothwell's choice was wise, if not tactful, since he and the pages would be considered the most expendable members of the group should disaster strike.

For safety they rode gently, single file and well spaced. Even so, the ice seemed to vibrate with the weight of their horses and sometimes they stood still while it crackled alarmingly.

Assured by Bothwell that such sounds meant nothing, at last Tam felt Ajax's feet touch the solid mass of the island. Turning, he breathed a sigh of relief, counting the riders as they came safely ashore.

The six pages, the Queen, her Maries and Bothwell.

Twelve. With himself that made – thirteen riders.

Thirteen! He hoped and prayed that the Queen had not been counting. What would her reaction have been had she noticed this unlucky number at the outset of their journey as they gathered in the courtyard to leave the castle?

From all accounts, she would certainly have considered it an ill omen and decided that they should postpone this particular journey until later. Which would not have been a bad thing, in Tam's opinion. And he suspected that others besides himself would have preferred their warm beds to facing the Queen's whim of a long ride in the icy dawn.

There was no going back now, though, and the deadly number of riders was not commented upon. Perhaps he was the only person who had bothered to count, he thought, as they rode into the shadows of a rose-tinted morning, the silence broken by birds' gentle twittering and a cow lowing.

It was a scene of enchantment, a serene world where what remained of the priory after the Reformed Church's orgy of destruction took on the semblance of an enchanted cathedral rising from the slowly lifting mists.

The Augustinians, now depleted in numbers to six canons who strove gallantly to hold on to their lost world, came forward to greet the royal party. They were somewhat taken aback to discover the real identities of the 'gentlemen from the court' at Stirling Castle they had been told to expect.

The Queen, taking Bothwell's hand, jumped down lightly from her horse and swept off her bonnet.

Recognizing his royal visitor, Canon Malcolm bowed low and made to kneel before her: 'God bless your Grace.'

She put a hand on his arm. 'Do not kneel to me, reverend sir.' She laughed. 'Do you not remember how kind you were to your Queen when she was a little girl, long ago?'

He took her hand, kissed it. 'You blessed us with your presence, Your Grace. There never was a lovelier little princess.'

'Walk with me, if you please,' said the Queen, and she took the old man's arm. The pages were directed towards the stables with the horses, while the Queen and her Maries followed Canon Malcolm into the church, where a Mass was said for them.

As Bothwell and Tam prepared to remain outside, they were tactfully ushered into a vaulted room off the cloisters, made welcome by a great fire with food and ale on the table.

At Tam's side one of the younger canons said, 'Ours was once a silent order, our hermitic lives similar to those of monks. But of late we are less strictly enclosed and thus able to serve as parish priests on the mainland.' Smiling, he added, 'This is the warming room, so called because it has the only fireplace in the priory. In stricter times it was the one place where fires were allowed, even in winter. Here conversation was permitted and we were allowed to welcome guests.'

Tam felt reassured that others besides himself were grateful on such a morning for bodily comforts and for that huge log fire, crackling in the hearth. When the royal party returned from Mass they too eagerly warmed their icy hands before it.

Canon Malcolm said grace and with his juniors joined them in a plain but wholesome breakfast of freshly baked bread and cheese and ale.

Appetites satisfied, they were beckoned to follow the Queen and the old man through the cloisters to where the day stair curved upwards into the west range. There the Queen indicated that she wished to go on alone.

Marie whispered to Tam and led him outside. She looked up at the latticed windows above them.

'That is the Prior's lodging, where Her Grace stayed when she was a child and her mother feared for the future of Scotland and for her daughter,' she said as the Queen leaned out, and smiling, waved to them.

Moments later she emerged and walked over to where Marie and Tam were waiting. 'I wished to see it once more. Unlike the rest of us, it has remained unchanged.' She sighed wistfully. 'As for my lovely lodging, time has stood still. The same books, the same bed I slept in. Even after twenty years and a few more trees, I can still see the bower where we used to play as small children. Do you remember, Seton?'

'I do indeed, Your Grace.'

She beckoned to the three Maries. 'Come with me.' She smiled and glanced over her shoulder toward Bothwell, deep in conversation with Canon Malcolm. She made a small gesture indicating that this sentimental pilgrimage would be of scant interest to him.

'You come too, Tam,' whispered Marie softly as they made their way across the ice-bound grass to a round hillock which thorn trees, interlaced overhead, had turned into a tiny bower.

'Long ago, before the blessed saints came to Scotland and brought their message of Jesus Christ and our salvation,' said the Queen, 'legend had it that this was an enchanted island and our little bower here a fairy ring.' Clasping her hands, she smiled. 'This was a place where spells could be made and wishes granted.'

'How we loved to play and pretend, Your Grace,' said Beaton.

'And tell each other stories,' said Seton.

'And try to guess what the future held,' said Livingstone, smiling contentedly from happy marriage and the fulfilment of motherhood.

'We went further than that sometimes, when we told each other's fortunes from the playing cards,' said Fleming, soon to wed.

The Queen sighed. 'God was good to us, for we knew little of what lay ahead. The bounds of our lives were on this island. Beyond the lake, on the other side of the water, the world seemed very big, very scaring, but in our magic bower we were always safe.'

'Protected by good fairies, some said,' Livingstone put in.

The Queen sighed. 'Protected by angels too.'

'Here we were safe with our dreams, Your Grace,' said Seton.

'Safe from our nightmares,' said the Queen sadly, and put an arm around her. Then with one last look and a deep sigh, she kissed her fingers to the little bower and, followed by the Maries, started back to the priory.

'A moment! I have dropped my glove,' said Seton at Tam's side. 'Come with me.'

Her look was an invitation and he guessed the loss was no accident, for she knew exactly where she had left her glove as she said, 'Thank you,' and on impulse stood on tiptoe and kissed his mouth. 'That will be my memory of Inchmahome,' she said softly, and he took her into his arms, held her tightly and kissed her deeply. 'And that will be mine.'

She smiled up at him, her heart in her eyes. 'I am glad, Tam. For I do not imagine I shall ever return here. I wish to remember it as a time in my life when I loved.'

'And when you were loved,' said Tam as he pulled her into his arms again.

193

The kiss with Marie clinging close to him lasted longer than he intended and when at last he released her she touched his cheek.

'Dear Tam, time is running out for us too, is it not?' She shivered. 'I can feel that even without Aunt Beaton's magic powers,' she said sadly. 'Soon we go our separate ways to our homes and families for Christmas. We all meet again in Stirling for Fleming's wedding on Twelfth Night. After that Aunt Beaton will take you back to Branxholm and who knows when we will meet again?'

Tam had no answer to that and asked instead, 'When do you leave for Seton? You will spend Christmas there?'

She looked at him and shook her head. 'That would have been so this year had my brother also been at home.' She hesitated. 'Her Grace goes to Drummond Castle, at Crieff. She wishes me to accompany her.'

'Is that your wish too?' he asked gently.

She avoided his eyes. 'Adam Drummond has specially invited me. I will enjoy being at Drummond again. We went often when I was a child.' Another hesitation. 'I like Adam very much, Tam,' she added frankly.

'Like?' Tam's eyebrows raised. 'Are you sure that is all, Marie?' He paused. 'I think he expects more of you than liking.'

She smiled. Tam's observation had pleased her. 'Yes, I believe you are right. I was always fond of him and it was the intention of our families that we should marry when we were old enough. But then I went to France with the other Maries and as I grew older and was ready for marriage with Adam, I changed my mind. I knew I never wished to leave the Queen's service and that I would stay with her as long as she needed me.'

Tam was silent and she took his hands. 'But my mind is changing yet again. And had I never met you, Tam, I think I would gladly marry Adam Drummond.'

'You have answered my question, Marie. Escape to Drummond. Have a new and fulfilled life. You were made to be a wife and mother. Be like Fleming and Livingstone. Follow their example. You need not leave the Queen once you are wed.' He put a hand on her shoulder and said earnestly, 'Dear Marie, you deserve a bright and happy future. Take the opportunity that is being offered you.'

Even as Tam advised her, he was aware that he had not read that future in her hand. There was a long life-line, many lovers, but no marriage. But palmistry could lie, he told himself. He wanted her happiness and security above all things, the happiness and security he could never give her.

Her face was sad and she sighed deeply as he continued, 'Our ways will part, Marie. As you said, I am for Branxholm with your Aunt Beaton. I am her servant, my life is hers to command. I have no other life.'

He felt that Marie was unconvinced. Standing on tiptoe, she kissed his lips gently.

'Whatever happens, Tam, we can keep this, our one moment of magic. Nothing will ever spoil it.'

'Nothing,' Tam promised, and picking up the bonnet which had slipped off during their embrace, he stroked her hair and said, 'But you must move on, Marie. Marry this young man who loves you.'

'Tam—' she began to protest, and he cut her short.

'Listen to me, dear one. Whatever lies ahead, I can never make you my wife, we both know that. There are many reasons. Firstly, I have nothing to offer you, even if by some miracle your family would permit our marriage.'

And Marie bit her lip, knowing it was true, remembering the harsh lecture from her uncle, Sir Anthony Pieris, who had seen them not so innocently intentioned at the Queen's birthday.

'I do not know what my life was before – before the night Lady Buccleuch rescued me from her grounds. Do you not see that when my memory returns, I might even have a wife – God knows, even a family of young children.'

Marie raised tear-filled eyes. 'And I do not care a fig about that, or about being your wife. At this moment all I know is that I love you. That I seem to have loved you always, there was no beginning to it.' Her eyes explored his face and she shook her head sadly. 'For you are like no man I have ever known in my whole life.'

Tam could think of no reply to that as she put her arms around him, laid her head on his chest. 'There are other ways of being together besides marriage, as you well know, Tam,' she whispered.

'Not for you, Marie Seton,' he said firmly. 'You know you must wed according to the wishes of your family, some suitable man of noble birth equal to your own. A man like Adam Drummond.'

Her tears overflowed then and he kissed them away gently. 'If you love me, Marie, promise you will make a good happy marriage. Promise.'

She put her arms around him once more. 'My head knows you are right, Tam, but my heart – and my body – ache for you. Whatever the future holds for us both, you will always have a place in my heart.' Again she shivered, staring intently up into his face. 'Who are you, Tam? If I think too much about that, it scares me, and I do not know why. I only know I was carefree before I met you as I shall never now be carefree again.' Tearfully, she broke away from him, then said, 'It was so unfair of God or destiny, whatever we might call it, to let you come into our lives like this and change them. And then go away again.'

Silently he held her. There were no words for either of them.

At last Marie regained control over her tears. Blinking them away, she said, 'Before we join the others, there is something I want to show you.'

Taking his hand, she ran lightly across the grass, through the cloisters and opened the door into the chapter house. She pointed to the grave slab of a knight carrying a spear and shield. 'That is Sir John Drummond, Adam's ancestor. The family were important benefactors of the priory. His father, Sir Malcolm, gave it his estate of Cardross in thanks for his release from English captivity.'

Among the stone coffins of long-dead crusaders and priors lay a double effigy of a knight and a lady, their arms entwined, feet resting on a lion and a dog.

'He is Walter, the first Earl of Menteith,' said Marie, 'and Mary, his Countess. They died three hundred years ago. As small girls, we all loved to come here, fascinated by them lying there still so much in love, in that last embrace for all eternity.'

As they turned to leave the chapter house, Marie paused before Sir John Drummond's grave slab and looked up at Tam. 'I am glad we saw this together – that love can last for all eternity. A good omen, for the Drummonds are good people. They have always had close royal connections. Margaret Drummond was the favourite mistress of Her Grace's grandfather King James the Fourth. Rumour had it that they were secretly married and she bore him a daughter. Alas, she and her two sisters, Euphemia and Sibilla, were poisoned, probably by those who saw her as an obstacle in the way of the King's more expedient political marriage to Margaret Tudor.'

'Where did all this happen?'

'At Drummond Castle one Christmas, I believe.'

Drummond Castle didn't sound a happy or safe place for Mary Stuart either, Tam thought, asking cautiously, 'Is Lord Darnley to be there?'

'No one knows. He has not accepted the invitation.'

'And Lord Bothwell?'

'He goes to Liddesdale, I believe.'

A sudden crash from the outside, the sound of heavy stone falling against heavy stone, as if masonry had collapsed. A shout.

'Dear God.' said Tam. 'What was that?'

Taking Marie's hand, he ran lightly back over the grass to join the others standing outside the chapter-house wall.

Bothwell staggered over towards them, stared upwards, white-faced. The Queen rushed forward and cried out his name.

Bothwell looked dazed. 'A stone fell. There – ' He touched it with his foot. 'It missed me by inches.'

Eyes turned to the piece of masonry, which had cracked in two. No one could have survived its impact.

'An accident, my Lord. Most unfortunate,' said one of the canons. 'The building is sadly in need of repair. The winter weather, the freezing and thawing, affects the old cloisters. But repairs of such magnitude cost money and our coffers are empty.'

From the direction of the ferry landing, the sound of a horn indicated that the pages were waiting with their horses.

Bothwell said, 'That is the signal. Madam, we must leave now. Soon it will be dark.'

At Tam's side, Marie whispered, 'I fear Her Grace has forgotten she has to give final audience to the ambassadors before they leave tomorrow.'

The short winter day was drawing to a close, the sun sinking towards the horizon. As they walked towards the waiting horses, Bothwell took Tam aside.

'A word with you. I have just seen Will Fellows.'

'Will Fellows, my Lord?'

'Aye. The same, or his double.'

At Tam's incredulous look, he said impatiently, 'There is naught wrong with my eyes, Eildor. I ken what I saw. I tried to follow him and that was when the stone fell. Someone tried to kill me, let us make no bones about that. It was no accident.'

'A moment, my Lord.' Tam was bewildered. 'Did you say Will Fellows – here?'

'Aye, the same lad, I'd swear, that rescued me that night at Craigmillar. Dear God, if only he had waited. I meant him no harm.'

It was impossible, but Tam could hardly suggest that Bothwell had become obsessed with the disappearance of Will Fellows, whom he had met only once and briefly in gathering darkness outside Craigmillar Castle, and had described as having a bonnet down over his eyes. He could hardly point out without causing offence that any youth similarly muffled against the cold might resemble him.

Tam had his own theory that the six young pages left to their own devices had been capering about to keep warm, exploring the ruinous extents of the priory buildings. A worn stone had been accidentaly dislodged. By merest chance, Bothwell had been walking beneath at that moment, and no real surprise that the culprit had not rushed forward to confess either.

A more unhappy thought, nothing to do with Will Fellows, was that the page might have been bribed to follow Bothwell and, awaiting opportunity, hurl a loose stone down on him.

From Bothwell's confused and angry expression, Tam realized that the same thought had struck them both.

'Did you observe this lad among the pages who accompanied us, my Lord?'

Bothwell shrugged. 'I take little note of servants. It was dark, all were swathed in black cloaks. Besides, I am not on the lookout for likely young pages. My name is not Henry Darnley,' he added scornfully.

The Queen and the Maries had reached the waiting horses at the edge of the ice-bound loch, followed by their hosts. Canon Malcolm gave his blessing for their safe return to Stirling.

'Dear God,' muttered Bothwell, looking back to the priory, now silhouetted against the darkening sky. 'If only we could stay and I could find that lad again. We must keep this from the Queen – at all costs, d'ye hear, Eildor?' he added sternly.

Once again in single file, they prepared to cross the ice to the other side of the loch, dimly blue in the already fading light.

'As before, you lead with the pages, Eildor. I will bring up the rear again,' said Bothwell.

This suited Tam's purpose very well. More confident than he had been on the first crossing and safely on solid ground once more, he turned his horse and counted the riders.

Behind him the pages, followed by the Queen, her Maries.

He counted. One, two, three . . .

Bothwell came ashore. The last rider.

Twelve.

Twelve. When there should have been thirteen.

'Are we all assembled?' asked Bothwell.

'Are we sure no one is missing?' asked Tam.

Heads were shaken all around.

But one was missing, someone none of the party had particularly observed when the journey began in the dark before sunrise.

A torch-bearer. One of the pages was missing.

Tam stared back at the black silhouette of the now distant priory.

Where was he? His absence suggested that Bothwell was right, that this was another attempt to kill him. Was the would-be assassin still on the island in hiding somewhere?

It was then that Tam saw a rider leaving the loch some two hundred yards to the north of them. At that moment, he had just reached the shore and was disappearing into the woods.

Tam realized that whereas they had ridden slowly, carefully, in single line for safety, the rider had galloped fast across the ice. He had gained time and would soon be well ahead of them on the Stirling road.

'Tam?' Marie was at his side. 'What is it? Why do you hesitate? Is something wrong?'

Tam realized the folly of involving Marie in any of these sinister happenings, but said, 'We are one short. One of the pages rode on ahead. He took a path higher up the loch.'

Marie smiled. 'Oh, he will be safe enough. The ice will hold him. The Queen awaits.'

About to move forward, he took her rein, said, 'Would you recognize any of the pages again?'

'The stable boys, Tam?' Marie laughed. 'They all look exactly alike to me. I'm afraid I never know one from another. We are brought up to avoid eye contact, you know,' she added primly.

As she rode off, Tam glanced towards Bothwell. Deep in conversation with the Queen, he had not noticed and Tam felt disinclined to draw the missing rider to his attention.

Doubtless Bothwell's reply would be the same as Marie's. That he did not know one stable boy from another. Yet he thought he had recognized Will Fellows.

As for the missing rider, whatever his identity, they had little hope of meeting him on the road. If he was behind what had happened back on Inchmahome, a clumsy accident or another unsuccessful attempt on Bothwell's life, the lad would be safe back in Stirling and invisible once again long before they reached the castle.

Watching Bothwell riding proudly ahead, laughing with the Queen at some private joke, Tam was glad of the pistol at his side. Thankful, too, that my Lord Bothwell was not being carried back to Stirling on a litter.

A dead man.

The thirteenth rider arrived back well ahead of them and watched their approach from a high window in the castle. It would have been quite satisfying if the little procession below had included my Lord Bothwell being carried on a litter.

In pain and agony, with a few broken bones.

But not dead. Not yet.

Chapter Eighteen

Thursday 19 December 1566. Evening

Darkness had fallen when they reached the castle. Tam led Ajax towards the royal stables, hoping to discover the identity of the page who had been the thirteenth rider and his reasons for choosing to ride back to Stirling alone.

Candlelight and laughter led him to the horse-keepers' saddle room, where five heads turned quickly towards him. There was no need to introduce himself. The lads at the table rose from their repast and bowed. Clearly astonished that they should receive a visit from Lady Buccleuch's steward, they exchanged glances.

Could he have read their thoughts, Tam wondered, would their anxiety have related to Lord Bothwell's misadventure with the fallen masonry at the priory and the search for a scapegoat?

He tried to put them at their ease by saying how well the day had gone and thanking them for their part in making matters run so smoothly. The sighs of relief were almost audible. They relaxed.

'But you are one short,' he continued amiably. 'There were six of you?'

Looks were exchanged. Silence. Then the oldest

said; 'He came along at the last minute, sir, just as we were leaving.'

'Indeed? His name?'

Again looks were exchanged, cautious this time. Heads were shaken. 'He never told us, sir.'

'No, sir.' Eager this time. 'He kept himself to himself.'

'Didna seem to want to join in,' put in the first lad.

'Aye, a bit above the rest of us, if ye ken what I mean.'

'Oh,' said Tam. 'In what way?'

This question produced an uncomfortable silence.

'He hinted that he was sent by Lord Darnley to make sure that Her Grace travelled in safety and that no ill befell her.'

Tam nodded grimly. That was not quite the kindly interpretation most folks at court would have put upon Lord Darnley's husbandly care. A much more sinister one came to mind.

'Is the matter urgent, sir? Can we help you?'

'Only by telling me where I can find him.'

Doubtful looks across at Tam clearly indicated their concern. Was this man questioning them about a secret spy sent by the Queen? Rumours were rife. Now what was he asking?

'Were any of you in the vicinity when that piece of masonry fell? There was nearly a very nasty accident.'

They had been talking about that among themselves before this man arrived. Heads were shaken. 'No, sir. The five of us were playing dice, over by the horses at the ferry landing.'

A shudder of apprehension went through the little

group as Tam asked, 'So this other page wasn't with you, and you have no idea who he was?'

'No, sir. We do know that Lord Darnley favoured him,' came a somewhat reluctant whisper from the eldest and bravest of the group.

'How do you know that?' asked Tam.

'Angus here saw him leaving the King's apartments very late one night – did ye not?'

The lad addressed as Angus said shortly, 'That is none of our business, Jock. There could have been a lot of reasons.'

Another of the lads laughed coarsely. 'But not for such a pretty lad. The King's taste is well known.'

'That is enough. Enough, I say,' said Angus. And to Tam, 'Take no notice, sir. Such gossip is dangerous.'

Tam made reassuring noises and left them, frustrated by another path into the labyrinth leading nowhere. But the odds that Darnley was behind the attempts on Bothwell's life were increasing. Perhaps it was not too remote a possibility that the thirteenth rider, favoured by him, had been sent to Inchmahome to spy on the Queen and arrange a convenient accident.

Deep in thought, Tam made his way to Janet Beaton's apartment, where the candles had been lit for some time. As he entered, she turned to him angrily. 'Jesu, where have you been? You have taken your time. I heard the Queen and Bothwell ride in hours ago. Dallying with Seton, once again, were ye?' she sneered.

Bad moods seemed to be the order of the day. Something had upset Janet Beaton too. Before he could utter a word of explanation she demanded sharply, 'Did ye have a pleasant day? I hope none of you die from the effects of creeping about that priory in the freezing cold.'

Tam decided he had best soften her mood by telling her of Bothwell's accident. It was a mistake.

She heard him out and said, 'Jesu, Tam, has the man no sense at all? The place is in a ruinous condition and if, as ye suggest, the pages were running about, trying to keep warm no doubt, a stone could easily have been dislodged. As for Will Fellows – ' with a heavenward sigh – 'surely my Lord Bothwell is allowing his imagination to play tricks on him – again?'

Quickly realizing that Janet was running out of patience and sympathy, Tam explained about his search for the thirteenth rider and his recent visit to the stables.

'That is why I am late, Janet. I suspect a plot against my Lord Bothwell – at the instigation of the King.'

'God's love, Tam, how can ye be so naïve?' Janet thumped her fists together and regarded him savagely. 'A stone falls from ancient masonry and your missing rider – who was somewhere in the vicinity – feels guilty. And afraid. With good reason,' she added grimly. 'Would ye want to be taken to task and face Jamie Hepburn's anger, if ye had narrowly missed killing him? A man of power and influence. The lad would lose his situation – and be lucky if that was all his punishment.'

At any other time, Tam felt, Janet would have been more concerned about Bothwell's safety. He was soon to learn why she was not on this occasion.

'And did Lord Bothwell return with you?' she demanded suspiciously. When Tam said he did, she went on bitterly, 'He had best make the most of the next few days, before Her Grace goes to Drummond. Not having been invited, he plans to take his much neglected wife, Lady Jean, as second best, to Crichton Castle. To his sister Janet's home. A very pleasant family reunion,' she said sarcastically. 'The lass is a firm favourite with Her Grace, seeing that she is married to her father's other bastard, Lord John Stewart. Ye havena' met him, but he's a charming man, loyal to Her Grace. And a very different prospect to our scheming, ambitious Moray.'

'No doubt Lord Bothwell will find such society a pleasant change after the intrigues of the court.'

But Tam had said the wrong thing again and made Janet scowl more than ever. 'Ye're missing the point, Tam. I fancy this will be a much sought after conjugal reconciliation. Despite his protests that he cannot bear to touch her, that he loves only me, I ken Jamie Hepburn better than he kens himself.' She sighed deeply. 'His intentions run towards the urgent need of an heir – a legitimate one would be very desirable,' she added drily.

'I am sorry, Janet,' said Tam.

Suddenly her mood changed. She smiled with all her customary radiance. 'Never mind, Tam, we still have each other for consolation,' she said, with a wicked glint in her eye which Tam could not fail to misinterpret. 'Especially as Her Grace is taking Seton to Drummond with her.' She poured some wine, handed him a goblet. 'This missing page ye are so concerned about, this thirteenth rider – perhaps he had his own innocent reasons for riding ahead of ye to Stirling. Nothing to do with falling masonry. Do not ask me what they were – I canna cope with the ways of young pages – or the King's catamites.' She shrugged. 'Perhaps he was better acquainted with the area and just kenned a quicker way back.'

Tam was not convinced, but there was another more pressing matter. 'This strange and sudden illness of Seton's maid? You examined her, I believe.'

Janet regarded him, hands on hips and laughed. 'Tam, Tam – Bess was merely succumbing to a middle-aged woman's trouble. Does Seton not ken such things?'

'She made it sound very sinister,' said Tam.

'Sinister!' Janet laughed. 'God's love, Tam. The poor woman has floodings with her monthly courses which are getting steadily worse. Maybe she was too shy to discuss such matters with young Marie. Perhaps she only confided in me in desperation, knowing that I might have herbs which can help.' She shook her head. 'But she needs to rest on such days. A man might not realize, but being maid to any of the Queen's Maries is very demanding and exhausting.' Pausing she looked at him, then said gently, 'And so you thought she was being poisoned?'

'There is a lot of it around,' said Tam soberly. 'But I should like to talk to the maid, recommended to Marie by Lady Jean Gordon.'

'So?' queried Janet.

'I have been thinking about those poisoned sweet-meats.'

'And?' Janet's smile was mocking.

'Do you not see?' he said desperately.' This new maid who was with her at the time, possibly from her own household, could have been well acquainted with my Lord Bothwell's habits.' Pausing to let this sink in, he said, 'It would have been possible for her to set the trap for him – at Lady Jean's command.'

Janet frowned. 'Is Seton aware of the poisoning attempt?' When Tam shook his head, she went on, 'Are you sure you want to involve her in all this, Tam?' She paused. 'If she discovered something dangerous, a plot that Bothwell's enemies are anxious to keep secret, have you considered that you might be putting her life in peril too? By taking advantage of her affection for you.' And seeing his expression, she laughed. 'Oh, I ken all about it, and so does everyone else at court. She is not very good at concealing her feelings is our Mistress Seton.'

'Not for much longer, Janet. When she returns from Drummond after Christmas, I have a strong feeling that she will be ready to announce her betrothal to Adam Drummond.'

'So-o,' said Janet significantly, 'that's the way of it. And will that please you?

Tam shrugged. 'It is the best thing for her.'

'But not for you, I fear.' She looked at him intently and, leaning over, stroked his cheek. 'Ye're a strange and curious man, right enough, Tam Eildor. Different from any others I have met in my long experience.' Smiling, she added, 'No wonder women find you so interesting, such a challenge.' Then, regarding him narrowly, in the same words Marie had used on Inchmahome, she whispered, 'Who are you, Tam?'

'I have not the slightest idea, Janet. But if I ever find out,' he said, grinning, 'be assured, you will be the first to know.'

She laughed too. 'Meanwhile, we have each other for Christmas.'

'Branxholm, is it?'

'Nay. We stay in Stirling, but not here in the castle. Ye'll have seen it down the road. Mar's Lodging. Not as grand as this and Lord Erskine plans to tear it down and replace it with a grander, more modern palace. But we'll be comfortable there, as it is tolerably well furnished. Lady Morham will be with us. She is here for Fleming's wedding. As you know, they have always been close.' Frowning, she added sharply, 'Her main reason is to see her son, who will not be here, a sadness for her, but she was overjoyed to accompany Mistress Sinclair and travel in a litter.'

'Mistress Sinclair is staying in Stirling?'

'Aye, she has a widowed sister, Mistress Else Mowat, who lives in Bow Street. They are spending Christmas together.'

So he was to meet Anna Throndsen's sister at last.

But more immediately, he was summoned by the Queen. Her Grace wished him to sing for her.

Janet's eyebrows rose in mocking despair as he hurried across to the royal apartments, where the Queen had just received a very important visitor who made himself known long before he reached her door.

Tam had a glimpse of the ugly little Prince yelling lustily in his nurse's arms, his gnomish face not made any prettier by being bright scarlet, clearly in a very bad mood.

The Queen, however, clutched him to her as if he was the most beautiful, most saintly small creature in the whole world. She cooed over him, kissing the tear-stained face.

At last she was aware of Tam and, smiling, regarded him with an expression of bemused preoccupation.

Anxious not to interrupt one of her rare moments of well-deserved bliss, he felt that competition with the infant Prince was to be avoided at all costs. Especially any bright suggestion that might occur to Her Grace of calling upon him to sing a lullaby. Bowing himself out, he lingered in the antechamber on the off chance that the Queen might remember the reason she had summoned him. And that Marie Seton might put in an appearance.

As he loitered, Livingstone came over. 'Seton has gone with Fleming to discuss matters regarding coifs for the wedding. It seems to be a matter of urgency.' Seeing Tam's confusion, she smiled. 'Her Grace might be some time. Small babies can be very demanding, especially this one. And Her Grace has an audience with the ambassadors within the hour. I presume it is Seton you await – or is there something I can do?'

Thanking her, Tam bowed and exited quickly. It would seem that there were no secrets between the four Maries and that his dalliance with Seton was common knowledge.

Before departing for Drummond, the Queen was to make dramatic political moves which would have far-reaching consequences. Decisions perhaps also dictated by a mood of Christian charity as the season demanded, that would receive a mixed and often heated response from her subjects, as well as those with her best interests at heart.

First of all, a lavish grant to the Protestant Church, an effort to seek their support and secure the religious tolerance which was her ultimate desire for Scotland. Three days later, she returned to Archbishop Hamilton the necessary powers to see through her divorce from the King – a move calculated to ease proceedings which would have encountered considerable obstacles in acquiring a papal dispensation. This also greatly pleased the Hamiltons, traditional enemies of the Lennox family, whose dearest wish was to see Henry Darnley brought low and deprived of all kingly power.

Most surprising was Mary's acceptance of her half-brother Moray's long-sustained request that she put the past behind her and pardon the murderers of David Riccio.

This move, although going against her own feelings of revulsion, would guarantee Moray's support for the divorce and, more importantly, return Morton and his fellow conspirators from exile, where she could keep an eye on their activities. If they remained in England, it was certain that they would be sought by any who plotted against Mary.

And that included the wily Elizabeth of England, who had always shown herself eager to make welcome to her realm any enemies of her cousin Mary of Scotland.

Chapter Nineteen

Mar's Lodging. Christmastide 1566

Tam observed with amazement the great clamour of activity which attended the Queen's progress from one residence to another. Although her stay at Drummond would be brief, it was accompanied by an army of retainers and even some favourite items of furniture.

He had not seen Marie alone since they parted on Inchmahome and he hoped an opportunity would present itself before she left with the Queen. He realized that Marie and her three companions would be very much in demand at this time, but he could not overcome an uneasy feeling that she was avoiding him.

Perhaps that was for the best, even though such noble feelings were tinged with regret and his last sight of her was at Adam Drummond's side, as the young man came proudly to escort his royal guests.

Tam stayed out of sight, but he need not have done so, for watching the animated conversation between the two as they rode out of the courtyard, he did not think his absence was noted.

Meanwhile, Janet kept him occupied with Branxholm's legal documents, forever creating new clauses and adding new claims. Their compilations were never-ending, complicated by the demands, legacies and entitlements of six children from Janet's three marriages.

She was looking forward to the move to Mar's Lodging, frustrated by the draughty castle and the eternal quest to keep warm. The tall houses, some four storeys high, lacked the elegance of the nobles' town residences in Edinburgh. This omission, however, did not greatly concern Tam.

'What we lack in style, we shall more than make up for in comfort,' said Janet.

For once the royal parties had departed, there was little attempt to look after any guests who lingered. Despite Janet's complaints, servants stayed invisible.

Lord Darnley was the last to leave the castle, having been successfully avoided by the visiting ambassadors in whose ears he sought to plant a sinister catalogue of his wife's misdoings.

Despite a pretence of approval that she had forgiven Morton and the murderers of Riccio, he was outraged at his family being insulted by her concession to Archbishop Hamilton. Had he known the real reason that a royal divorce was behind the proceedings, it would have merited more than the heated and vindictive argument with Her Grace before she left, in which he contrived to humiliate her in front of the Maries, before huffily departing to his father's Glasgow home. Without, it was noticed, ever showing the slightest interest in his infant son's first Christmas or taking him into his arms for a proud father's kiss.

In the days before they moved from the castle, despite

being constantly at Janet's beck and call, and rallying to her uncertain moods, Tam still found time to write down, in case any accident befell him, all that had happened to Lord Bothwell since the first attempt on his life at Craigmillar Castle.

If Lady Jean Gordon were the guilty party, then Tam had a horror of hearing of some fatal misadventure at Crichton. He felt it was imperative to have documented all the details so far, not only for his own satisfaction but that so doing might also give him clues to those events that concerned threats to Bothwell's life.

He wrote:

1. Craigmillar, the attack by an unknown woman with a dagger that Bothwell suspected had been a gift made specially for Anna Throndsen's protection, while they were living together in Brussels.

2. The subsequent disappearance of his rescuer, Will Fellows.

3. The unresolved matter of Ben Fellows, who might be a relative of the missing man. His dead body claimed with suspicious alacrity by 'a fine Edinburgh lady' to be taken to Greyfriars kirkyard for burial. Purporting to be Fellows' niece, her description fitted that of Bothwell's assailant. The red-headed carter who assisted her was (according to the woodcutters) one of a notorious thieving family named Crozer.

4. The discovery of Ben Fellows' corpse, brought up by fishermen from Duddingston Loch wrapped in the cloak Bothwell had given to Will Fellows.

5. The subsequent disappearance of Archie Crozer, perhaps explained by impending marriage and fatherhood rather than something more sinister. Such as the body of a drowned young man recovered from the Nor' Loch as the Queen and Bothwell passed by on their way to Stirling.

6. The poisoned sweetmeats in the Queen's apartment in Stirling. By someone aware of the Queen's aversion to marchpane and Bothwell's weakness for it. Bothwell was kept in ignorance of this possible attempt on his life and the true facts concerning the poisoning of the Queen's favourite dog.

7. An arrow at the royal hunt had 'misfired', missing Bothwell by inches. Lady Jean Gordon had been following the hunt. Where was she when this incident took place?

8. The loose stone in Inchmahome Priory. A stranger to the other pages, who was the thirteenth rider so anxious to avoid their company on the way back to Stirling?

Tam then made a list of possible instigators of these crimes, real or imagined, by Bothwell:

Lord Moray, the Queen's half-brother,
Lady Jean Gordon, Bothwell's estranged wife,
Lord Darnley, the Queen's estranged husband.

Their instruments were a mysterious woman and, in Darnley's case, one of his catamites, if the stable boys' information was correct.

And in theory, according to the promptings of Lord Bothwell's guilty conscience, the woman was Anna

Throndsen, to whom he had been betrothed in Copenhagen in 1562. He had taken her dowry, then deserted her and their child.

When Tam had completed his list, he had come to some curious conclusions, fantastic but within the bounds of possibility.

He must talk to Dorothy Sinclair. It was imperative that he find out what she knew of her sister's movements and whether she was still in Norway.

They met finally on Christmas Day in her widowed sister's house in Bow Street. Smaller and vastly more welcoming than the rather sombre Mar's Lodging, it was pleasantly furnished with rich panelling. A broad oak staircase led into rooms hung with tapestries and chairs in Spanish leather, softly cushioned. A long refectory table hinted at lavish feasts.

Both sisters were seated by the fire when their visitors entered. They rose and curtsied immediately. Both wore white coifs, their hair hidden above bare brows in the fashionable manner. Else was fair in the Scandinavian manner, her eyes pale blue, whereas Dorothy's eyes were a striking rich hazel. Within minutes of that first encounter, Tam also realized that Dorothy was by far the prettier, her personality the more dynamic of the two.

He had been introduced by Janet as 'Master Eildor, my most trusted servant and master of the household at Branxholm'.

Lady Morham, who had arranged the meeting, peered at Tam. Her eyes seemed more filmed over than ever and Janet confirmed that she would soon be blind.

218

'Welcome, Master Eildor, we have met before. Your voice has a pleasant timbre, one not readily forgotten.'

Tam was introduced to Mistress Mowat, who stared at him rather coldly. Perhaps unsure whether one curtsied to a titled lady's servant, however trusted, she merely inclined her head.

'And this is my dear companion. Mistress Sinclair, of course, whom I believe you met at Morham.'

Dorothy Sinclair had no such misgivings as her sister about etiquette. She curtsied prettily. Tam bowed over her hand and she looked up at him with those large, brilliant eyes that dominated her face.

'Alas, Master Eildor, we did not have that pleasure.' And to Lady Morham, 'Remember, dear madam, I was in Edinburgh.'

Lady Morham nodded vaguely. 'You were indeed, my dear. My memory is not what it was.'

'I met your little nephew William, Mistress Sinclair,' said Tam.

She smiled. 'A dear child. We are all devoted to him.'

'He is not with you?' queried Janet.

'Alas – for ourselves, that is,' sighed Lady Morham.

'He was specially invited to Traquair,' put in Dorothy Sinclair. 'It is a favourite place of his, for there are many other children for him to spend Christmas with. The prospect of Stirling and a wedding have little appeal for a child. Master Eildor.'

'And he already spends far too much time with grown-ups,' said Else Mowat, who had contributed little to the conversation so far.

She seemed ill at ease and a little withdrawn. Tam noticed her anxious looks in her sister's direction, as one who fears some indiscretion. Perhaps she found Dorothy's easy manners towards a servant forward rather than friendly, and Tam got the idea that the invitation to Lady Buccleuch had not come from her.

Mistress Sinclair, however, was clearly enjoying the pleasure of having company. She talked of the Queen, asked about her health and was interested in her visit to Drummond Castle.

'She has my sympathy, such a dreadful husband,' put in Else. 'Royal he may be, but he is the talk of every tavern-keeper in Stirling. Such behaviour!'

An uncomfortable silence followed and there seemed no suitable reply to an observation so close to home regarding badly behaved husbands.

At last Lady Morham said sadly, 'My son is not with you. I was hoping he would spend Christmas with us, but he has gone instead to his sister at Crichton.'

'I am hoping he will take the time to visit William,' said Mistress Sinclair. 'He looked in on us briefly but, alas, Else and I were visiting friends.'

Looks of sympathy were cast in the direction of Lady Morham, the much neglected mother, and Tam felt that the details of Bothwell's shocking behaviour were a constant talking point with the two sisters during her absence.

The conversation then turned to Fleming, the reason for Lady Morham's presence in Stirling.

As he listened, feeling somewhat bored by a topic seemingly so inexhaustible and exciting for the four women, Tam realized there was no way he could tactfully introduce Anna Throndsen into the conversation.

At last, as they prepared to leave, he resolved to choose a more opportune moment to call on Mistress

Sinclair again. Her manner towards him already suggested that he would not be unwelcome.

'We return to Morham as soon after Marie Fleming's wedding as the weather will allow,' she said in reply to Janet Beaton's question.

'I will see Lady Morham safely home. She has a town house in the Canongate, rarely used these days, alas.' The look she gave in her old friend's direction spoke volumes of compassion. 'She has most kindly put it at my disposal when I need it for urgent matters – relating to William.'

'I understand you wish to adopt him,' said Janet.

'That is my most earnest hope, to make a home for my little nephew. And to ensure his future happiness.'

'A matter that has been sadly overlooked by his father,' was Else's acid rejoinder as the guests took their leave. And they could but agree with her on that issue.

Chapter Twenty

Mar's Lodging. New Year 1567

For Tam the year of 1566 slid pleasantly and uneventfully to a close, and eased itself quietly into the New Year. Soon the royal party would be leaving Drummond and returning to Stirling to celebrate Fleming's marriage on Twelfth Night to William Maitland of Lethington.

For Tam, this interlude at Mar's Lodging was a purely domestic time of escorting Janet Beaton to visit friends and her many relatives by marriage. Often invited to Else Mowat's home, they played cards with Lady Morham and the two sisters. While their social circle grew wider, Tam also became better acquainted with Mistress Sinclair.

Janet Beaton, who had an eye for such things, observed that she seemed to seek his company. Twice they met by accident. Once he found her alone in the busy marketplace, unattended by a maid.

When he remarked upon that, she said, 'Such an unnecessary indulgence,' declining his offer to carry her basket back to Bow Street. 'I am quite capable of taking care of myself. I have been doing so for a long while now, Master Eildor. In Shetland women are more independent, less reliant on men. It is a harsh life, connected with the sea, a cruel ruler of men. Women are used to loss, to being widowed young.' She sighed. 'Many take consolation in having their children by them. I, alas, was not so fortunate. I was left alone and I found the prospect of a bleak, cold, harsh life very unpleasing. I longed for my own kin and you know the rest. I sought out William and my sister Else. And Lady Morham has been like a mother to me.'

On the second occasion, he had ridden down to Stirling Bridge and was returning through the royal park. Dorothy Sinclair was ahead of him, riding alone and fast. He hailed her and she reined in, waited for him.

'How good to see you so unexpectedly, Master Eildor. Shall we race back to the castle?'

He laughed and told her she would soon outride him, that he was a very inexpert horseman.

She looked puzzled. 'I find that hard to believe, Master Eildor. You seem so very accomplished at everything.'

He patted Ajax's neck. 'You are very kind, but this is not one of my skills. And that I manage at all without disgracing myself is thanks to this good beast's tolerance and patience.'

She sighed. 'I love riding. I love the speed and the exhilaration of being free in the open air. Perhaps one day you will come to know that marvellous feeling.'

He bowed. 'Perhaps. Meanwhile, please continue without me. I shall not be offended.'

She laughed. 'As you will, Master Eildor. I will bid you adieu until we meet again. Soon, I hope.' And she was away.

He watched her go. 'Riding like the wind' was the phrase that came into his mind. Glorying in movement, free from the convention that demanded a lady be accompanied out of doors.

He decided then and there that Dorothy Sinclair was a most refreshing acquaintance and a day came when he called on her and found her sister absent. Her greeting included a cheek to be kissed in welcome.

'Am I being too forward, Master Eildor?' She smiled at him. 'It seems right and natural to kiss you, for you are so good to all of us. And I feel that there is a bond of friendship between us in the short time we have known each other.' She stood back and looked at him gravely. 'You have the face of a man I would trust. A good friend – and a bad enemy.'

Tam bowed. 'I will endeavour to remain the former and never the latter.'

He liked her and the friendship was true for Tam. It seemed as if he had known her a long time. Such had been his feelings with Marie Seton too. But this was different. There was no danger to be encountered here. Dorothy Sinclair was a mature woman who knew her own mind and, as he had observed, possessed an independent spirit. Cultured, well spoken – a charming voice with only the faintest hint of an accent – more knowledgeable than her sister Else, who, he gathered, had lived a more restricted life.

When Dorothy's husband was alive, she had travelled with him to many places in Europe. Resourceful, she relied on no one, a trait Tam admired and one, he was certain, that belonged to the more enlightened world temporarily lost to him.

One day she told him that Else, who tended to

avoid their company was perhaps jealous of their easy ways with each other.

'Else was always awkward with men. Her marriage was not successful and her husband had left her poorly off.'

Dorothy then rather triumphantly confided, 'I believe she has formed an attachment for you, Tam.'

Tam was surprised, since they had hardly shared more than a few polite words and when he arrived she immediately absented herself.

Dorothy laughed. 'That is her way. As I told you, she is very shy with men and unused to being in their society. We come from a large family of daughters and she did not have good fortune as I did with my suitors.

'You were both more fortunate than your sister Anna, I believe.'

She sighed. 'So you know all about poor Anna. My Lord Bothwell gave her no respite in his wooing. He was determined to have her and he was – is – a man of considerable charm when he chooses to exert it on ladies. And it was the dearest wish of our father, the Admiral, that we should all marry Scotchmen. So, of course, there was rivalry among us when the Lord Admiral of Scotland came to our home. We heard a cruel rumour later, when it was too late,' she added bitterly, 'that it was Lord Bothwell's boast that he could have had any one of us in his bed. But Anna had most to give, the largest dowry, and she was the cleverest and the most exciting.'

Looking at her and remembering Bothwell's description, Tam said, 'I find that hard to believe.'

'It is true, believe me. Beside Anna, the rest of us were pale shades.'

Perhaps if they were all as colourless as Else, she might well be right, thought Tam.

'I understand he abandoned her after William was born and she went back to Norway.'

'He abandoned her – and William – and stole her money,' Dorothy said heatedly.

'Have you seen Lord Bothwell since you came to Scotland?'

'No, and I have no desire to,' she said sharply. 'I shall avoid meeting him face to face at all costs. When he came to see his mother, I hid in a closet,' she said. 'The way he treated poor Anna was despicable and unforgivable.'

'She has never returned to Scotland to see her son?'

Dorothy gave him a strange look. 'There was another child, a girl, conceived shortly after William was born and when Anna still had hopes of being his acknowledged wife. The little girl was frail and she took ill. Anna implored his help. She was alone in a strange city where she knew no one. She made the journey from her lodging to the court at Holyrood, but he refused to see her or the babe, or even to get help from one of the royal physicians. He turned her from the door and the child died.' She was silent for a moment and then she shook her head. 'That was the cruellest blow of all. Anna blames him for their daughter's death. She will never forgive that.'

An appalling story, right enough, but Tam thought that the child might have died anyway. Infancy was a tenuous business, mortality in the first two years of life common evidence in any kirkyard.

'Do you hear from your sister?'

'She keeps in touch with me by letter, but Scotland has bad memories for her.'

'When did you last see her?'

Dorothy frowned, remembering. 'We used to meet while she still had hopes of Lord Bothwell being true to his vows. When she visited Scotland, he would put her on a Norwegian ship that briefly sailed into port at Lerwick. She would visit us then.' She sighed. 'But there is no reason for her to come here now.'

'She has not been back in Scotland?'

'Not since our father died and our mother, who is something of an invalid, needed Anna to look after her and run the household. She was very good at that, and had helped our father with his business dealings during his illness.' Pausing she gave him a shrewd glance. 'You have asked me at least twice if Anna has been back in Scotland. Is there some reason for your curiosity?'

Tam considered whether he should tell her about the mysterious woman who had attacked Bothwell. He decided there was nothing to be lost and that in fact there might be something to be gained by this confidence.

'There have been several attempts on Lord Bothwell's life – here in Stirling and earlier at Craigmillar Castle. We suspect that they were the work, or at the instigation, of some person who knew him and his habits intimately.'

She looked at him wide-eyed and laughed. 'And you suspect Anna? How incredible!'

Tam shrugged. 'Not so. A thwarted woman seeking vengeance.'

But the idea that the two gently reared sisters,

Dorothy and Else, had a sibling capable of plotting murder did not seem so plausible any more.

Again Dorothy laughed. 'What a strange idea! Anna would have to be a very clever woman indeed. Tell me, how did you arrive at such conclusions?'

'A description given to Lord Bothwell by a young man who rescued him at Craigmillar from a woman who was about to plunge a knife in his back. He showed Bothwell the dagger he had seized from her hand and Bothwell thought he recognized it.'

Dorothy smiled. 'It does not sound a very likely story. Daggers are not unique, not even a lover's special gift.'

Their conversation was interrupted by Else's arrival and, under that cold watchful stare, they parted, with hopes from Dorothy that he might visit her in Edinburgh before he returned to Branxholm with Lady Buccleuch.

'I have recently rented a small house on the outskirts of the town. I feel the air will be purer for William, and if it suits me I will consider taking up permanent residence there.'

'Will he not miss his grandmother?' said Tam, remembering the bond between them.

Dorothy nodded. 'I will make certain that there is room for her too. Morham is too large, too cold and isolated, for her poor health. Else suggested this arrangement and I saw immediately the advantages of a small, comfortable house. I am taking Lady Morham to see it on our return. I think she will be charmed with the idea. And perhaps you, Master Eildor, will come with us?'

When Tam said he would be delighted, she continued, 'Doubtless a man's hand will be needed.' She laughed impishly and touched his arm. 'And you need have no fears that I will not be adequately chaperoned.' she regarded him seriously. 'For I should not like to feel that this was to be the end of our acquaintance. You can be free with me, Master Eildor. We are experienced people and visiting a widowed lady will not do irreparable damage to either of our reputations.'

Chapter Twenty-One

Monday 6 January 1567. Morning

As Janet prepared to leave for Fleming's wedding in the Chapel Royal, Tam realized that this serene and happy time at Mar's Lodging, undisturbed by plots or counterplots and with the pleasing addition of Dorothy Sinclair's company, was almost at an end.

Splendid in russet velvet, happy and excited, Janet sighed. 'Next week at this time we will be home in Branxholm. This is my last social occasion and I am not sorry.'

'Will Lord Bothwell be at the wedding?'

Janet scowled. 'I doubt that. Matters at Liddesdale keep him fully occupied. He's a Borderer, like myself. Glad to be free of the court and all its intrigues.' Adjusting her coif, framed in pearls and garnets, she considered her reflection and added, 'Have you heard that Lord Darnley was taken ill on Christmas Eve, the very day he reached his father's house in Glasgow? It is said he has smallpox, but that I fear is an innocent diagnosis of the disease.'

Tam frowned. 'Innocent?'

'Aye, Tam. It is syphilis. And all things considered, God may relieve Her Grace of this loathsome burden of a husband without the necessity of a scandalous divorce, if she has patience to bide her time a little.' At the door she turned and smiled. 'You had best say farewell to Mistress Sinclair, Tam, for there will be little opportunity of meeting her once we get back to Branxholm. Ye'll have plenty there, I dare say to keep yer mind off any budding romance.'

Tam's eyebrows raised. 'I was not aware—'

Janet laughed shortly. 'Then ye're a fool, man. Anyone can see that the lady is smitten with ye. Look at the way she seeks out your company.' And with a coy smile, 'Aye, and ye're not averse to that, I fancy.'

She put a hand on his shoulder. 'It's a grand thing for a young man like yerself to have a mistress.'

'Madam,' said Tam indignantly, 'we are far from that.'

Janet shook her head. 'Not too far – yet, Tam. Anyway, a widowed lady like Mistress Dorothy Sinclair is a better prospect than Seton. I'm pleased that ye didna take advantage of her infatuation. And that ye kept her at a distance – at least most o' the time,' she added with a laugh.

'No fault of mine,' Tam grumbled. 'I had little option in the matter. You have my word that I am deeply fond of Marie Seton and, had we been equals in social standing, I would have wished to make our relationship a lasting one.'

Janet smiled at this self-righteous pronouncement as he went on, 'But there are promises I might not be able to keep, as you well know.'

'Aye, Tam, better than most.'

'I cannot commit myself to any woman, only to find in the fullness of time that I am a bigamist.'

231

'Perhaps a father too, Tam, although I have noticed little paternal about you,' said Janet as, leaning over, she kissed him gently. 'Such sentiments do ye credit It doesna worry some men – Jamie Hepburn included,' Janet added bitterly and sighed. 'I ken only too well that our time together is limited. That is all that concerns me, but Seton has no experience in the ways of the world. Poor lass. Although, her betrothal to Adam Drummond would be an excellent move and would receive the blessing of both Setons and Drummonds. They're a fine family, well thought of and close to the Queen.'

'And yourself, Janet. Would you approve?'

'Aye. Not that my opinion would be sought.' Sighing, she stretched her arms above her head. 'But let's get Fleming's wedding over and leave as quickly as we can.'

A quick kiss and she was gone.

Tam had time to deliberate on Janet's words. With no opportunity to talk to Marie alone since he watched the royal party ride in two days past, he had not been at all surprised to see Adam Drummond riding at her side. The young couple looked happy, totally involved with one another. Tam was glad for them both. And rather more selfishly for himself.

Matters had moved swiftly since Marie went away and he had spent a great deal of time in Dorothy Sinclair's company. A remarkable woman, clever, intelligent and attractive.

He recognized that here was the kind of woman he could love and respect. Her Viking inheritance, her life in Shetland, had bred a stronger version of woman-kind than he'd encountered at Mary's court.

He spent the evening playing cards at Bow Street. Neither of the sisters had been invited to Fleming's wedding and Else seemed a little distracted, her attention constantly wandering from the cards. At last, complaining of a headache, she excused herself and retired.

He had given up trying to understand Else, who remained an enigma. The very opposite of her sister, she was nervous and ill at ease in his company. He wondered why she disapproved of him. Despite Dorothy's assurances that she had an attachment for him, this was not the behaviour of a love-smitten female. That idea did not ring true. There was something else, deeper and more disconcerting, about her behaviour in his presence.

This was not the first time she had left them together on the flimsiest excuse and Tam exchanged a glance with Dorothy who merely smiled knowingly. Had Else's action been kindly meant or even suggested by Dorothy? For both realized this was to their advantage, aware that once Tam settled in the demanding atmosphere of Branxholm, as Janet had warned him, he would have little excuse to visit Edinburgh and their meetings would be few indeed.

When their ways parted Tam would be truly sorry, his memories of Stirling as a pleasant interlude of warm friendship with Dorothy Sinclair.

He would carry in his mind the vivid picture of her riding fearlessly, and alone, never afraid to be solitary, scorning dependence upon anyone, a free spirit unshackled by the strict rules and conventions dictated for well-born females of the time.

Also in her favour was her total disregard for the superstitious beliefs and fears that dominated so many lives, from which even the the Queen of Scotland was not immune.

'We make our own destiny, Tam. We are not play-things of the gods. We all have it in us to fulfil our ambitions and desires, if we are strong enough to take fate by the throat. When we are young, young as the Queen, we are vulnerable. But later, we discover that life itself shapes us.'

Tam smiled, said teasingly, 'And yet even you did not wish to have your fortune told?'

She turned and stared at him, remembering the evening they had spent together and her indignant outburst when Lady Morham had been eager to have Tam read the cards or her hand.

'I know my fortune,' Dorothy had said shortly. 'I know what life holds for me. Why should I be confused by the foolish revelations of a pack of cards?'

'Do you not believe, then, that our lives might be mapped out in our hands?' Tam asked.

'That our lives are written the day we are born?' She made a gesture of dismissal. 'I think it is highly unlikely and totally against my rigid Protestant up-bringing. Our dear father, the Admiral, taught us by his own example to be practical people.'

'Your sister Anna was hardly a good example,' Tam reminded her gently.

'Anna was very young, very foolish. She had a soft heart and could not recognize a man who wanted only her fortune. Nay, Tam, superstitions are only for ignorant peasants. For those of us who use our heads, not our hearts, we know differently. We know that we can shape our destinies.'

'Yet even our Queen is swayed by omens.'

She shrugged. 'Incredible, is it not? As a Catholic and one who regards herself as God's anointed, she should surely have more faith in His divine will.' Without awaiting his reply, she smiled: 'Let us trust that time will teach her better wisdom, or I fear it will be the worse for us.'

When he told her about the Queen wishing to turn back after encountering the drowned man at the Nor' Loch, and how glad he had been that she had not counted thirteen riders as they crossed to Inchmahome Priory, Dorothy's reaction was one of incredulous amusement. 'I wish I had been there, Tam. It must have been a remarkable day. Did you ever discover the identity of the missing page?'

Tam shook his head and Dorothy, like Janet, suggested that the thirteenth rider had some better prospect in mind than riding home in stately fashion with the Queen.

'And on such a cold day too, who could blame him?'

Loving islands, even the small ones, she wanted to hear more about Inchmahome and talked enthusiastically of Norway and the fjords and the ancient sagas.

Tam knew he would miss her conversation most of all. She had an amazing knowledge, doubtless based on her earlier travels with her husband. It extended beyond travel, to literature and art. She also dabbled, she said, in painting.

When he expressed a desire to see some of her

work, she laughed. 'Some day, when I have leisure, I shall paint you.'

He was sorry when the evening was over and Lady Morham returned to Mar's Lodging in a flutter of happy exhaustion. As Dorothy hovered over her anxiously, the romantic sentiments she carried from Fleming's wedding were again satisfied at finding her dear friend alone with the personable Master Eildor.

Tam fancied she was already hearing another peal of wedding bells, although she sighed and said, 'My dears, I am just tired – and too old for such great events. At one time I could have danced with the best of them.' She sighed. 'But that was long ago.'

Dorothy removed her old friend's shoes and set her feet upon a stool. 'Tell us about the wedding.'

'A splendid occasion, but somewhat pale and insignificant after the wonders of the little Prince's christening. A little lack-lustre, I fear, if unfair comparisons should be made. It had the appearance of a purely family event, for close friends and kin.' Then, sitting up in her chair, she leaned forward excitedly. 'But I must tell you, Marie Seton was there with that delightful young man Adam Drummond. He had come to Stirling especially to escort her to Fleming's wedding. Now, what do you think of that?' she asked, her eyes gleaming. 'Watching them together, I think we might well have high hopes of another wedding soon. Perhaps when she takes him to Seton, he will ask her brother for her hand.'

Chapter Twenty-Two

Wednesday 8 January 1567. Morning

Tam was pleased that as soon as opportunity permitted, Marie came to Mar's Lodging in search of him.

'Tam, I can only stay a moment. Adam is waiting for me,' she added breathlessly. 'We are riding out to Stirling Bridge.' She smiled, took his hands. 'It is good to see you again. I missed you at Drummond.'

'Did you indeed?' Tam's eyebrows rose at that. 'But you had young Adam, who has not been far from your side since your return to Stirling.'

'He came only for Fleming's wedding.'

But Marie blushed prettily as Tam asked gently, 'And have you news for me?'

She frowned. 'News, Tam? What sort of news?'

He held her hands. 'The best possible, Marie. Are you not to be betrothed to Adam? There have been hints—'

'From Lady Morham, no doubt. She is most anxious to marry all of us off as speedily as possible.' But her smile suggested that such rumours were not entirely displeasing. A moment later, suddenly solemn, she sat down on the window-seat. 'I know not what to do, Tam. Adam wishes us to marry, but I am not certain.

I think I love him enough and he would be a most suitable choice, since my family regard him very favourably.' She sighed. 'But I am in no hurry. As I told you, the Queen will always come first with me, and I cannot leave her service until her divorce is complete and I see her life settled more happily.'

She looked up at Tam, who made no reply. 'You will have heard that Lord Darnley is ill. I wish I could find it in my heart to pity him, for something brought about by his own folly.' She shook her head. 'His illness, serious in other men's eyes, is not enough to keep him from plotting. As you know, the Queen restored Archbishop Hamilton's powers. The Protestants took this as a dangerous threat and even Lord Moray warned her that she must immediately revoke his powers. The Hamiltons are the hereditary enemies of the Lennoxes, since time immemorial, rivals over the fiefdom of Glasgow. And so Lord Darnley regarded this and any favour bestowed on them as a personal insult.'

She sighed. 'What a Christmas this has been, Tam. One not easily forgotten, this time of peace and good-will to all men. A joyful celebration of Christ's birth indeed, with news constantly arriving of the King stirring up plots against Her Grace. He wrote to His Holiness the Pope, to the King of Spain and to the King of France, saying that she was dubious in the faith for showing preference to Protestant nobles and clergy in her court. He complained about the state of the country, which was out of order, he said, all because the Mass and Popery were not again elected. And giving the whole blame to Her Grace for not managing the Catholic cause aright.'

Marie looked around nervously, as if afraid of being

overheard. 'She read us a letter from her ambassador in Paris that it was openly spoken of by persons who loved her that the King, with assistance of some of the nobility, should take the Prince their son and crown him. And being crowned, his father should take upon him the government. We all recognized that it was in her own interests and those of Scotland to forgive Morton and the Scottish lords she exiled for poor Davy's murder, and to recall them, when she would have preferred never to set eyes on them again.'

'A practical move,' said Tam. 'Easy to see, from her point of view, that they would be safer out of England and the web woven by Queen Elizabeth, who would use them for her own ends.'

'I agree,' said Marie. She hesitated, then added, 'Alas, there is a matter even more hateful to her than recalling poor Davy's murderers, Tam.' And wrinkling her nose in a gesture of distaste, she explained. 'It seems that she has no other option but to seek a reconciliation with her husband and resume their marital relations. How she wept, our poor lady, when she received news from France that on no account must she proceed with the divorce, as this would alienate the English Catholics, who would then transfer their support to Lord Darnley.' She shuddered. 'And then, because she is Queen first and woman second, she realized that this drastic measure, however repellent to her personally, would make certain that she could extend her influence over Darnley once more. And destroy her enemies' power to use him against her, as she did after Davy's murder.'

'Unpleasant or not, it is certainly the wisest action,' said Tam.

Marie looked out of the window. 'I must go. There is Adam, patiently waiting for me,' she said tenderly. As though aware of her, the young man looked up, smiled. She waved to him. 'No need to stay out of Adam's way, Tam, or fear his jealous wrath. I have told him all about you, that you are my dearest friend.'

'And always will be, dear Marie,' said Tam.

At the door she hesitated. 'I would love to see you again, Tam. May I write to you at Branxholm?'

He kissed her outstretched hands. 'I would be honoured.'

Janet was in her apartment, walking the floor impatiently. 'Delays and more delays. Once again we have to await the Queen's pleasure, for she intends to take Prince James back to Edinburgh with her, away from his scheming father's clutches. I trust that she will have no further need of me at Holyrood and that I will be allowed to return to my own home,' she added sourly.

Tam learned that Dorothy and Lady Morham would be leaving ahead of the royal party. Wishing them Godspeed, he was kissed by Dorothy, the gesture of a trusted friend rather than a passionate lover. He did not let his lips linger, wishing to avoid any display of emotion or arousing false hopes. Mostly his own.

'Once I have seen Lady Morham safe home, I will be returning to Edinburgh,' Dorothy told him. 'Who knows, maybe we will meet again sooner than we thought.'

Watching the cavalcade make its way down the steep street, it seemed a long time since he had first encountered Dorothy Sinclair, his only interest then what she might tell him of her sister Anna Throndsen. And even longer since he had cared about solving the identity of Lord Bothwell's would-be assassin.

Part Three
Kirk O'Field

'The matter of the King's death is so horrible and strange and we believe the like was never heard of in any country. He was slain with such a vehemence that of the whole lodging, walls and other, there is nothing remaining not a stone above another, but all carried far away, or dung in dross in the very groundstone. It must have been done with the force of powder and appears to be a mine.'

– Mary Queen of Scots to Ambassador Beaton in Paris,
10 February 1567

Chapter Twenty-Three

Beaton House in the Canongate.
Friday 31 January 1567

Janet's plans had once more been frustrated by fate, this time in the shape of her favourite daughter, Alice, taken seriously ill in Blackness.

With Branxholm further away than ever, Janet decided Tam would remain in her family's town house. As there were legal settlements to be drawn up for two of her remaining children and properties to be acquired in Edinburgh, he could make that his goal until Alice had recovered sufficiently for her mother to take her departure.

'There should be enough to keep you busily occupied,' said Janet. 'Once these settlements are agreed, they will need to be copied and witnessed. Take them up to Walter Pax, near the castle.'

Tam's eyebrows raised at that. Walter Pax had a reputation as a scheming lawyer and hints that he was an expert on forgery were confirmed by Janet's next words.

'You have a good legal head, Tam, but your writing is intolerable. We need fair copies of these documents.'

Preparing to leave the house once again, she said,

'The Queen will be returning from Glasgow bringing Lord Darnley to convalesce at Craigmillar. It is all in readiness for him, well away from any contact with the little Prince at Holyrood. I hope Her Grace will excuse me from being in devoted attendance on this particular invalid,' she added wearily. 'I hear he wears a taffeta mask to cover the pustules on his face. Curing the pox is beyond even my herbs.'

Now in Edinburgh and with time on his hands, Tam decided to call on Dorothy Sinclair. Directions from Janet's servants were that the district of St Mary's was readily accessible.

'It is just inside the city wall, sir, overlooking the Cowgate. The whole area is called Kirk O'Field, because of its connections with what was an ecclesiastical foundation before the Reformation.'

The old servant paused, wondering perhaps whether Master Eildor looked kindly on the ruinous conditions that had been visited upon Catholic churches and abbeys by religious intolerance.

'It is on slightly higher ground than the Canongate. There are some pleasing gardens as I recall, and there is less noise than we have to suffer.'

As it was surprisingly mild considering the date on the calendar, Tam decided to leave Ajax in the stables behind the house and go on foot. Fresh air and exercise would not come amiss.

Edinburgh's shrieking winter gales were absent and the sun shone thinly but benignly as he made his way through the Netherbow Port. Away to the south of the city, the summit of Arthur's Seat was, for the first time, almost clear of snow.

His passage into the open country was marked by farm dogs that ran out to greet him and hens that dispersed from his path, clucking anxiously. Overhead the black shapes of corbies hovered, their raucous cries filling the air, lulled by the mild weather into a belief that mating time was at hand and their huge untidy nests were due for another noisy brood.

The tall trees stretched skeleton-like branches into a blue sky and, at Tam's feet, the first fragile snowdrops brought the promise of renewed life into the black tangle of winter hedgerows.

He breathed deeply. Soon it would be spring and the anniversary of the evening when he had opened his eyes in Janet Beaton's garden. He was still no nearer to solving the mystery of his own identity, but a year's passing had changed his frantic efforts at remembering.

Let life drift along, he decided. His present existence was pleasant. He was happy, even content, regarding the gaps in his memory, as a man who loses the use of an arm or a leg comes to term with the fact and learns to live with the inconvenience.

Climbing the gentle incline leading to St Mary's, he found himself in a pleasant rural scene, dominated by the ruined church from which the district took its name.

Among the houses clustered around a quadrangle was the old Provost's House, a substantial building on the south side where the ecclesiastics who served the foundation once lived. Behind it lay the Flodden Wall, with a narrow passage or court between and through the town wall, a postern gate leading out into the country.

The next building, property of Robert Balfour, was the new Provost's House at the south-west corner. Two tall mansions, almost hidden by high walls and at a short distance from one another, belonged to the Hamiltons and the Douglases.

All this information Tam was to obtain later from Dorothy, who had made a careful study of this desirable area when she rented St Mary's Lodge, with a view to taking a permanent lease of some suitable property.

He approved of her choice, observing that the area had the peaceful feeling of a cathedral close, protected by the city wall, and beyond it rural scenes of gardens and orchards. This would be the perfect place to bring up her young nephew.

An enquiry of an old man smoking a pipe in the sunshine indicated there were few newcomers and therefore considerable interest in any new arrivals. He pointed out the house where Mistress Sinclair lodged in St Mary's Close, one of three small cottages, set at right angles to the quadrangle and once reserved for the lesser clergy.

Tam had some difficulty making his escape from what promised to be a lengthy discussion about the inquitous decline in conditions within the city since his informant was a lad! At last he walked across the grass to the house with pantiled-roof, crow-stepped gables under dormer windows and a turret housing a turnpike stair.

Opening the gate of a tiny garden which would be pleasant in summer, with birds twittering in the fruit trees, he walked up the path and tapped on the door.

A moment later, Dorothy's familiar face appeared,

astonishment mingled with other emotions. She stammered a greeting, taken aback to see him again. 'Tam, what brings you here?' she demanded. 'I thought you to be away back to Branxholm by now.'

For a moment, as he began to explain, he thought she intended to keep him at the door. Then at last, a smiling welcome. 'Do come in.'

He followed her through a long, narrow reception room, perhaps the original dining room for the clergy, and up a turnpike stair into a pleasant chamber with deeply embrasured windows, but somewhat sparsely furnished.

'As you will realize, this is only a temporary abode, until I complete negotiations to settle here. But I like this area. The air is more pleasant and wholesome than in the city.'

Tam agreed and she went on, 'When next you visit me, I hope to have rugs on the floor and some tapestries for these rather bleak walls. There is much to do. Even for a short stay, I like my home to be comfortable.'

Although she talked at great length, full of apologies, charming as ever, he had an extraordinary feeling that their former closeness had somehow evaporated. Her voice was strained, her manner distracted – as once her sister Else's had seemed.

When he asked after Else, and whether she would be visiting, Dorothy gave him a startled look. 'She has no plans at present. At least not until I have a more permanent residence.'

As he watched her smiling, her wandering gaze hinted at anxiety and he wondered if his call had been particularly ill-timed and she had – or was expecting –

a more important visitor. A lover, perhaps. Tam was aware that he would be sadly disappointed if that was the case.

So certain was he of having her at a disadvantage, he mumbled some excuse about having to leave directly.

She laid a hand on his arm. 'No, Tam. You must not go so soon. Now that you are here, I insist that you sit down and take a glass of claret with me. I am afraid . . .'

Once again, that searching glance around the room, followed by apologies.

'I am afraid that the house is not quite what I would wish to show to visitors. But it will serve my purpose for the present. If all goes according to plan, I have hopes of making it my home once William is with me. And it seems I have made my choice of a place to live at the right time.' She smiled. 'I am to have a royal neighbour. None other than the King himself. He is to move into the house across the quadrangle. For a few days only, I believe, while he is still convalescent.'

This was news to Tam. Obviously Dorothy Sinclair's information was more up to date than Janet's. Not wishing to contradict her, he marvelled at the lightning speed with which rumour, however inaccurate, travelled.

Henry Darnley was preparing to leave his father's house near the Bishop's Palace in the precinct of the Drygate in Glasgow. News had arrived that the Queen, saddened by her husband's illness, was arriving within the hour.

He watched the servants frantically rushing

around, heard his father's shrill commands. He didn't feel up to any of this. Sick, feverish and still quite ill, he did not relish the journey to Edinburgh, which his suddenly thoughtful wife implored him to make.

He found her insistence that they should resume their marital relations and 'all be as before' rather touching, this appeal to his wounded pride and his sick body. There was, however, as always seemed to be the case in anything Mary suggested, a slight impediment. Until he had made a full recovery from his 'smallpox', as she politely called it, fulfilling to the letter the time of quarantine, he could not possibly stay in Holyrood. When he protested, she said gently that this was not for herself, but for their son.

'I do entreat you, husband, to give this your careful consideration. Sickness and plague do not spare even infant princes.'

What did she mean by plague? How could she be so tactless? But he dare not risk the Prince, whose survival was crucial to his own ambitions, his secret plans.

'I suggest that we stay in Craigmillar.' And, ignoring his sullen, mutinous expression, 'It is for a short time only. The air there is pure and should help restore you speedily to the fullness of health – which will be of benefit to us both,' she added smoothly. Did he detect a sly smile?

Craigmillar. Darnley tried to avoid the mirror, where the grotesque reflection of the taffeta mask, with its sinister round holes for eyes and mouth, was his protection from the world's view of the pustules that marked his disease.

Craigmillar?

*

And he hardly listened to Mary, remembering the letter his valet, Taylor, had brought a few hours earlier. It was from Edinburgh. From Ned, the youth he loved to distraction. Ned wrote in a beautiful hand, his writing exquisite, like everything else about him, but one word: 'Craigmillar' leapt out at him.

'Sire, you are warned to avoid Craigmillar. This would not benefit your best interests.'

He had re-read the letter, cast it aside impatiently. He was apprehensive enough without Ned's warning, wondering had he confided too much in someone who had failed him so far.

He thought of the fiasco of that night in Stirling, when Ned fought off his kingly advances by whispering that he must be excused as he was presently suffering from an unfortunate condition.

'You did not get it from me then,' said Darnley in righteous indignation since the consummation he had longed for was not forthcoming. Then there was the matter of Ned's twin sister. He would rather not brood on that.

But all had ended well. The sole possessor of Ned's secret, implored not to reveal it, Darnley had realized the power it gave him. He had found a useful ally and, since his identity was unknown, he was free from the scrutiny of jealous lords. Aye, Ned was proving useful as a spy, moving from place to place, from household to household, in the guise of a servant.

Darnley recalled their last meeting, their conversation in his apartments at Stirling Castle. The last of the fireworks marking the events around Prince James's christening had faded, leaving only the acrid fumes of gunpowder thick upon the frosty air.

As the wooden fort disappeared in smoke and rubble, that was when the remarkable uses of gunpowder first occurred to him. Here was a more efficient way of disposing of one's enemies than the overworked royal methods of poisoned wine or a bloody knife. There were no mishaps with gunpowder, no witnesses remained to make accusations.

Ned had sat at his feet listening. There was a saying he had overheard, allegedly from the Earl of Morton: 'the king is sic a bairn that there is nothing told him, but he would reveal it.'

Realizing the truth of this, Ned was clever and, with no secrets between them, Darnley confided that his dearest wish was to rid himself of Mary and Bothwell, whom he hated and despised.

Ned whispered that his mother had a small farm on the outskirts of Edinburgh, near a place called Kirk O'Field. There were many old houses in the quadrangle of the ruined church. His mother had worked as a servant long ago in the old Provost's House.

Darnley listened intently.

Ned's mother had told him that because of the uneven foundations of the area with its many hills, the lower level of this particular house, once a receptory of the ecclesiastical buildings, was built across vaults.

Ned paused and gave him a significant look before adding carelessly, 'Vaults have certain uses and they can be undermined.'

With gunpowder. That was the unspoken thought in Darnley's mind. But how was he to convince the Queen to choose such a humble dwelling?

Ned smiled. 'Tell her that you have heard the air is good and wholesome and will speed your recovery. Tell her that you long for peace and quiet – and reconciliation with her, away from the court.' His glance lingered on the taffeta mask. 'And from men's vulgar curiosity, sire.'

Darnley gave him a sharp glance, but Ned continued. 'Once she is in agreement, you must then play your part well, sire. That you still love her to distraction. She will forgive the past. I hear from my sister, she who is maid to Mistress Seton . . .' Pausing, he gave Darnley a coy look which changed the snort of indignation into laughter. 'I am told that Her Grace is soft-hearted, ready to forgive her enemies, saying Masses for their souls. Take advantage of that, sire.'

Darnley sighed. 'God knows, I have tried, with little success.'

'Try once more, sire,' Ned insisted. 'There is much to be gained. Once you have her to sleep in the house, – drugged with wine if necessary, for such matters can easily be arranged,' he added smoothly, 'your horses in readiness, you slip out and your servant, Taylor, whom you can trust, and myself will light the fuse.' Ned clapped his hands. 'Boom! It will be all over and you, sire, will be Scotland's rightful King.'

Darnley had put the plan to his father, with some diffidence. But Matthew Lennox, after a certain amount of frowning, biting of lips and exclamations of consternation, doubt and fear, agreed.

He could rely on the support of the Lennox clan to further his son's legitimate right to the throne and to their own advancement,

The matter was urgent, since the infant Prince had

been removed from the nursery at Stirling to the safety of Holyrood. Mary had learned that the Lennoxes had a ship anchored in the Clyde watching her movements and in readiness to remove Prince James from her custody at Darnley's instigation.

Lennox nodded. 'Kirk O'Field. I know the area you speak of. Perhaps it is a good choice for our purpose, The Provost's Lodging would suit us well. The Balfours own several of the houses and Sir James is in charge of the arsenal at the castle.' He rubbed his chin thoughtfully. 'Balfour owes me a debt of gratitude,' he added grimly, 'and he is no friend to Mary, although she believes so, which is greatly to our advantage.' He shook his head. 'To my mind, the house has only one disadvantage. It is dangerously close to the cursed Hamiltons and you well ken, son, that we have no reason to love one another.'

Darnley nodded, having been brought up from his earliest days to appreciate the reasons for this feud, stretching back over many generations, when the Hamiltons had considered themselves the rightful lords of Glasgow.

Treachery and murder had followed, on both sides, with little to choose between who was right and who was wrong, but such doubts were not permitted to the young Henry Darnley.

'The matter needs more thought. But I agree, son; in principle, that is,' Lennox said cautiously. And, watching the Royal party gather in the courtyard below, 'Agree with her. Say you will go to Craigmillar. Then, when you are in sight of Edinburgh, change your mind. Tell her you have been recommended to this house at Kirk O'Field, that it is in the country and will speed your recovery.' Putting his hand on his son's shoulder, he added grimly, 'Leave the rest to us and, by this time next week, you will be King of Scotland.'

Chapter Twenty-Four

East Lothian. Friday 31 January 1567

Even as Darnley and his father plotted in Glasgow, there was another conspiracy afoot under the wintry trees in the gardens of Whittingham, the Douglas stronghold, where Bothwell, newly returned from Liddesdale, had been summoned by the returned exiles, Morton, his cousin Archibald Douglas and Argyll, husband to Mary's half-sister, Lady Jean Stewart.

Recently pardoned by Mary, they still smarted under their betrayal by the King over their part in Davy Riccio's murder, and were determined to have their revenge. They were joined by Maitland of Lethington, his absence from the court conveniently excused by his recent marriage and honeymoon.

There was no mincing pretence at diplomacy here. The lords were forthright, outspoken, with only the corbies high in the trees and the seabirds patrolling the skies to hear their voices.

Their verdict was unanimous. Henry Darnley, he who would be crowned King of Scotland, must die.

'There might still be a divorce,' whispered cautious Lethington.

'Divorce?' They turned on him angrily.

'Divorce is too mild, too many complications,' said Morton.

'As long as Darnley exists, he will scheme against her,' said Argyll.

'Aye, and mark it well, my lords, against us,' said Douglas. 'Our heads will sit uneasily upon our shoulders.'

'Think of the advantage of being rid of him, having him disposed of permanently,' said Morton, nodding in agreement.

'The man is diseased. In a few years he will be dead or insane,' said Bothwell hopefully.

'Are we to wait that long?' said Morton. 'Such a crowned king, such a consort even, is a blasphemy before God. Aye, and consider what is in it for yourself, Bothwell.' He paused before adding softly, 'We are your men – we all ken how matters go apace with Her Grace and yourself, and there is no better man to sit by her side and rule Scotland.'

'Aye, who better?' echoed Argyll enthusiastically.

Bothwell listened but little, well ahead of them, his own secret plans already made as solemnly they put their hands together and swore to rid Scotland and the world of Henry Darnley.

All that remained was how to achieve this worthy goal.

Next morning news had just reached Bothwell that Darnley, *en route* for Edinburgh, had been refused lodging at Holyrood Palace by the Queen's command.

With no plausible argument against her excuse that smallpox might affect the infant Prince, even though both were aware of the real nature of his disease,

Darnley had reluctantly agreed to go to Craigmillar Castle. Then, within sight of Edinburgh, he had panicked. He hated Craigmillar, he said, it was his turn to protest and make excuses. The royal cavalcade stopped, bewildered. Where was he to go?

He had an answer ready for them. He wished to be taken to a house that had been recommended to him for its good clean air. It was on the outskirts of the town at a place called Kirk o'Field. The tantrums of a sick man were beyond the doctors who accompanied them. With no other option, they had to agree.

Bothwell reported this latest turn of events to the conspirators, adding, 'And the house is the property of Sir James Balfour.'

The lords exchanged glances and could hardly restrain a certain amount of gleeful hand-rubbing.

'Holyrood would be impossible for our plan. Dangerous too. Wine and long knives can go wrong, can lead assassins to the scaffold instead of the intended victim. We do not want another fiasco like Riccio's murder.'

'This time we will not choose the dagger or the pistol.'

And into all their minds came the whispered thought: gunpowder. Blow up the entire house. With Darnley in it.

'You are Sheriff of Edinburgh, Bothwell. Consider the convenience for the man who has the keys to the castle arsenal at his disposal, who can give orders with no questions asked.'

'But Darnley plans to have the Queen living there with him. If she has given her word,' Bothwell protested, 'then she will stand by it.'

Gunpowder was not his way. He would have preferred single combat, the Border justice.

'She can forestall him, man, deny him access. She is good at that. Good, I hear, at making excuses to keep him out of her bed,' said Maitland, avoiding Bothwell's eyes.

'Is she to be privy to our plans?' was Bothwell's next question.

Looks were exchanged. Would that be advisable? Even though she wished to be rid of her husband, she doubtless hoped that natural causes, like the pox, would remove him from her.

They remembered her well-known hatred of violence, oft-declared, that she 'would rather pray with Esther than take the sword with Judith'.

'I will not have her put in any danger,' said Bothwell.

'You are right. We will warn her. That should be enough,' said Argyll.

'You, Lethington, let her know that she would be ill-advised to sleep in the house with Darnley. Any excuse will do,' said Morton, then, turning to Bothwell, 'Doubtless, you will think of something when the time comes. You have her trust.'

'Now let us be practical,' said Douglas. 'Are there any events by which we can be certain she will be absent for several hours?'

'There is Sebastian Pagez's wedding next week, on the ninth of February,' said Lethington. 'He is her favourite servant, a talented lad, and she has promised to be present when he marries her maid Christina Hogg.'

'Excellent!' Heads were nodded eagerly.

Only Bothwell looked doubtful. 'I have your solemn word that the Queen will be in no danger?'

'Not one hair of her head,' said Morton as again they clasped hands, the pledge made anew.

As Bothwell left them, Morton said, 'Do not be tempted to let your wife warn her too clearly, Argyll. Nor you, Lethington. It is best that she remains in ignorance. Although, with God's help,' he added piously, 'some day she will live to thank us for ridding her of Henry Darnley.'

Bothwell was uneasy. He feared that Mary, knowing him so well, loving him so well, might see the dreadful deed that was planned reflected in his eyes. And he doubted his own abilities to be natural with her, for he was not good at dissembling.

But though it was in Mary's and Scotland's own interest, her name and his own must not be linked to her husband's murder. He knew from experience that there were people in Edinburgh, simple people not expected to understand the whirligig of power, who would be shocked at the killing of this outwardly golden youth.

Their King, twenty years old, whom they saw roaming the streets of the town at night, the proper consort for their lovely young Queen, and father to the future King of Scotland.

Ordinary folk, Bothwell knew, were sentimental about royal personages, holding them in awe and seeing only the glossy exteriors of God's anointed, unaware of the corruption within. The lives of those born royal, he decided, were like fairy-tales and people hate to be disillusioned, awakened to the terrible reality.

He feared that the death of the young King, his murder suspected, might see Mary's popularity diminished, and with it an end to his own ambitions.

He must warn her.

He made haste from Whittingham to Holyrood and, seeking an audience with Mary, was received almost immediately. As the door closed, he took her in his arms. She made no resistance but clung to him, tears welling in her eyes.

'It has been so long, so long,' she sighed.

'Not much longer, my love,' he whispered.

She sprang away from him, 'The divorce?'

He shook his head. 'No, Madam. Something more permanent,' he added grimly.

Horrified, she stared at him, hit his chest with her clenched fists. 'No, James. No,' she whispered. 'I absolutely forbid that!'

He seized her hands, held them tight. 'Then think of Scotland, I have information that he means to kill you.' He paused, watching her face grow paler. 'You know only too well that it is true and will happen, as God's in His heaven, if you do not strike first.'

She was trembling in his arms. 'For God's love, Madam, will you throw your beloved Scotland to a diseased boy who will die insane in a couple of years?'

Released, Mary sat down, her shoulders drooped, her face in her hands.

'And when Darnley is gone, what of your son? I beg you, if you cannot think of yourself and your own safety, think of the son of your body you have given to Scotland, who must rule this kingdom after you.

'And think of the jealous lords, the Lennoxes, Arrans and Hamiltons, who will fight like lions over him to gain power, to satisfy their own ambitions, caring naught for this country's future. And think of your half-brother Moray, who will sell out to England if it suits his purpose.'

Mary shuddered. 'I will not be involved in murder,' she whispered.

Kneeling before her, he stroked her cheek. 'You will not even know about it, my love. An unfortunate accident that will be over before he knows it. He will not even suffer.'

She put a hand to her mouth. 'Not like Davy, for God's sake, No daggers.'

'No daggers.'

'No poison.'

'No poison. We will be merciful to him, more than he would be to you. Never forget that he plans your death and this will be his second attempt. He tried the night he killed Davy, hoped you would lose the child, and your own life. And that he would be King. Have no doubts on that score.'

She looked at him, knowing it to be true, as he added grimly, 'We plan to thwart his attempts, hoist him with his own petard, before he can do any more damage.'

Then, caressing her cheek, he leaned over and kissed her. 'But we will need your help to accomplish this matter.'

Frowning, she bit dry lips as he continued. 'You

must accede to his requests. You must play the part of the loving, compassionate wife.'

'No, James. Never that!' Her eyes flashed anger.

'We do not intend you to share his bed, if that is what you fear. Do everything save step between his sheets. To the world a loving, tender companion at his sickbed each day. Let him and his family believe he is secure. And that you are falling into the very trap they have set for you.' He stood up, drew her to her feet. 'Then, when the time is ripe, we will give you warning – ample warning. Once you receive it, you must not delay. Not for one moment. You must fly.'

Chapter Twenty-Five

Beaton House. Monday 3 February 1567. Morning

Tam realized, by the number of mosstroopers bearing the Hepburn coat of arms riding up the Canongate towards the castle, that Bothwell had returned from the Borders. Doubtless news had reached him of Janet's sojourn in Edinburgh.

He did not long delay in calling on her, somewhat dismayed to discover Tam in residence and learn from him that she was not at home.

He talked pleasantly with Tam about Stirling and his stay at his sister's home at Crichton over Christmas. Tam gathered that there had been no incidents of a sinister nature, no more mysterious attacks or attempts on his life, while he was on his home territory in the Borders.

This information was sufficient to confirm his suspicions that since such incidents had taken place in Craigmillar, Stirling and Inchmahome, the assassin must have been able to move easily, unrecognized, in the anonymous mass of servants that followed the Queen's progress from one castle to the next.

Listening to Bothwell, Tam mentally crossed off Lady Jean Gordon, since Bothwell had survived unscathed from Crichton, where his wife would have had ample opportunity to dispatch her unsatisfactory husband.

That left his two other suspects, Lord James Stewart, the Queen's half-brother, and her husband, Lord Darnley, as those who might have in their influence and pay the 'Spanish lady' and the thirteenth rider.

While they were talking, Janet returned and welcomed Bothwell warmly with whispered words and embraces.

'I cannot stay long,' he said. 'We are escorting Her Grace back to Holyrood from Kirk O'Field.'

'Can you come back later – this evening?' said Janet.

Bothwell shook his head. 'She visits her husband twice a day. I have little free time.' He sounded annoyed.

'So, they are reconciled,' said Janet.

Bothwell's laugh was sardonic. 'Ye might call it that. On the surface, they present a picture of wedded bliss. Even to Her Grace spending the occasional night under the same roof.'

'Matters have progressed,' said Janet.

'Under the same roof, but not in the same bed,' said Bothwell shortly.

Suddenly aware of Tam's presence, Janet handed him a sheaf of documents.

'There are the property settlements and my son-in-law's will. I need to have them copied immediately. This is a matter for the professionals. Take them up the Canongate to Walter Pax. He has scribes for just such work.'

'Walter Pax, eh' Bothwell said grimly. 'Among his less salubrious occupations he is reputed to be a spy for Lord Randolph, who eagerly passes on information to his English mistress, Elizabeth. Are ye sure he is the right man for your documents?'

It was her turn to be amused. 'Pax is not a man to fall foul of, but my family papers will tax even his imagination. There is nothing in them that might tempt Elizabeth to waste her time reading. I guarantee she would be asleep within the hour.'

Bothwell laughed as she continued. 'They are mere domestic matters, but we are in such a tangle of affairs at Branxholm, so threatened by legal intricacies, that I can let nothing go without making doubly sure I have documentary evidence.'

She looked at Tam. 'You will be grateful for my trouble, I assure you, when you are steward once again. Now you may leave us.'

Tam walked up the High Street thoughtfully. As it was market day, the luckenbooths at St Giles were busy, the odours of flesh, human and otherwise, strong indeed.

Pushing his way through the crowd, he suddenly found himself face to face with the last young woman he ever wished to see again. A never-to-be forgotten cloud of red hair. Jenny Crozer.

There was no possibility of avoiding the encounter, although he would have turned on his heel and fled if he had dared. As she scowled at him, he noticed that in the huge basket over her arm, with its ribbons and fairings for sale, there also nestled a newborn baby.

Tam bowed politely, making way for her, his hopes

that maybe she did not recognize him doomed when she smiled.

'Aye, 'tis yersel', the bonny man who didna want to marry me.'

Tam was spared the embarrassment of thinking up a suitable answer, when another bright red head popped out of the crowd, leading a horse-drawn cart laden with vegetables. Dear God, the Crozers were here in force, he thought, as Jenny pointed to the newcomer.

'There's ma man. He got held up, but he was in time to make our hand-fasting legal, and to get me ma granny's legacy.'

So this was Archie, alive and well, thank God, thought Tam fervently. But his belligerent scowl spelt trouble.

Tam peered into the basket. 'That's a fine wee lad,' he said pleasantly.

'Lass,' Jenny corrected as Archie loomed large.

Tam bowed. 'My compliments to you both.' And, aware that there would never be a better opportunity to question Archie about the Spanish lady and Ben Fellows' reappearing corpse, he asked, 'Will you take a pot of ale with me?'

Archie needed no second bidding. Telling Jenny to look after the cart and see no one stole any of the vegetables, he followed Tam into the tavern across from the church.

With ale in front of them, Tam said, 'I wonder if you can help me?'

Archie stared at him suspiciously and Tam realized this was not going to be easy. 'I am looking for a lady.'

Archies eyes widened. 'A lady?'

'Aye. One that you took into Edinburgh in December. My cousin,' Tam added hastily, accompanying that lie with a silver coin slid across the table.

Archie pocketed it first, then said with a coarse laugh, 'I'm no in the business o' pimping, if that's what ye're after. At least not for a paltry coin.'

Tam shook his head. 'You misunderstand.'

Archie prepared to stand up. 'I dinna misunderstand. I ken what ye're on about. I dinna ken any ladies.'

'I think you will remember this one. My cousin was taking an uncle of mine for burial from Niddrie, where he died, to Greyfriars kirkyard.'

Archie's expression changed, his face wiped clean of all expression. 'I ken no such lady. I know nowt about taking corpses anyways.' And, leaning towards Tam in a threatening manner, 'How d'ye ken it was me? Did she tell ye?'

'Archie!' Jenny was at the door, shaking the basket and trying in vain to quell the baby's roars, out of all proportion to its minute dimensions. 'A laddie has run off wi' some of the vegetables. He wouldna pay me. Ye'll have to come. I canna tak' care of everything.'

Conscious that Archie was regarding him narrowly and the suspicious scowl was not in any danger of disappearing, Tam watched them leave and quickly followed, immersing himself in the crowd. Hopefully before Jenny could give an account to her angry husband of their first meeting.

Doubtless the story she had originally told showed Tam as a pathetic coward, a poor weedy specimen and he feared there might be domestic strife ahead when

Archie realized that his wife's account differed from the evidence of his own eyes.

Tam's second encounter that day was even more disconcerting. Walter Pax's tall house near the castle with its windows staring over the city, must have given Pax's spying activities a useful vantage point, he decided as he climbed the stairs. After some little time he was admitted to an antechamber hung with portraits and tapestries that produced the illusion of a wealthy private residence. A clerk appeared regarding him with suspicion, until he uttered the magic words 'Lady Buccleuch'.

Another short wait and he was led into the room he had observed overlooking the street. On three walls, shelves overflowing with documents went high to the ceiling, the lower reaches lined by scribes at work, to the ceaseless scratching of quill pens.

As Tam explained Lady Buccleuch's wishes to Pax, the man's bland countenance gave nothing away, its grey complexion showing a remarkable likeness to a slate wiped clean. Shrewd heavy-lidded eyes, however, belied his nondescript appearance and Tam was aware that one of the pens nearby had ceased its scratching, its owner's face poised in his direction.

As he turned, the youth was walking quickly towards the door, his manner so furtive Tam could only conclude that he did not wish to be seen.

For an instant Tam thought he recognized the face beneath the well-turned-down velvet bonnet and, as the door closed, he interrupted Pax, who asked rather irritably, 'What is wrong?'

'That young man. I thought I knew him. What is his name?'

Pax frowned. 'Ned Wells.'

Tam shook his head. 'Does he live hereabouts?'

Pax froze. If his face was capable of any expression, then it would have been distrust. 'I know nothing of his whereabouts, sir. He is merely an apprentice who looks in from time to time when I am overburdened with work.'

Tam realized that was all the information he was likely to receive. He left, suspecting that Pax knew more than he was giving away with good reasons for keeping his own counsel.

In that conclusion Tam was right. Pax had indeed far-reaching plans for this particular apprentice. He had already entrusted him with confidential, nay, even treasonable, material purchased at considerable cost from an unknown woman. Heavily veiled, she was anxious to keep her identity secret.

A man of few emotions, he felt a thrill of excitement at letters which were addressed to Lord Bothwell from a passionate Norwegian lady and from the Queen herself. Valuable properties which met with such approval from his employers that rarely opened purses were eagerly brought out.

He watched Eildor from the window, frowning. Perhaps Lady Buccleuch's servant was also a spy. And he was not prepared to take chances that might put his own head on the block.

Janet was absent when Tam returned to Beaton House and he took the opportunity to examine the secret

271

document he had been preparing on the mystery sur-rounding the attacks on Bothwell.

Since the red-headed carter involved in the disposal of Ben Fellows' corpse in Duddingston Loch was now alive and well, he could not be the drowned young man whose recovery from the Nor' Loch had so upset the start of the Queen's journey to Stirling.

Tam could only conclude that his original premise had been correct and Archie's services had been hired by the 'Spanish lady'. When Jenny had put in an appearance so inopportunely, he was still hoping to obtain some answers to that riddle. But as Archie was obviously terrified of the consequences of his actions, and had doubtless been paid well to keep silent, Tam realized he could have little hopes of any useful infor-mation from that source.

To his account of events, he added further obser-vations regarding Walter Pax's shy apprentice and one or two suggestions which, although fantastic, might eventually throw out possible leads.

By the time he had finished, it was growing dark and, suddenly bored with the prospect of yet another evening of his own company, he decided to visit Dorothy Sinclair in her new home.

Aware of the dangers of cutpurses and worse in the twilight hour, he knew he should take a link-boy or torch-bearer if he was to go on foot. But the distance seemed too little to go down to the stable in the mews at the back of the house and saddle up Ajax. Besides, he enjoyed walking. He would take a chance on the criminal fraternity of Edinburgh being still heavily engaged spending their market day's cache of ill-gotten gains.

The approaching evening was pleasant indeed. A sunset and the first stars in a clear sky above the quadrangle of houses at St Mary's suggested a peaceful place forgotten by time.

In the tall, imposing building that was Hamilton House, candles were lit in the window. The windows of the Provost's House were similarly lit and there was a scene of activity, of arrivals and departures outside, of torches visible through the long, low building which led from the living quarters into the courtyard.

He remembered why. The King was now in residence.

Wheels rumbled on the narrow wynd behind him. Too late to step aside, he held up a hand in warning. The carter, distinguished by the red hair escaping from under his hood, was undoubtedly Archie Crozer, heading straight towards him.

Archie stopped the cart just before the horse's hooves made contact with Tam, who had leapt aside and stumbled to the ground, his hands over his head.

Leaning over, Archie yelled, 'Are ye bad hurt?'

Tam picked himself up indignantly. 'No thanks to you. You are in a terrible hurry, man.'

Suddenly he recognized Tam's face staring up at him.

'Ye're the mannie Jenny telt me about. Ye tried to bribe me.' He looked at the King's house in terror. 'Are ye wi' them?' he whispered. 'Is this yer doing?' he added, pointing to the cart. 'Have they sent ye to spy on me?'

Tam saw that vegetables had now been replaced by two large trunks and a barrel.

Archie had leapt down in an agitated manner. 'I'll

have nowt to do with this. I'm just a carter, I'm not a traitor. It's just one more delivery for me. I have my orders – from the castle,' he added proudly. And with this acknowledgement of importance, he anxiously regarded his load. Carefully examining and tightening the cords that bound them together was a matter of serious concern.

Tam felt he should offer to help, since he had been partly responsible for this upset.

'Where are you off to with that load, at this time of night?'

Archie gave a grunt. Without deigning to reply, he sprang aboard the cart again. As it shot forward, a thin grey trickle of dust was deposited at Tam's feet.

He picked up a few grains, sniffed it.

Gunpowder.

Tam ran after the retreating cart, keeping at a safe distance. Its destination was the King's lodging, where it disappeared through the narrow gateway and headed towards the low building to the right.

On the evidence of fine folk arriving and leaving through the postern gate in the town wall, the Queen would be visiting her convalescent husband. According to Bothwell, she went twice a day. And with the Queen, the Maries.

Marie Seton might well be in danger.

His heart beat faster. He must tell her. He must warn Bothwell. And Dorothy Sinclair should be aware of the dangers of gunpowder in the vicinity of that quiet cathedral-like quadrangle, with its ruined church and its air of antiquity.

But Dorothy Sinclair was not at home. Tam decided she could wait. She was not in any immediate danger.

If only he knew where to find Bothwell.

His progress across the courtyard was challenged by a sentry.

'I wish to see Lord Bothwell. It is a matter of urgency.'

Looking past the man, he saw the Queen's horse being saddled. And fortune was with him. At that moment Bothwell emerged from the house, hurrying across the yard.

'My Lord, a word with you.'

Bothwell stared into the gloom, recognized him and came forward.

'Ah, Eildor. Will this take long? The Queen awaits me.'

'A word, my Lord. Outside, if you please,' said Tam desperately. 'A matter that concerns Her Grace.'

Bothwell followed him into the lane, where quickly Tam told him about Archie Crozer, the red-headed carter, who had not drowned in Duddingston Loch.

'Just moments ago, my Lord, he drove a cart – which I have reason to believe contained gunpowder – towards the low building at the side there.'

Bothwell looked in the direction Tam indicated. 'The *salle*, it's called – where the Queen receives her courtiers, before they're admitted to the King's bedroom.'

Tam watched Bothwell's reactions. Even in the dim light, they were not as surprised and shocked as he had imagined they would be by such news.

'The Queen, sir.'

Bothwell sighed, put a hand on his arm. 'The Queen is in no danger, Eildor. You have done well to warn me, but you have my *word* on that.'

Tam remembered the conversation he had overheard between Bothwell and Janet.

This was no time for delicacy.

'Her Grace visits Lord Darnley each day. Is it not true that she spends the night with him?'

Bothwell winced at that. 'She does not sleep in the same chamber, Eildor. She returns to Holyrood most nights.'

He put a hand on Tam's arm, said gently to him, 'I do entreat you, forget all this nonense about gunpowder, put what you think you have seen out of your mind. Rest assured, Her Grace is in no danger and will not come to any harm.'

And suddenly, sickeningly, Tam realized that there was before him a plot to kill the King. And Bothwell was part of it.

He wished he could tell Janet, but it was unlikely she would return from Blackness before morning.

He stared after Bothwell. He had to tell someone. To warn Marie Seton.

Chapter Twenty-Six

Wednesday 5 February 1567. Morning

Tam slept little that night. By morning Janet had still not returned and, fearing the worst, he hurried down the road to Holyrood, narrowly escaping a heavy shower of sleet and rain.

He hoped that this early in the day he would be sure of an audience with Marie. When he was announced, she rushed out and greeted him warmly. She was dressed for outdoors and explained.

'I am glad to see you, Tam, but we are about to leave on our daily visit to Lord Darnley.'

Sighing as if the prospect did not give her much pleasure, but remembering the conversation he had overheard between Janet and Bothwell, Tam said, 'I understand that matters are now harmonious between them.'

Marie regarded Tam gravely. 'It is beyond belief, a miracle to those of us who know them, what marvels the King's illness has worked upon their marriage. Her Grace has always a tender heart and they are on the most cordial terms. Lord Darnley is almost pathetically pleased to see her each day. She never leaves his bedside, plays cards and reads to him. Twice she has slept in the room below, and he is to return with her to Holyrood at the end of the week when the period of his quarantine is at an end.'

Fear gripped Tam's throat as he asked, 'Do you sleep there also?'

'Nay, he will allow none of us to accompany her. She has the little room below his own. You can see it from here. There are a few steps down to it from the *salle*.' Marie paused and added significantly, 'She has promised to be his true wife again, in bed and board. And truly it seems to us, watching them, as if they had turned back the clock and matters were again with them as they were before – before last year at this time.'

He realized she meant when Riccio was murdered.

She continued, 'He leaves here on the morning after Bastian Pagez's wedding to Christina Hogg on Sunday.'

The night planned for Darnley's murder, thought Tam grimly. But how could he begin to tell Marie that he had reason to believe the house was mined with gunpowder. What of the panic that would ensue? He might even be arrested himself.

No. He must rely on Bothwell to tell the Queen the truth. He could not bear to entertain even the slightest suspicion that she might also be involved. And he thanked God that none of her Maries ever stayed with her at the King's lodging.

He realized he was hardly listening to Marie any more, as she said, 'All has worked out very well, after the great fuss Lord Darnley made about not going to Craigmillar.' She sighed. 'The move to Kirk O'Field caused everyone a great deal of trouble.'

'In what way? Surely they were prepared for him?'

Marie shook her head. 'Not at all. His last-minute decision was very inconvenient. Craigmillar was in all readiness. Then on the very outskirts of Edinburgh he suddenly decided he wanted to go to this place away on the south side of the city, right in the country. Everyone tried to dissuade him, but he was determined. So beds and furniture had to be hastily removed from Craigmillar for his convenience—'

'A moment, Marie. You mean that he did not know before he left Glasgow?'

'No. Maybe he brooded about that horrible raven that followed his litter all the way from his father's house. Maybe that stirred his guilty conscience and made him fear Craigmillar, where all had been prepared for him.' She looked at Tam. 'I wonder if ravens have souls?'

'Why do you think that?'

She shuddered. 'Because the horrible bird refuses to leave him. It has settled on the roof of the Provost's House. It might well be poor Davy come back to haunt him.'

'Seton, Her Grace is ready.'

Summoned, Marie took her departure.

He bowed over her hand and she whispered, 'Come again and see me, Tam. Once the Queen is back in Holyrood, we will have more time at our disposal.'

Deep in thought, and none of it agreeable, Tam was walking past the gates of Greyfriars when he saw a woman emerge from the kirkyard. A woman in deep mourning, wearing a hood. But despite her back being turned towards him, some ten yards away, there was something in that walk, in the proud carriage, that he recognized.

He began to run towards her, shouted, 'Dorothy!'

She turned and gasped out, 'Tam!'

'I thought it was you, but I have not seen you in mourning before. I called at your lodging,' he began, and then said, 'I trust this is not a sudden bereavement.'

She sighed deeply, recovering her composure. 'Sadly, this is the anniversary of my dear husband's death, Tam.' Her eyes filled with tears. 'I always bring out my mourning again. It is what he would have wished.'

Tam was surprised. This was far from the convention-defying he had come to expect from the unsentimental Dorothy.

'He is buried in the kirkyard here,' she said.

'I understood he drowned at sea.'

She smiled sadly, wiping away a tear. 'That is so, but his body was washed up at Leith. His boat sank in a storm offshore, when they were making for Edinburgh.'

Tam took her hand, which trembled in his. 'My condolences, Dorothy, on your sad day.'

'Yes, it is sad, Tam.'

'May I escort you back to St Mary's?'

'My thanks, but no.' She brightened. 'You must excuse me, but I am in a great rush. I have my lawyers to see. Little William's adoption. There are always more papers to sign. The procedure seems endless.'

As their ways parted, Tam watched her walk across and disappear down a close. Curiosity led his footsteps into the kirkyard.

He could see no stone that might relate to John Sinclair. And then he felt a certain compassion. Perhaps having a monument was more than his widow could afford. He had presumed, wrongly, it seemed, that she had been well provided for, a woman of property.

Retracing his steps, he remembered the version of the tragedy related by Lady Morham: a ship sunk after being attacked by English pirates off the Scottish coast. Maybe it had survived long enough to continue its voyage before the storm . . .

Suddenly he stopped. He had reached the infant's grave he had stood by that first day when he came in search of Ben Fellows' burial. How long ago that seemed.

'Magdala, beloved daughter of—and sister—'.

He paused in front of the stone with its mutilated inscription, remembering how cruel it had seemed. But the morning's rain had restored some of the lost names, which now stood out boldly:

He crouched down to read them.

The parents' names remained barely decipherable, but as he looked bleakly into the falling dusk he knew who it was he had seen earlier that week in Walter Pax's office.

Chapter Twenty-Seven

Kirk O'Field. Sunday 9 February 1567. Morning

Tam arose early that morning and was already outside the Provost's House long before the church bells in Edinburgh had begun their weekly summons.

Unable to sleep, his thoughts had returned repeatedly to his last meeting with Bothwell and the latter's insistence, when he tried to alert him to the possible danger threatening the house, that the Queen was in no danger.

If this was so, as Bothwell had assured him, then the target was the King. And tonight was the last chance. It had been carefully planned for when the Queen would be absent at Pagez's wedding and was unlikely to return to sleep in the King's lodging, on whose roof the raven had taken up permanent residence. A mournful sight, its cawing echoed through the daylight hours as it hopped back and forth along the apex of the pantiled roof, resisting every attempt to scare it away and leading a charmed life. For it had become target practice and the object of many bets from those on sentry duty.

But oblivious of pistol shots from keen marksmen, it merely cawed indignantly, took off into the air and, before they could give a dissatisfied grunt, settled back to its hopping, minus one or two floating feathers that drifted groundwards.

Observing the latest attempt by the soldiers on its miserable life, Tam decided there could scarcely be a greater foreboding of disaster, But what was he to do about it when the signs were that a worse human tragedy was in the offing?

He was in a dilemma of his own. He could scarcely spend the entire day vigilant in the open air, chilled to the bone by a brisk north wind with flurries of snow, keeping an eye on the house before him, so still and silent on a Sunday morning.

Shivering, he realized the necessity of finding some sheltered place, preferably indoors, from where he could keep watch and be ready to warn the Queen.

The obvious place was Dorothy Sinclair's lodging, so it was at her door he presented himself.

Dressed for the outdoors in her furred cloak, she seemed a little taken aback to find him on her threshold. Her welcome lacked its usual warmth. Had Tam been less preoccupied with more urgent matters, he might have considered it cool in the extreme. Hardly what he had been led to expect by the close friendship that had existed in Stirling and the eager invitations to extend their relationship once Dorothy settled in Edinburgh.

'What can I do for you, Tam?' She sounded a little impatient, a busy woman harassed by a hundred household tasks.

'Alas, Dorothy, I must throw myself on your mercy. I have had a difference of opinion with Lady Buccleuch over some documents which were entrusted to my care. Two have gone a-missing.' He paused, shrugged significantly. 'Accusations have been levelled at me. It is intolerable. I am afraid I have walked out on Her Ladyship.'

Dorothy regarded him solemnly, then said slowly, 'This is serious indeed. Where will you go?'

Tam gave her his most endearing smile. 'I have no home in Edinburgh and no money either. I am utterly dependent on Lady Buccleuch's charity.'

'I can offer you money.'

'I could not accept money. But I would be most grateful for your hospitality.' Ignoring her sharp intake of breath, the refusal he felt was certain, he continued rapidly, 'I am certain that Lady Buccleuch will repent of her anger, given time to consider her ill-advised words. She has a hot temper but is forgiving by nature.' He paused, smiled. 'All I require, Dorothy, is a very temporary refuge – a day, at most two – until such time as her temper cools and I can appear in her house without some destructive object being again thrown at my head,' he added, touching his forehead and an unseen scar ruefully.

Dorothy continued to watch him, her expression unreadable.

'You are a good friend,' he said desperately, 'the only one I can turn to in my present grievous plight.'

Recovering, she smiled, but sadly. 'You would be most welcome, Tam, but I am hourly expecting my sister Else for an extended visit.' She emphasized the last two words. 'I had a message only yesterday. She is most anxious to come to Edinburgh. There will not be beds enough in my little house—'

'Dear Dorothy,' Tam interrupted eagerly, not wanting to let this opportunity slip. 'I promise not to be in your way. I can sleep anywhere. I am no stranger to hard floors.'

He realized that she did not care for the idea, but by being so accommodating he had given her little option to refuse.

'Then you had best come in.' A forced smile and she stood aside, allowing him to pass along the corridor into the room beyond. 'I shall be absent most of the day. After morning service at St Giles, I shall be visiting friends of Else's and I shall wait with them for her arrival.' She paused. 'I trust you will manage on your own?'

'I will indeed. My needs are slight and I am grateful indeed for your hospitality.'

She held out a cool hand. 'It is the least I can do for my friend.'

Watching her ride out, he climbed the stairs to an upper chamber with a vantage point overlooking the King's lodging and the *salle* with its vaults. Before settling down, he went through the sparsely furnished house and carried out a minute search for something that he felt sure should be present.

His thoroughness was rewarded and, with a feeling of some satisfaction, he settled down to what promised to be a long and uncomfortable vigil. But one infinitely preferable, in tolerable comfort, to lurking about the chilly closes of St Mary's until nightfall.

He had not long to wait before being alerted to activity from the two houses on either side of his lodging.

Apparently not everyone went to church on Sunday, and about a dozen men, by their watchful attitudes obviously soldiers but in no sort of uniforms, moved constantly back and forth across the quadrangle to the lower regions of the house opposite.

They did not take their horses, stabled in the mews behind the three houses where Dorothy kept her own horse, but went on foot. Each carried a large sack, trying with indifferent success to assume the look of tradesmen or artisans going about their legitimate business.

Tam guessed that they were unlikely to be delivering their burdens in the servants' quarters and the busy kitchens on the floor below the Queen's bedroom. Their most likely destination was the *salle* with its vaults as it had been earlier for Archie with his delicate cartload of gunpowder.

From his vantage point, the nearest house, also owned by Sir James Balfour's brother Robert, was the new Provost's House at the south-west corner. The lofty mansion of the Hamiltons was perhaps a hundred feet away, and beyond it, at an angle, stood the Douglases' house. Of these, only the roofs and upper floors were visible over high garden walls.

At last his patience was rewarded by the sight of the royal party riding through the postern gate. Seizing his chance, he hurried down the stairs and across the quadrangle as they approached the courtyard.

Before he could be challenged by the sentry, he was observed by Marie Seton, who waved him over and said, 'How good to see you, Tam. You received the message left for you at Lady Buccleuch's?'

Tam mumured a reply which Marie didn't hear, bending over her horse's neck to keep him still. 'Her Grace wishes to have a word with you.'

The Queen was dismounting when Tam went forward, bowed deeply.

She smiled at him. 'Master Eildor, well met indeed. We are somewhat at a loss for entertainment for our poor invalid. He wearies of my reading. When Seton mentioned that you were at Beaton House, she suggested that you might sing for us.'

Tam was delighted at the unexpected prospect of seeing the inside of the King's lodging.

'While I am attending my husband's bath, may I leave you in good Seton's care?'

Tam followed them through the *salle*, a long, narrow room that was a grander, more elegant version of the clergy's original receptory. A separate hall linked the west and east wings of the house and was joined by a turnpike stair which gave access to the two royal bedchambers, the lower the Queen's, the upper, as he learned from Seton, Lord Darnley's.

As the Queen went ahead of them, Marie paused by a pleasant window with a gallery projecting to the south, resting on the city wall and looking across to Arthur's Seat.

'Lord Darnley will allow no other than the Queen to handle him in his bath, a daily necessity for his present condition,' she added, repressing a shudder. 'He has so many other whims too, especially for furniture and ornaments that will hardly fit into this temporary lodging, which, by his command, had to be furnished as regally as Craigmillar. The fuss he made about a black velvet bed, saying he could not abide to sleep in it. He had to have the violet one, Her Grace's gift to him last summer, brought over especially from Holyrood.' She sighed. 'If you could see Her Grace's humble bedroom, down there.' She pointed back the way they had come. 'It is so tiny, with only a little green and yellow bed and a furred coverlet to keep her warm.'

'Need she sleep here, with Holyrood so near?'

'Lord Darnley insists upon it. The room is cold and damp. She is far from well and it will do her ill. But she insisted on pleasing him by staying here, although it so uncomfortable, and against all our wishes and entreaties.'

She hesitated, as one in danger of saying too much, and Tam asked, 'For her health?'

'Nay, Tam, for her safety,' she whispered and gave him a candid glance.

'You think she might be in danger?'

Marie nodded. 'We fear for her every moment she is out of our sight and under the King's roof. He refuses to allow her Maries, as he calls us, in attendance. Insists that our chatter disturbs him and makes his head ache. It isn't true, since Fleming is still on honeymoon and Livingstone is with her baby at present.' She shrugged. 'I am the only one he looks on favourably. Apparently I do not laugh loudly or a great deal, as he claims Beaton does. Not that I find anything to laugh about in this situation,' she added unhappily. 'But he tells Her Grace she may "bring the solemn one". Do you think me solemn?'

'Not in the least,' said Tam.

Marie shook her head. 'He is rather like a sick and spoilt child recovering from illness. He must have his own way in all things or he screams and yells and throws things. And curses our poor dear lady. It is intolerable.' She looked out of the window. 'And yet, as matters have worked out, we all have to agree that Kirk O'Field was a wise choice. Far enough from Holyrood and the city for the real nature of his illness to be kept secret. And it is a quiet, secure place, remote from any dangers, lying as it does just within the Flodden Wall.'

'Dangers, Marie? Did he have reason to believe he was in danger?'

'Nay. But since matters are now so harmonious between Her Grace and himself, he did warn her of a plot against her. Saying that she must beware of those persons who sought to make mischief between them, and that it had been suggested to him that he should take his wife's life,' she whispered, her eyes wide in horror.

'Did he give any details of this plot?' Tam demanded sharply.

'Not one. He refused to say more, on the excuse that even to think of such a vile and wicked deed made him feel faint and ill.'

Such fineness of feeling did not quite equate with the Lord Darnley Tam had learned to know and distrust.

The echo of bells continued, drifting across from the city.

'This is Carnival Sunday,' Marie explained. 'A time for celebration, the last Her Grace can enjoy before Lent begins. 'There is to be a wedding at Holyrood. Bastian Pagez marries Christina Hogg, one of her Grace's favourite servants. After the ceremony there are various ambassadorial engagements which she has to attend, but nothing must interfere with her daily visits to Lord Darnley. We are due to return here at

289

nine, when Her Grace would like you to be present to sing for us.'

'Seton!' A servant appeared on the stairs from Darnley's room. 'Her Grace awaits you.'

Marie curtsied, turned to go.

'Marie!' said Tam, his voice urgent.

'What is wrong?'

'Does Her Grace sleep here tonight?'

Marie nodded. 'That is the arrangement. Lord Darnley insists that she spends this last night here with him before they go to Holyrood.'

The servant hovered impatiently.

Tam watched her go. What could he say? How could he whisper a warning, details of a plot that he only suspected on the flimsiest of evidence?

If it was all in his mind, wild imaginings, then he might find himself on the rack in the torture chamber of the Tolbooth.

He had spent the day productively by making some careful notes and observations in the unhappy eventuality that he fell victim to whatever the coming night at Provost's House held in store.

These he took wrapped around a package for Janet at Beaton House. She had not returned from her own vigil with her sick daughter.

Retracing his steps to Dorothy's lodging, he resumed his watch at the window until darkness rendered the King's lodging invisible and, through the postern gate leading from Holyrood, a torch-lit procession bearing the Queen and her courtiers appeared.

As he walked across the quadrangle to join them,

the night was bitterly cold with yet more flurries of snow and the promise of worse weather to come.

The sentry was accustomed to Tam now and he was directed to the *salle*. Already sounds of merriment issued forth from the long, narrow hall, its walls agleam in the radiance of torches and candlelight. The air was heavy with the smell of hot wax and the smoke of many candles as the courtiers waited, in attendance on the Queen and her nobles. Some of the ladies in brilliant costumes were already masked in readiness for the event of the evening, when they would return to Holyrood for Pagez's wedding masque.

At one end of the room was a raised dais fringed in black velvet, but the Queen was not in evidence.

Tam's arrival was expected, so he was ushered through the room and into an antechamber where Marie waited to take him up the stair, past the window where they had paused together earlier that day, and into the King's bedroom.

Smiling a greeting, she whispered, 'Only a very few, the very privileged, are allowed into the King's bedroom. This way.'

A torch-bearer led them through an anteroom hung with tapestries showing the rabbit catchers and called 'Hunting the Conies', where the royal commode stood in isolation. Upholstered in velvet, it was fitted with twin pans and surmounted by a yellow silk canopy with a red and yellow fringe.

To Tam's startled and amused exclamation, Marie whispered, 'It once belonged to a cardinal – alas, he is no longer with us.' She opened the door into the King's bedroom.

The atmosphere took Tam's breath away. A small,

hot, stifling room in which, it seemed, the windows were seldom opened. It was well lit by candles in sconces in the walls.

Sitting on velvet cushions, the very privileged – Bothwell, Huntly and Argyll – were playing dice at a table with a green velvet cloth. They were also in costume, masks laid aside, Bothwell splendid in the black velvet and satin doublet, trimmed with silver, Janet Beaton's gift.

He looked surprised to see Tam and, beckoning him over, said cheerfully, 'Will you join us, Master Eildor, for a game?'

'He will not, my Lord.' This from the Queen, who had watched Tam enter. She laughed. 'Master Eildor is required by the King.'

Tam approached the bed where, on a high chair, upholstered to match the violet bed, the Queen was seated. She had drawn it close to the bedside, over the little Turkey carpet provided to keep Lord Darnley's feet warm when he left his bed.

Tam saw that she was holding her husband's hand, talking to him softly. As he bowed low to them both, he could not see Darnley's expression, hidden by a taffeta mask, with holes for eyes and mouth to conceal the ravages of his disease.

A wasted, pathetic sight, thought Tam, in sudden pity. I should not like to have the blood of such a one on my hands or on my conscience. And looking at the Queen, so happy-seeming, he could not in his heart bear to think that under that smiling exterior she was cold-bloodedly planning her husband's murder.

'Master Eildor will sing for you, husband. Would you like that?' Her tone was caring and anxious.

Darnley grunted a reply and she leaned forward to listen.

'Some of the English ballads you brought with you from Yorkshire? That would be splendid,' she added, beckoning to a page who sat in the window with a lute. She rustled through some papers on the bedside table and said, 'Here are the words for you, Master Eildor. "My love hath my true heart". Nick here will accompany you,' she added, clapping her hands for silence.

Tam sang as requested, was applauded. Sang again and received further applause, although there was little indication from the invalid slumped against his pillows of what he thought of the arrangement. Nor did he show the least interest in the merry little party of dice-players.

At last Marie Seton leaned over to the Queen, trying to attract her attention.

Darnley observed her, withdrew his hand from his wife's grasp and demanded, 'What is it you are whispering about, Seton?'

Marie curtsied politely. With a swift glance in Bothwell's direction, she said, 'I am but reminding Her Grace, sire, that she has promised to go to Bastian's wedding masque at Holyrood.'

This brought an angry exclamation from Darnley. He leaned forward from his pillows, thumped his fists on the coverlet. 'This is intolerable, Madam,' he shouted at the Queen. 'I had your word that you would spend the night here. All has been made in preparation for you. Your room is in readiness.'

'Do not distress yourself, husband,' said Mary softly. 'Remember that tomorrow ends your quarantine. From tomorrow we will no longer be parted, not even for one single night.' She smiled, pressing his hand.

'Tomorrow, Madam – it is *tonight* that I am talking about. *Tonight* that is important to me. Not tomorrow,' said Darnley, a desperate note in his querulous tone.

Tam gazed anxiously at Bothwell, who, dice in hand, was listening intently to this very private conversation which all the room could hear.

Tam noted that Bothwell was very still, watching Mary take a ring from her finger and put it into Darnley's hand.

'This is my pledge,' she said softly. 'Until tomorrow.'

Marie curtsied, the men bowed and all left the room, Tam following. Darnley, glaring at them, furious at being left, shouted, 'You – Eildor, stay a while. I would hear more of your songs. The same as before. Tonight I have a longing for my own land.'

Tam bowed, singing two more ballads unaccompanied, when a servant arrived.

'Sire, your three great horses are in readiness for the morn.'

'They will be there at five?' Darnley demanded.

The servant, Taylor, bowed. 'As you have instructed. At five of the clock, saddled and ready.'

Darnley slumped back against the pillows. 'You may leave us, Eildor. We wish to sleep.'

Tam walked down the turnpike stair very thoughtfully, out through the gate leading across the quadrangle. He was trying to work out some logical reason why Darnley should require three great horses saddled and ready for departure hours before dawn.

The indication was of a long pre-dawn journey to

be undertaken at the start of what promised to be a bitterly cold February day.

Preoccupied, he paid little attention to a figure in a long black cloak, the hood drawn well down, who stood hastily aside and melted into the shadows to let him pass.

Dorothy Sinclair's lodging was in darkness. She had not returned from meeting her sister and, although there was no message, someone had thoughtfully left bread, cheese and a flask of wine.

Tam was grateful. And he sat at the high window, hungrily consuming the food, but prudently taking only a sip or two of the wine. He longed to drink more, but, not having eaten all day, he needed his mind sharp on what lay ahead in the hours of darkness at the King's lodging.

He leaned forward, frustrated at the scant illumination afforded by a shaft of moonlight that revealed little beyond swaying torches signalling late-night revellers near the house he had just left.

But the late-night revellers were involved in a grimmer activity. A band of frustrated conspirators who realized that their plans had gone seriously wrong.

The Queen's death was their target. The carefully made plan was that she should be safely abed and asleep in the room below the King. Then at five in the morning, when the town slept in darkness, he would depart in all secrecy with his great horses.

That was the signal. Once he was through the postern gate, the gunpowder stored beneath the *salle* would be ignited, the house blown up, with the Queen still in her bed.

Darnley would meanwhile be heading along the Glasgow road to meet his father, Lennox, chief of the conspirators, who had already left his home and would be heading towards Edinburgh to triumphantly crown his son King.

After, of course, publicly comforting him for this shocking bereavement, this wicked murder of his wife, of the anointed Queen of Scots.

At the same hour, a little distant from the King's lodging, there was an emergency meeting of a second group of conspirators, this time led by Bothwell. The plot to kill the Queen had reached his ears. A frightened servant of Darnley's, persuaded by threat of torture, had sobbed out the King's plan.

At that, Morton and Douglas nodded heads in agreement, their consciences appeased. There was now only one way out. Darnley must die. The fuse must be lit by one of them.

'I will do it,' said Bothwell. 'I have a score to settle.'

The scene in the cellar, the frightened servant and his subsequent dispatch – for none could remain alive to reveal the identities of the men concerned – had been witnessed.

Ned Wells, who had access to the King's bedroom by royal command at all times, ran unchallenged up the turnpike stair.

Darnley's arm was seized, he was shaken into wakefulness from an uneasy sleep. He hated having to rise before dawn and was having a bad nightmare. And now Ned was telling him it was no dream.

'My Lord, you are in mortal danger. You must escape – this instant. The house is to be blown up. Bothwell is at this moment gone to attend to it.' And, cutting short Darnley's queries and protests, 'There is no time, sire. Your plans were made known. Your trusted servant talked – and was slain. You must go. Now.'

Taylor appeared at the door, candle in hand, awakened by their voices. 'The house is to be blown up,' said Ned. 'Make him understand.'

Darnley shook his head, like a man not properly awake, then demanded, 'Where are my clothes?'

'Tell him to hurry, Taylor.' And to Darnley, 'There is no time to call servants to dress you, sire. Go as you are. Do not delay an instant, or we will all be blown to kingdom come with the house.'

And so it was that Darnley took fright and in his nightshirt clambered down through a window into the garden, accompanied by Ned, who assisted the King, with Taylor, his faithful servant. The latter thoughtfully carried a chair and a rope in readiness to descend the city wall. And with further consideration for his royal master's modesty and dignity, he threw a furred robe over his shoulder to conceal his nakedness.

Ned watched them as they ran, two stark white figures in nightshirts, until they were out of sight, stumbling barefoot across the snowy grass towards the safety of the city beyond the garden walls.

Bothwell's work was similarly at an end with the lighting of the fuse as the air was split apart and the King's lodging crumbled like a house made of cards, rising in the air to collapse into nothingness, a pile of rubble flattened to the ground.

The explosion, like that of thirty or forty cannons fired in a volley, as it was later reported, shook the houses of Edinburgh to their very foundations.

Many believed this was the end of the world and arose from their beds in terror, those whose consciences irked them frantically praying.

The Queen who had returned from the wedding revelries was awakened by the noise that rattled all the windows in Holyrood. 'What is that?' she demanded. 'What has happened?'

Tam Eildor, who had fallen asleep on a chair at the upstairs window across the quadrangle, was hurled bodily across the room as the windows shattered. He staggered to his feet, dazed and bruised.

What time was it? Still dark.

He had not intended to sleep. His head felt like lead – as if he had been drugged.

Drugged. Aye, that was it. The wine he had sipped.

He staggered down the turnpike stair. Part of the timbered roof had collapsed, but mercifully the front door was open, blown off its hinges by the blast.

He scrambled across the stones and planks of wood and into air thick with the acrid fumes of gunpowder. But the scene he remembered had changed out of all recognition, for where the Provost's House had once stood there was not one stone still standing upon another. All had dissolved into a smoking pile of rubble.

As he made his way carefully and unsteadily across

the debris littering the quadrangle, he heard muffled voices calling out, calling for help.

Dear God, could any have survived?

Several of the town watch who patrolled the city gates of Edinburgh each night, and had been in the vicinity of the Netherbow Port, were already there, searching through the ruins.

'The King?' Tam said.

They looked up at him, shook their heads grimly. None could have survived the rubbish heap that had once been the old Provost's House.

Suddenly a shout nearby, from one of the searchers.

'Over here!' Stones were pulled aside and a mutilated body revealed, a blackened face unrecognizable. A hand appeared, another victim, a servant's body eased out of the fallen debris.

Torches were held, but the rescuers stared into dead faces.

A sigh went round the group. Neither belonged to the King.

Another shout from the garden to the south side of the town wall. Tam joined the others as they raced across the icy lawn.

'The King is found!' someone called.

An orchard with a few bare trees.

Tam stared down at the naked figure of a young man in a crumpled nightshirt. His eyes were closed.

A few feet away. Another body of an older man.

The King and his valet.

They were dead. But Tam pushed the town watch aside.

'Let me pass. I am a physician to the Queen,' he added.

They held torches above his head as he knelt and examined the two bodies. There was no mark on either of them. No bloody wound, no singed hair or cloth.

To the anxious questions, he confirmed that they were dead. But he did not add what troubled him most. These two men had been running away from something. They had not died in the explosion that had destroyed the old Provost's House. His guess was that they had been strangled or smothered.

Behind him, the town guard had produced the board on which they carried dead men from the scaffold for burial. And the King was placed – reverently – on the same last resting place of the bodies of common criminals by which he was to be transported to Holyrood.

After they had gone, Tam remained at the scene. Someone had left him the torch he requested and carefully he searched the now crushed grass for evidence of the King's murder.

All he found was a chair, a rope, a furred robe, a dagger and one slipper. He sat back on his heels, considering.

Such items and two naked men indicated swift flight, possibly a descent from a high window. Only a terrified man would have rushed out into the snow of a February night attired in just a nightshirt. Someone had warned Darnley in the nick of time.

But his would-be rescuer had not bargained for others who waited and how his escape from one kind of death had delivered him into yet another. Which seemed remarkably like execution. And the executioner?

Bothwell? Was it Bothwell?

Tam stood up. Perhaps. But he felt certain that Bothwell would have used a sword.

Still horrified by the tragedy he had suspected but had been unable to prevent, he walked back through the garden and began to pick his way towards what had been, until an hour ago, the courtyard he had watched from a window across the quadrangle.

All seemed silent. But there might be other victims.

He listened. And into the silence, a small sound. He followed it.

'Help me. Help me, for pity's sake.'

He knelt down, moved the choking dust and rubble from a figure wrapped in a black cloak.

A white face, blood-streaked, looked up into his own.

His heart hammered against his ribs.

'Help me.'

Chapter Twenty-Eight

**Beaton House. Monday 10 February 1567.
Before dawn**

As Tam rode up the High Street with his unconscious burden, the whole of Edinburgh was in uproar, people rushing to and fro, shouting questions for which there were as yet no answers.

Janet was in her night-robe, alarmed. She had been awakened by the blast. She was not alone. A young man stood by the window.

'My son-in-law, Hamish,' she told Tam. 'What has happened?'

'The King is dead,' said Tam.

But their immediate concern was for the injured page Tam carried into an upstairs bedchamber. They were followed by Hamish, who had paused to summon a maid to bring hot water and linen.

'We are fortunate indeed. Hamish is a physician, on his way home from a learned gathering in York,' said Janet.

Leading the way downstairs, she demanded to know what had happened to Darnley.

'Strangled!' she exclaimed, upon hearing Tam's news. 'Murdered in the garden?'

'He did not die in the explosion, that is for sure,' said Tam.

Drinking the goblet of wine she poured for him, he took her quickly through his rough awakening in Dorothy's lodging by being hurled from his chair by the force of the explosion, to his part in the discovery of the bodies of Darnley and Taylor.

About to tell her of his rescue of Hamish's patient, how he had seized a saddled horse which had bolted from the King's stable and told sentries at the Netherbow Port that he was physician to the Queen, with an injured victim needing immediate attention, he got no further than the first sentence when a servant curtsied at the door. 'Dr Fenwick wishes to see your ladyship.'

'I'm coming too,' said Tam.

The page lay against the pillows, face half-concealed by a bloodied bandage.

'Well?' demanded Janet.

Hamish shook his head gravely. 'Apart from that deep cut across the forehead, there may be permanent damage to the legs, as well as possible internal injuries. I have done all I can. The rest is up to you, good mother.'

'Poor lad, so young,' said Janet.

'Your poor lad will need careful nursing.' And Hamish smiled at her wryly. 'Especially since he happens to be a lass.'

'A lass! But who?' Janet went closer to the bed, stared at the bandaged head and turned swiftly to Tam, who had remained silent throughout.

'You knew who it was,' she said accusingly and he nodded.

'Dorothy Sinclair.'

Chapter Twenty-Nine

Monday 17 February 1567

Tam had rarely left the house during daylight hours. On Monday Janet handed him the package he had left at Beaton House before the fatal night at Kirk O'Field.

'I read what you had written, Tam. A wise move. It was as well one other person knew the truth,' she said as they both listened to the unabated uproar up and down the street.

While the search for the King's murderers continued with arrests and merciless questioning of any survivors and witnesses, Tam had prudently remained indoors and spent many hours sitting by Dorothy's bedside.

Occasionally her eyes opened, but she did not know him, sometimes calling out in pain. He felt helpless, unable to do more than force sips of water between her dry lips.

'Will she ever recover?' was his anxious question.

'Many women would have died, but she is strong and making good progress,' said Janet.

'Is there nothing more you can do for her?'

Janet smiled. 'Nothing my magical powers can perform, if that is what you mean. Hamish and I have done all we can for her bodily ills. We must leave that to time's healing hand, if God so wills. But there are other sicknesses I cannot cure.'

Then, later that morning, she reported, 'Take heart. Tam. She has spoken to me.'

'What did she say?'

'Only that she wishes to return to Lady Morham, who will be anxious about her.'

Janet put her hand on Tam's shoulder. 'It is time we were leaving too. I cannot protect you from the wolves much longer.'

'Wolves?'

'Aye, Tam, wolves. Ye've heard all the noise outside, seen the placards. The people are righteously angry. Their dissolute young King, not yet one-and-twenty and deified by death, has been slain. They are looking for a scapegoat at every turn.' She sighed. 'They have even been at this door many times, asking if I knew the identity of one who calls himself the Queen's physician. I cannot hide ye much longer.'

'But I have done nothing!'

She smiled grimly. 'I am aware of that, but once they have you, they are not averse to putting innocent men to the torture in their anxiety to discover a culprit. Believe me, once the rack and the thumbscrews have done their work, you will be ready to confess to anything. Anything at all.'

The noises outside grew louder and she went over to the window.

'More placards, more images of our beloved King, foully murdered. Today the Queen made a proclamation.'

'How is she taking it?'

'Shocked, they tell us, poor lady. It was Bothwell's duty as sheriff to awaken her in the middle of the night and tell her the bad tidings. Her reaction was shock. I am told the doctors fear for her, have advised her to leave the city immediately the King is laid to rest.' She shrugged. 'There might be good reason for that.'

'This proclamation. Surely she is innocent?'

'A copy was thrust through my door. Here you are, read it for yourself.'

'We know not yet who is responsible for this vile deed, but it is certain that with the diligence our Council has begun already to use, the same being discovered, we hope to punish the same with such rigour as shall serve for example of this cruelty to all ages to come. Always who ever have taken this wicked enterprise in hand, we assure our self it was addressed always for us as for the King, for we lay the most part of all the last week in that same lodging, and was there accompanied with the most part of the lords that are in this town that same night at midnight, and of very chance tarried not all night, by reason of some masque in the abbey, but we believe it was not chance but God that put it into our head.'

Tam looked across at Janet. 'These noble lords she mentions. What of Bothwell, Janet?'

Janet shuddered. 'Aye, Bothwell. Where was he the night the King was slain? That is what everyone asks. And where was her loving half-brother, James? Very conveniently absent – away visiting his wife, who had suffered a miscarriage.'

'Bothwell, has he not visited you, then?'

Janet laughed bitterly. 'Need you ask, Tam? I tell myself it would be too dangerous, that it is his good sense to keep away from Beaton House in case I am further implicated.' With a sigh, she added, 'He was seen repeatedly by many witnesses in the vicinity of the King's lodging. If he is a guilty man, then he needs some lessons in dissembling, since he identified himself readily enough according to the sentries' evidence.

'As Sheriff it was his duty to lead a party of soldiers from Holyrood to where the King's body had been carried into a house nearby. Here it would be inspected by surgeons, but while members of the Privy Council were being summoned, the general public were allowed in to have their vulgar curiosity satisfied.' Janet paused. 'That was how the news was spread that the King had been strangled, the means left to everyone's imagination. By his own belt, his nightshirt sleeves, a serviette, even a napkin soaked in vinegar, so rumour has it.'

Tam had told her about the array of objects he had seen lying near the two corpses and she said, 'When you opted for the nightshirt sleeves, you, were probably right, for this is where you came, or rightly did not, come in.'

She was silent for a while, then, 'The town watch related how the King's body had first been discovered by one calling himself the Queen's physician. Why was he not present? Why had he not declared himself and why did no man know his identity? "Bring him forth here!" was the cry then. And still is,' she added grimly. 'Ye ken the rest. The King lies in state, his body embalmed at Holyrood. In a few hours he will be buried in the vaults of the Chapel Royal. But that ceremony is not for the likes of us.

'My continued presence here is no longer necessary. Alice will recover, thanks be to God and the gift of herbs He gave me. So we must think of ourselves, Tam. We must make haste to be well clear of Edinburgh before the people give rein to their emotions, stirred on by Knox. And by some women who lived nearby and have gained temporary importance as witnesses to the explosion by allegedly hearing the King's last cries: "For the sake of Jesus Christ, who pitied all the world, have pity on me, kinsmen."'

'Kinsmen?' said Tam.

She gave him a significant look. 'Aye, his mother was a Douglas, a political marriage to heal old grievances.'

'So we are going to Branxholm at last?' said Tam, relieved by Janet's decision to leave.

'Nay. That is the first place they would look for us.'

'Surely you are not included?'

She laughed. 'I was one of the first. There is a placard only yards from this window, nailed to a wall, naming Sir James Balfour and Bothwell and saying that the Queen was privy to the King's murder, influenced by a known witch, the one called Lady Buccleuch.'

'Where will we go?'

'I have a small house near Haddington, bequeathed to me by a cousin who was priest at the church there. It will suffice until we learn how matters proceed with the Queen.' She nodded towards the ceiling. 'And I'm curious to know why Mistress Dorothy was lurking about Darnley's lodging dressed as a boy that night.' Her hard look invited comment.

Tam remained silent. He knew most of the answers already, but the puzzle was still incomplete although the mention of 'kinsmen', suggested that Darnley had fallen foul of his hereditary enemies.

Chapter Thirty

**East Lothian. Thursday 20 February 1567.
Morning**

Janet and Tam, with Dorothy in a litter, joined the royal party as it wound its way towards Seton. The Queen was accompanied by her physicans. In accordance with their examination, she was 'in great imminent dangers of her health and life, if she did not in all speed break up that kind of close solitary life and repair to some good wholesome air'.

Their advice had been emphasized by all who knew how she had endured great anguish since Darnley's murder, as reports reached her from Edinburgh, of angry and menacing crowds with their placards that accused Bothwell and herself of murder.

Tam managed to ride alongside Marie Seton, who confirmed their worst fears. 'She sits for hours at her bedroom window, white-faced and trembling, without a word or a morsel of food passing her lips. All of us who know and love Her Grace fear that not only her body but her mind also will break down,' she added in a fearful whisper.

This Marie, in deep mourning, as were all the court by Mary's orders, was very different from the happy, laughing Seton he had left such a short time ago, excited and more than a little in love with Adam Drummond.

When Tam asked after Adam's health, Marie said sadly, 'I believe he is well. He wishes us to marry as soon as the Queen's mourning is ended and her health permits. But, alas, marriage is further than ever from my thoughts now. Since this terrible tragedy the Queen needs me with her more than ever.' She shook her head. 'My place is at her side, ready to comfort and reassure her. She relies on me.'

'Then follow the examples set by Livingstone and Fleming, who married and remained in her service.'

'You do not understand. If I marry Adam, it is to be his true wife and mother to his children, the future heirs of Drummond. And that is to be my only home. The break with the Queen must be complete. It is Adam's command and I well know and understand that such is the one condition of our marriage. I must be lady of his house. He must be my first allegiance and I must have no other.'

'Is he not proud that you should serve the Queen?'

'He says I have spent all my life serving Her Grace and it is now time that I served a husband. He is quite right, Tam. He has asked me to make a choice, a decision. I must think well upon it.' She shrugged. 'But you see the state of my poor lady. How can I of all people, her most trusted servant and childhood friend, desert her now when she needs me most? How could I be happy as Adam Drummond's bride with such matter on my conscience?'

'What of Lord Bothwell?' asked Tam, remembering the rumours hinting that he had murdered the king, intending to step into his shoes and rule Scotland at Mary's side. And that they were already lovers.

Marie gave him an unhappy glance. 'What indeed? Her Grace refuses to believe that he had any part in the King's murder, but who knows? She relies on him, trusts him. Pray God that her trust is not false. But I think she is a little afraid of him.'

Within sight of Seton, Marie turned to him and said, 'Dear Tam, I am afraid.' She closed her eyes tightly. 'Afraid that I may never see you again. Tell me that my fears are foolish.'

Tam reached out for her hand, aware that his murmured reassurances were lies. When their ways parted, his heart felt like lead, as with Janet, Dorothy and their escort they continued towards Morham. Tam thought of Marie's words concerning Bothwell and the Queen's fear of him. Was it with greater cause than she would admit even to her close and loving companion Seton?

At Morham, Bothwell's mother came out to greet them, her anxiety all for her dear friend Dorothy.

Servants helped her out of the litter and one of the men carried her up the steps and into the house.

From the garden the small figure of William appeared and rushed towards her, seizing her hand, crying one endearing word, to which Janet reacted with some surprise.

'I had not realized matters had so progressed.'

Lady Morham smiled. 'So touching, is it not? He holds her in such loving regard.'

They paused briefly to take refreshments. Eager to reach Haddington, Janet did not contradict Lady

Morham, who assumed that they were heading back to Branxholm.

'It will be good for you, my dear, to be home and at peace after all these dreadful days in Edinburgh. Rumour has reached us, of course, but to have lived through such dangerous times.'

Tam wondered if rumours concerning her son's part in the King's murder had also reached her, but that seemed unlikely, as she discussed the tragedy as if it had already happened long ago.

With so much personal tragedy, these matters failed to touch the life she had made for herself here in Morham, mere pebbles skimming the smooth surface of a lake.

Dorothy was carried to the bedchamber she had occupied since her first days at Morham, with William at their heels, holding tightly to her hand. She smiled at him and whispered a grateful thanks to Tam and Janet. Then wearily she closed her eyes.

Tam escorted Lady Morham downstairs, leaving Janet to give instructions to those who were to look after Dorothy.

When she joined them again after taking some refreshment, she indicated to Tam that they should leave.

'I expect my son will be looking in to see me on his way to visit his dear wife,' said Lady Morham. 'Lady Jean is gravely ill, we hear.'

This mention of her daughter-in-law's illness seemed to affect her little more than reporting that of a stranger or a servant on the estate. For Tam it all added to the picture of Bothwell's sad lack of filial affection for his mother and responsibility for his son.

'James will no doubt bring us all the latest news of what is happening in Edinburgh,' Lady Morham continued. 'All these terrible riots. Ordinary people are so unfeeling. We can only thank God that Her Grace was not in danger and has been spared to us.'

At the door Janet paused. 'Will you give Lord Bothwell a message from me?'

'With pleasure, my dear.'

Janet handed her a letter. 'He will ken where to find me.'

And to Tam, as they rode away, she explained, 'We spent many happy days at Haddington when Jamie was being sought by his enemies. They never thought to look for him in a church house belonging to a priest.' She sighed. 'How long ago it seems, but we loved each other deeply. Handfasted, it was a kind of extended honeymoon.'

Tam regarded her nervously. He trusted she was not expecting a second honeymoon with himself as a reluctant successor to Lord Bothwell.

But his main concern was for Lady Jean Gordon. Although he refrained from mentioning it to Janet, he wondered if her thoughts were the same as his own.

Could it be that Bothwell, if he were guilty of the King's murder, was also in the process of removing yet another obstacle to the fulfilment of his secret ambition, marriage with the Queen?

Chapter Thirty-One

Morham. Friday 7 March 1567. Afternoon

The priest's house on the river by the great church of St Mary's at Haddington was pleasant enough, but their stay was brief. Janet, often absent from the house visiting acquaintances, as well as many of her kin within an hour's ride, was aware that Tam was ill at ease.

His relief was evident on the day she announced that they would be returning to Branxholm, for, according to reports which had reached her from Edinburgh, they were no longer in any danger. They had been forgotten as the angry citizens vented their hatred on Bothwell, adulterer and murderer.

These events were a far cry from the threats to his life from an unknown woman which had begun that night in November, at Craigmillar Castle, events to which Tam now had the key.

There were only one or two missing links in that chain and only one person could fill them in for him. It was becoming a matter of urgency and if that person still lived, he had a feeling he would be sent for.

He hoped it would be soon, as he was aware that his own time was running out. Dreams that were not dreams any longer, but vivid presences with very clear instructions, urged him that his mission was ended. It was almost a year now, soon after Riccio's murder, that he had arrived in Janet Beaton's garden. Now, as they prepared to depart, Janet mistook his silence for apprehension and spoke reassuringly.

'Have no fears, Tam. The Scotts will protect their own. And there's an army of them around Branxholm,' she said grimly. 'Morham is on our road, shall we see how Dorothy fares?'

Lady Morham's welcome was warm as ever, but she was unable to conceal her anxiety. Her dear friend Dorothy was far from well.

'She will be glad of visitors, for her mood is very melancholy and she is sometimes in great pain.'

They followed her upstairs, to where Dorothy leaned back against the pillows, William playing with a wooden toy at her side.

Lady Morham said to him, 'It is time for your lessons, my dear. Your aunt needs to rest.'

Clambering over Dorothy, William did not notice how she winced. He kissed her and she hugged him briefly, told him to be a good boy and heed his tutor.

As the door closed, Tam and Janet moved closer to the bed, both aware of how greatly she had changed, and not for the better, in the short time since they had brought her from Edinburgh.

She looked exhausted, drained. And Tam felt compassion for the ghost of the Dorothy Sinclair he had known in Stirling, that strong, independent woman of great spirit. With considerable tact, Janet pressed his shoulder, indicating that she was leaving them alone.

Tam took her hand and asked. 'How is it with you?'

'I survive, as you see.' She smiled wanly. 'I am glad you have come, Tam, to see your poor Dorothy.'

He was silent for a moment. 'What do I call you now? Is it Dorothy, or Ned, or Will?'

She shook her head. 'It is Anna. Anna Throndsen.'

'William told us that.'

'William!' At her startled gasp, he added, 'He called you Mamma when we brought you here.'

She smiled. 'My son – I could not bear him to call me his aunt.'

Tam knew he would never be able to think of her as Anna, although he had known her real identity since Kirk O'Field, and guessed at it even longer.

She looked at him. 'So you are for Branxholm, Tam? I think you will not come this way again, and if you do, that you will not find me here,' she said sadly, pressing his hand. 'This will be our last meeting.'

Before he could reply, she said, 'I want you to know the truth, Tam. I missed William and only left him in Scotland believing that he would have a better future with his father, who would care for him, than in a house of women in Norway, with an ageing ailing mother who needed my constant attention. But I was wrong.'

And Tam remembered those few visits to Morham and how Bothwell preferred to forget he had a son.

'It all began when I came to Stirling to visit Else after her husband died. I still have a passport to Scotland and I've always loved horses – it is the only safe and comfortable way for a woman to travel, preferably in men's clothes, unless one is to be formally received. So I bought a docile horse and made the journey to

Edinburgh, dressed as a man, much to Else's horror. I took a room in a tavern, useful to my purposes later, in the High Street.'

She stretched out her hand and touched the toy William had left. 'First, I was to visit Magdala's grave in Greyfriars. I named her for my younger sister, an unusual name and in despair. I could not find the headstone. Then I saw that someone had defaced the inscription. A vile cruel deed, no doubt by James's orders, part of his refusal to acknowledge our children. Weeping, I left the kirkyard and stood aside for a procession of riders. James, and at his side the Queen. How proud he was, laughing and happy, and I was so miserable and alone. Our eyes met – he looked through me – and in that instant I knew he did not recognize or even remember who I was.

'I could not blame him for that. I had been well fleshed, with the womanly curves James found so pleasing. Now my body was flat and shapeless and I was dressed as a boy.' She moved thin shoulders. 'In that moment, watching them ride out of sight, I swore to destroy him to avenge Magdala's death, for I held him responsible. A woman beside me said the royal party were heading for Craigmillar Castle. I decided to follow them.

'I joined a group of packmen bound for Wooler. Near Morham I left them, rode in and said I had a message for Her Ladyship. Directed to the gardens, there was my little William, playing with a puppy.' Her face softened, smiling at memory. 'In nearly three years how he had grown, a handsome little boy. I ran over, put my arms around him and said, "I am your Mamma, William."

'Amazed, a little afraid too, he pulled away from me. "You are not my Mamma, you are a man. And I don't like you." He sounded quite grown-up, so cross and offended. At that moment Lady Morham appeared, William ran to her and cried; "Send this nasty man away, grandmother." But before he could say another word I pulled off my bonnet, shook down my hair and said to him, 'Forgive me please, I always ride in men's clothes.'

'Poor Lady Morham, she was bewildered and rather shocked by my appearance. As she sent William off to play, I knew that, half blind, she did not recognize me as Anna either. I had changed so much my secret was safe. For suddenly I knew I did not want my son to know I was the mother he believed had abandoned him. But to be sent away, never to see him again! I had to think very quickly. I said, "I am Dorothy Sinclair, Anna's sister. I have been visiting our sister Else in Stirling."

'Lady Morham was delighted. She called William back and explained that it had been just a pretend game. When William eagerly accepted me as his new aunt, his grandmother, lonely in a fairly isolated house, suggested that if I was not in any hurry to return to Shetland I might consider staying for a while. This was exactly the invitation I had been hoping for. Soon I was hinting that I intended to remain in Scotland and hoped to persuade Anna to allow me to legally adopt William.'

'Was she not curious about Anna?' Tam asked

Dorothy shook her head. 'After the first few days when I explained that I rarely heard from her, she did not bring up the painful subject of Anna's neglect of William again.'

Seized by a fit of coughing, she took a sip of water Tam gave to her.

'Is this too tiring for you?' he asked. 'You do not need to tell me any more.'

She took his hand. 'Dear Tam. I want you to know the truth. It is important that you do not judge me too harshly. I could have continued my deception indefinitely, but first of all I had to destroy James Bothwell. So, pretending I was going to Edinburgh to look at property, I headed to Craigmillar Castle. Stopping for refreshment at a tavern near Peffermill, I fell into conversation with a young Frenchman called Paris, body-servant to Lord Bothwell, who lodged at Peffermill House nearby with some of his mosstroopers. He was puzzled by my fine horse and accent, so I told him some story about tracing relatives in Scotland and that I was looking for employment. He suggested there was always work for a horse-keeper in the castle stables. His advice was correct and proved a good vantage point for observing James's habit of walking up the lane from Peffermill to the castle.'

'And that was when the idea of Will Fellows came to you,' said Tam. 'When you used this,' he added, throwing the dagger he had found in her lodging in Kirk O'Field on the bed.

She stared at it. 'How did you get it?'

'I searched the house while you were absent.'

'So careless of me and so very ungallant of you, Tam.'

Ignoring that, Tam said, 'That was your first mistake.'

'Mistake? How so?'

'In Stirling I confided in you about the attacks on Bothwell by an unknown woman with a dagger and you said, "Daggers are not unique, not even a lover's special gift." Read the inscription. "To Anna, a love gift from J. H." How did you know that? I certainly hadn't told you.'

'We all make mistakes, Tam.'

'Like getting rid of Ben Fellows' body in Duddingston Loch.'

'I can explain that. James giving Will his cloak with the Bothwell insignia was a grand gesture, but one that revolted me, 'she said with a shudder. 'I had to get rid of Will. When I overheard the carter – Archie Crozer – who brought logs to the kitchens, telling the horse-keepers that the old woodcutter Ben Fellows had died that morning, and I'd gathered from them that Archie would do anything without question if he was well paid, I became the old man's niece and paid Archie well to assist me. Taking a chance that a decomposed corpse being found much later wrapped in James's cloak would persuade him that his rescuer, Will Fellows, had also been murdered.' She paused, frowning. 'I was hoping that by then James would have remembered the dagger and that his guilty conscience would suggest the mysterious woman was Anna Throndsen.'

'Not his guilty conscience this time,' said Tam. 'It was Janet Beaton who put it into his head.'

She laughed. 'And unknowingly did me a great service. Did you believe her, Tam?

'I was not convinced. There were others with greater motives, including Lady Jean Gordon, his wife.'

Tam noticed how she winced at that, but he continued. 'Unfortunately for your plan, Ben Fellows' body was recovered almost immediately, while the wreckage of the cart, its live occupants, a woman and a horse had all vanished without trace. And I began to suspect that Lord Bothwell's rescuer and the would-be assassin were one and the same person.'

A bout of coughing seized Dorothy. Behind them the door opened and Janet appeared. Eyes closed, the sick woman lay back against the pillows.

'You must not overtire her, Tam. She must sleep. I have something here to ease her pain,' she whispered. Leaning over the bed, she said, 'This will make you feel better, Dorothy.'

A few sips. 'What a pleasant taste,' she murmured.

And as Janet moved away and Tam stood up to follow her, she said drowsily. 'Let him stay. Just a few more moments. Please stay, Tam. Promise.'

'I promise.'

Her eyes closed.

'Stay, Tam. You promised.'

Tam had returned to the bedchamber two hours later and, thinking Dorothy still slept, was about to leave again. Unaware that time had passed, she took his hand.

'I could have killed James the day he stood under Walter Pax's window in Edinburgh.' She looked at him thoughtfully. 'You were with him. Perhaps I should have killed you both.'

'Perhaps that would have been best.'

For a moment she stared at him, as if considering. 'I had become Ned Wells. I needed money desperately and some of my father's associates in Norway had trading agreements through Walter Pax. They were honest men, but they discovered that Pax was not. That he was a forger. I decided to pay him a visit. I wrote a good hand and I had to forge my father's signature often when his arm became paralysed and he left me in charge of his business ventures. He had debtors and was afraid of losing our home and leaving his family penniless.

'Pax was pleased to give me employment. I learned many things in my short time with him – that he was a spy in English pay. Part of one important document I managed to decode was a thinly disguised plot to kill the Queen.

'At Craigmillar even the horse-keepers had observed secret comings and goings that concerned Darnley and knew that Bothwell was involved. So I decided to visit the tavern at Peffermill, where I met Paris, who did not recognize the stable boy in the dim light as this fine lady of uncertain morals.

'Over his ale he became distinctly amorous, his confidential manner leading us to a very fine bed-chamber in Peffermill House, empty most nights since his master had better entertainment at Lady Buccle-uch's lodging. Paris was soon asleep and my virtue intact, since I carried a tincture for such matters which I added to his ale. In Shetland there are witches too, Tam,' she added.

'I set about searching through his master's pos-sessions, to see if there was anything that might be saleable to Walter Pax. I was surprised indeed and quite moved to find he had kept all my letters. I should never have thought him capable of such sentiment.

They were neatly folded in a casket I had given him, and there were also letters from the Queen. I realized their value.

'I knew from Paris that the Court was moving to Stirling and that suited me well. I had no wish to be deprived of tormenting him. I would stay with Else and take Lady Morham, who had been invited to Fleming's wedding.'

Her smile was weary. 'Then I met you. A very unexpected pleasure. We shared some happy hours together, did we not, Tam?'

'I remember one in particular when you were very upset about having your hand read.'

She looked at him without speaking for a moment. 'I was never quite sure about you, Tam. Who or what you were worried me. Had you really lost your memory? Or were you, as Else said, a creature of the devil's, conjured up, as rumour whispered, by the Witch Lady of Branxholm? I laughed at such foolishness.'

'But you did not think it was worth the risk, having your fortune told,' he said, and before she could reply, he added, 'I should have suspected. And the reason your sister was so uneasy is now perfectly obvious, aware that you were really her sister Anna, involved in some elaborate pretence she did not understand.

'I had to confide in her, but as little as possible.'

'Did that not concern you?'

She shrugged. 'It did. Else is not a very good actress. She was confused and could not get used to hearing me called "Dorothy".'

'I never quite believed it was because she had an attachment for me, as you put it. You were afraid that one day she would say "Anna" in my presence,' said Tam.

She nodded. 'A possibility very difficult to explain away.'

Tam smiled. 'As you did so many other things.'

'Poor Else. She is a very honest woman and a very conventional one as well. She did not like her sister Anna pretending to be a boy called Ned whose twin sister was maid to Marie Seton.' And with a sly look, 'Anything concerning Marie Seton's safety showed you up as a very poor actor, Tam.'

He ignored that. 'So it was your hand behind the poisoned marchpane?'

'As Ned, I made Abigail's acquaintance and discovered that, like so many maids, she was wildly in love with the master and he had made advances, promised her more favours than a few stolen kisses. Such as sharing his bed,' she added grimly and with a gesture of irritation. 'I suppose it was wicked of me and quite unnecessary to suggest the sweetmeats. I didn't want the Queen's poor dog to die. I love animals – in fact, I am quite besotted with horses and dogs. They are much more loyal and rewarding than humans.' She sighed. 'I told poor Abigail that this special marchpane had certain amorous effects on men which would be to her advantage. She was to lurk about when he left the Queen's apartment, and she immediately brightened at the thought of what was to follow. She was not very clever, alas, and panicked when she heard the little dog had died. Fortunately she was consoled by learning from Seton that it was a greedy animal and had died of old age and overeating.'

She put a hand on his arm. 'I was happy in Stirling,

ALANNA KNIGHT

and with you, Tam. I often forgot Anna and really
believed I was Dorothy Sinclair, with a handsome
suitor who was falling in love with me. I shall never
forget days we shared together.'

'And the ones we did not share? Like Inchmahome.'

She smiled. 'I had heard about the priory from Else
and I wanted to go there. When I was awakened by
the lads talking and saddling up, they were nothing
loath to let me carry one of the torches.'

'What were you doing on your own, wandering
about in the ruinous part?'

'That was of necessity, an urgent need for a private
place – to relieve myself. One of the reasons I did not
care to play dice with them and avoided too much
close contact which might reveal that I was a woman.
Suddenly I saw James walking below. I could not resist
that loose stone. The damage that could have done! I
could have hurt him quite badly.'

'You gave him a fright, that's for sure.'

She laughed bitterly. 'How happy that makes me.'

'And he thought you were Will Fellows.'

'He saw my face briefly. So I decided I had best
make my way back alone as I had an important assignation. With the King. The reason Ned had a room
above the stables.'

'The lads told me they did not know you.'

'Some of that was true. They did not care to talk to
a stranger – like yourself – about a page who was in
royal favour. Such gossip could be dangerous.'

'Could the King not have given you more comfortable accommodation?'

'He would have done so willingly. But I refused.
For the same reasons as I kept the stable boys at a

326

distance. And aware of the King's taste, I did not want him to take me by surprise! Besides, I had my nervous sister Else to deal with – and yourself.

'Life was becoming very complicated being Ned and Dorothy. At last, since having his amorous advances thwarted did not please the King, to keep his lust at bay, I had to confess that I did not have a twin sister who was maid to Marie Seton but that I liked dressing as a woman. How that small wickedness delighted him!'

Her laughter faded. 'I was summoned on the night of the fireworks after the Prince's christening. He had drunk too much and was very maudlin. He discussed in a casual manner what I thought about gunpowder used to better ends than fireworks. I knew he hated Mary and guessed what was in his mind when he said that castles were useless, with too many guards and sentries, as well as anxious courtiers. A small house would be more convenient.

'And I had the perfect place, in Kirk O'Field, a house James had rented from Robert Balfour. A safe distance, a short ride from Holyrood and his Border castles, suitable for his amours. He had installed me there when I was pregnant a second time, to keep me away from any social contacts at court. I was so unhappy – friendless, homesick for my loving family. My father the Admiral was dying, so I took William, returned home and had my baby.' She closed her eyes. 'Magdala was beautiful. I was certain James would never be able to resist her. We returned to Kirk O'Field and implored James to see us. He had us turned away like beggars from Holyrood, saying we were impostors, that he had no wife and no children. We were caught in heavy rain Magdala took a fever and died in my arms that night.'

Tam took her hands. 'I saw her grave in Greyfriars.'

Wild-eyed, she thumped her fists on the counterpane. 'May he rot in hell for that! May God forgive him, for I never shall! He killed our child. Now, by helping the King, I could have my revenge. The plot was to kill the Queen in the explosion and implicate the Earl of Bothwell, since the King loathed the mention of his name. He would be rid of both of them, and I knew enough of King Henry's vicious nature to guess that everyone who had opposed him in word or deed would go speedily to the executioner's block. And through her enemies, he would use my letters to James, which I had stolen and sold to Pax, to prove that his late wife the Queen of Scots had been Bothwell's whore.

'So I was Mistress Sinclair by day and at night I went across to the King's lodging as Ned Wells. The King's excitement was almost childlike. Unable to keep a secret, he confided in me and soon I knew all the intricacies of the plot. I even suggested Archie Crozer, whom I had seen on market days in Edinburgh, as the purveyor of the gunpowder from the arsenal at the castle.

' "Is he to be trusted?" was the nervous question. I assured him that money would buy his silence. And afterwards?

' "He will have to be disposed of, Ned. We can have no witnesses to this deed," was the grim reply.

'And so it was all arranged. The Queen would return from Pagez's masque and sleep in the room below. Before dawn, the King would slip out, his horses ready and waiting, the given signal for Taylor, his loyal servant, and myself to light the fuse. The house would be blown up and all of Scotland would mourn their dead Queen.'

In the short silence that followed, both gathered their thoughts, remembering the horrors of that fatal night, the enormity of all that had gone wrong.

'After the royal party left, there was silence in the house, the fuses being prepared under the *salle* in readiness for the Queen's return. And then, as I was making my way through the kitchens, I heard the sound of voices, screams of pain. Easton, one of the King's servants, was being questioned by James and others. Sickened by the scene, I heard him telling them all. And saw him executed, a knife in his heart as James said, "I will light the fuse."'

'I warned the King. Saw him climb down from the window with Taylor, run across the gardens. I waited no longer, but I was already too late. You know the rest.'

She smiled at him. 'You saved my life. Poor King Henry, I thought I had saved him, but instead he ran straight into the arms of the Hamiltons – or the Douglases. And now James will succeed in his ambition to marry the Queen and together they will rule Scotland.'

Tam was silent.

'Is that not what will happen?' And when he did not reply, she said accusingly, 'You know something, do you not?'

'I only know that what is about to happen will be recorded in history.'

'That is not a great deal of consolation to me.'

'What would be of consolation to you?'

Her eyes narrowed. 'If I were a Catholic and believed in Purgatory, in eternal damnation, I would condemn James to long and lingering death, so that he can be haunted by the ghost of Magdala, and by my hatred, like a thousand daggers in his immortal soul.'

'And what of you?'

She smiled, all hatred and anger gone as she looked at him. 'I am grateful to you, Tam, for rescuing me that night. I might have been just one more victim, but you gave me back my life. But I am not sure for how long. I am in great pain and I cannot imagine ever being free from it.'

Janet had told him that her injuries were serious, her legs affected.

'I fear not being able to walk or ride again. And that would be my answer, a living death.'

'Will you stay in Scotland?'

'I think not. If it is at all possible, I will go back to Norway. My mother needs me. And I will take William with me. An Earl's son or not, he deserves a better life. But what of you, Tam? Is it Branxholm?'

When he said yes, she was silent for a moment, then, straightening her shoulders, she said, 'I am very tired, Tam, and soon I must sleep again. Before we part, will you hold me in your arms, so that I might keep the memory of what could have been had we not been who we are and met when we did. One last embrace, Tam.'

He held her for a while, hearing her wildly beating

heart. Then he kissed her and she fell back against the pillows, closing her eyes. Her sigh, as he gently shut the door, was deep and happy, like that of a contented child.

Chapter Thirty-Two

Branxholm. Sunday 16 March 1567. Evening

Without a word being spoken between them, both were conscious that this was the anniversary of the night Janet Beaton had found Tam in her garden.

A messenger had brought word that day from Lady Morham. Her daughter-in-law, Lady Jean Gordon, had made a good recovery from her recent illness but, alas, her dear friend Dorothy was still an anxiety to them all, especially to little William, who wished to spend all his waking hours at her bedside.

As Janet cast the letter aside there was a feeling of new life, of spring and a world preparing for rebirth around them. Unseen, a blackbird tentatively tried out the first unsteady notes of what would be, one day soon, a rhapsody of joy.

Janet looked across at Tam. A quiet peaceful evening lay ahead of them, with his day's work as steward laid aside, like so many days they had shared since their return to Branxholm.

But Janet was uneasy. She had sensed for several days now that Tam was restless, withdrawn. How often mid-conversation his hand flew to the charmstone concealed under his collar. He reminded her of someone on the outset of a long journey, wondering anxiously whether he had with him all his goods and chattels.

As they sat by the window overlooking the garden, where dusk shrouded the trees and the blackbird's song grew stronger, he leaned across, took her hands and said gently, 'You know what I am going to say, do you not?'

'Aye, Tam. Ye're going away. That crystal ye wear . . .'

He nodded. 'I have no option.'

'Has your memory come back, then?' she demanded eagerly.

'Memory? What is that, Janet?'

Bewildered, she said, 'Tell me, Please tell me.'

He shook his head. 'I cannot. Just let us say that I have been summoned to return.'

'Return – but where, Tam, where?'

He shrugged. 'Whence I came, Janet.'

'What sort of place? You can tell me,' she insisted.

His head turned towards the window and he said softly, 'Where there is no memory, where all time – past, present and future – is as one.'

She frowned. 'I have never encountered such a thing, not in all my dealings with the occult, with the other worlds.'

'It is not occult, Janet. One day, when we are just a recorded fragment of history, men will have found the answer to all the things that the alchemists seek, things that will remain hidden for centuries to come, achievements and inventions that the world is not yet ready for but which men – and women – of the future will discover.'

She leaned forward. 'Tell me about them, Tam. Tell me what you know,' she insisted.

'Chariots on wheels that will travel without horses. Machines that will fly in the air, like our songster out there in the garden.'

'What else, what else?' she demanded.

'Machines that show pictures of what is happening on the other side of the world, in continents not yet discovered, in the universe and beyond the furthest stars. Machines that let us talk to people in lands far beyond our own.' He stood up, staring into the garden, hands resting on the window-sill, a listener. 'I must leave you now. It is imperative that I return by the same route, from the exact spot where you found me – out there.'

'Oh Tam, Tam. I shall miss you.'

'And I shall miss you.' He kissed her gently. 'But you must promise not to follow me and not to call me back.'

Holding him, she said, 'I promise. But, Tam, there is so much I want you to tell me of all these wonders of the future.'

He smiled. 'I have already told you too much.' And once more he kissed her, held her close. 'Who knows, maybe we shall meet again, in some of those other worlds.'

Tears welled in her eyes as he released her.

'Do not look. Do not watch me leave. Remember your promise. Close your eyes, Janet.'

She felt him kiss her eyelids and then the door closed softly.

For a few moments she remained where she was and then, unable to bear the tension any longer, despite her promise, she ran out into the dusk, to the place under the trees where she had found him.

The guard dogs had followed her and settled down a few feet away as she knelt and touched the grass. Her hand came away warm, as if a body had lain there, as had Tam's a year ago.

On her feet again, all around her the air was strange, almost menacing.

Nothing was visible but the first stars, a thin sliver of moon, far away, yet the atmosphere seemed to vibrate with unseen life, with some strange and terrifying quality beyond her comprehension, beyond her own certainty of other worlds.

She stood up, called out, 'Tam – fare thee well.'

But the garden was empty, the guard dogs had not moved and although the blackbird sang no more, there was just an echo of a name whispered in the wind: TAM – TAM EILDOR.

Afterword

Mary lost favour as in Edinburgh the scurrilous placards continued, depicting Bothwell and herself as
adulterers and Darnley's slayers, with lurid posters of
the infant Prince crying piteously to avenge his father's
murder.

Bothwell demanded that their instigator, Lennox,
take him to trial and make good his accusations, but
when the day arrived, Lennox failed to appear and
Bothwell walked free.

But the stigma remained. After her forty days of
mourning, Mary left the seclusion of Seton for Stirling,
to see her baby son, who on the death of his godmother
Elizabeth would inherit the English throne as James I.
They spent one happy April day together. He was ten
months old and they never saw each other again.

On the journey back to Edinburgh, Mary was met
at Gogar Bank on the outskirts of the city by Bothwell
with a group of armed men. He seized her bridle, told
her she was not safe to go further and that she was to
go to Dunbar with him.

Once there, according to the story put about, he
ravished her and she was forced to marry him. The
nobles did not want him as King either and public
opinion was soon stirred up against them, culminating

in the meeting of two opposing forces at Carberry Hill, more of a skirmish than a battle, where Mary's supporters, few in number, melted away.

Bothwell was eager to settle scores by single combat with the nobles, but Mary urged him to flee so as to live and raise an army to restore her to her throne.

This he solemnly promised to do, but fate ruled otherwise. They never met again. Loyal forces joined Mary in the struggle to regain her kingdom, but they were beaten. She was betrayed, sold over the border to Elizabeth of England, who had promised to help her dear cousin in her time of trial.

After eighteen years in prison, her continued presence an embarrassment to Elizabeth, the Casket Letters were produced, most written to Bothwell by the once lovesick Anna Throndsen, with Mary's own letters cobbled together with many discrepancies, in an elaborate forgery to prove Mary's guilt in Darnley's murder. Sinister plots to overthrow Elizabeth were also 'proven' and Mary was executed in Fotheringay Castle in 1587.

After Carberry, Bothwell had fled to the Orkneys, was refused entry and sailed on to Scandinavia in a valiant effort to raise money for an army. Taken hostage on a trumped-up charge of piracy, in desperation he appealed to Anna Throndsen to pay his ransom. She refused. Nine years later, in a Danish prison, chained like an animal to a pillar, Bothwell died. He was insane.

Anna had said, 'May he rot in hell.' She got her wish.

Her sister Dorothy's married name was Stewart. To avoid confusion with so many royal Stewarts, I have changed it to Sinclair, one of the few liberties I have taken with those who lived as depicted by history, biased or otherwise.

Anna vanished from historical records, but William was remembered as a beneficiary in the will of his grandmother Lady Morham.

Marie Seton never married. She stayed with the Queen as she had promised. Her lover Adam Drummond was my invention, but there are descendants of that same Drummond family, alive and well today, in Megginch Castle, Tayside. The eldest son and heir is named Adam.

Tam Eildor is fiction. His adventures have just begun.